A SA

WENT MISSING

CHRIS RILEY

Black Rose Writing | Texas

©2024 by Chris Riley
All rights reserved. No part of this book may be reproduced, stored in a retrieval system or transmitted in any form or by any means without the prior written permission of the publishers, except by a reviewer who may quote brief passages in a review to be printed in a newspaper, magazine or journal.

The author grants the final approval for this literary material.

First printing

This is a work of fiction. Names, characters, businesses, places, events, and incidents are either the products of the author's imagination or used in a fictitious manner. Any resemblance to actual persons, living or dead, or actual events is purely coincidental.

ISBN: 978-1-68513-365-8 (Paperback); 978-1-68513-369-6 (Hardcover)
LIBRARY OF CONGRESS CONTROL NUMBER: 2023943937
PUBLISHED BY BLACK ROSE WRITING
www.blackrosewriting.com

Printed in the United States of America
Suggested Retail Price (SRP) $21.95 (Paperback); $30.95 (Hardcover)

Went Missing is printed in Gentium Book Basic

*As a planet-friendly publisher, Black Rose Writing does its best to eliminate unnecessary waste to reduce paper usage and energy costs, while never compromising the reading experience. As a result, the final word count vs. page count may not meet common expectations.

PRAISE FOR
WENT MISSING

"An immersive, harrowing thriller of survival in the harshest wilderness. If Jack London had written a nail-biting thriller, it might be this story."
–**James Rollins, #1** ***New York Times*** **bestselling author of** ***Kingdom of Bones***

"Sam's brother goes missing deep in the Alaskan wilderness. Local search teams give up the search—but blood runs thick in the Nolan family and Sam soon finds himself tracking down what really happened to his younger sibling. The closer he gets, the harder it is to believe..."
–**Cam Torrens, award-winning author of** ***Stable***

Blurbs from other novels:

"Chris Riley's debut novel, *The Sinking of the Angie Piper*, does everything right: great-and-complicated characters, shining prose, and a story of emotional and physical conflict that will resonate long after you turn the last page."
–**James Rollins, #1** ***New York Times*** **bestselling author of** ***The Bone Labyrinth***

"Whether it's casual details about crabbing the frigid Alaskan sea or exploring the boiling maelstrom of the human heart, Chris Riley knows his stuff. The result is entertaining, illuminating and a fine ride."
–**Robert Ferrigno,** ***New York Times*** **bestselling author**

"Not since Robert Stone has a writer been so gripping or moving. *The Broken Pines* delves into danger, but at its core it is a novel focused on love and the power it wields. Everyone should read this book."
–**William Jensen, author of** ***Cities of Men***

To Jackson and Jessica, for all the memories...

*He who fights with monsters might take care,
lest he thereby become a monster.*
—Friedrich Nietzsche

WENT MISSING

PROLOGUE

It is in the far reaches of Canada's Yukon territory, a desolate land surrounded by cold mountain lakes and deep running rivers, encompassed by sparse meadows and endless forests, marshes and tundra, wildflowers and craggy mountaintops, the taiga of the great north, shadowed from a wilderness inhospitable to most any human being—it is in this land where a lone fisherman steps onto the shore of a hidden beach.

The fisherman's name is Bryson Nolan, and he looks at the pilot who has brought him here, a man with smiling eyes behind a face of gray hair, and then Bryson nods. "I'll see you later," he says.

The pilot extends his arm, they shake hands, and then he climbs into the cabin of his de Havilland floatplane and starts the engine. It is but minutes later that the pilot is halfway across the lake, two hundred feet in the air, and with the sounds from the single propeller engine now a fading hum across the water.

The fisherman watches as his ride disappears into the horizon, knowing he won't see the man, or any man, again for several days. He turns, picks up his gear—a large duffel bag and heavy-duty military grade backpack—and hauls them away from the shoreline.

He walks twenty yards and drops the items on the ground. He turns back toward the water and stares intensely, gratefully, at the vast wilderness surrounding him. At once he feels at home, here in this place, a place that is nearly the polar opposite of his other home, near Seattle, Washington. There is no metropolitan hustle here, no back-alley grime or crowded sidewalks. No rush hour traffic to contend with. In fact, there is *nothing* here, except for the earth and the trees and the quiet stillness of the lake...

Earl Lake.

There isn't a soul in sight. The landscape is bleak, lonely, and peaceful. The fisherman couldn't feel any more comfortable. He looks at the ripples on the surface of the lake and he imagines the size of the fish swimming in its depths. Several hundred yards away, the opposite shore is a dense thicket of stunted spruce and pine, and he studies it, wondering just how many large animals are presently roaming its shadowed pockets.

It is late May, and this is Bryson's second trip this year, out here in the bush. The first had been to another remote lake further north. The fishing had been great there, but a recon of the land resulted in a lack of evidence to warrant his moose hunt to be held later in the fall. His gut told him Earl Lake would be different. Looking around, he still feels this way.

The duffel bag at his side contains an inflatable Sea Eagle, 285 Frameless Pontoon Boat, which will take him less than fifteen minutes to make seaworthy. Bryson decides he will do that soon, and then take a casual trip out on the lake to fish, and to get a better lay of the surrounding shoreline. It is still early in the day, and he has little else to do other than make his camp. He picks up the bag again along with his backpack and walks further up the beach, looking for a suitable spot.

Twenty yards from the shore, he finds a small meadow on the fringes of an endless stand of trees. The ground is soft and sandy, mostly dry, and well enough for sleeping on. He sets his gear down and walks around, checking for bear sign. Finding nothing of significance, he returns to his gear and unpacks. In less than an hour, he has a decent camp set up, complete with a Quarter Dome 3-season tent, a fire ring made of local rocks, and a comfortable seat he'd fashioned from a fallen larch tree. Satisfied with his living arrangements, he uses nylon rope and hangs his waterproof sack containing all his food in a tall tree a few hundred feet away. Then he returns to his camp and puts together the Sea Eagle. Moments later, not much more than an hour after watching the plane ascend toward the horizon, Bryson is fly-fishing the great outdoors.

He catches a two-pound rainbow trout on his third cast. Then he catches another of about the same size, which he carefully releases back into the water. Throughout the rest of the day, he catches eight more fish, all the while observing the surrounding shoreline, looking for moose and other big game. For a long while, he observes a gaggle of geese resting on a flat of grass, and often, he hears what sounds like the slap from a beaver's tail somewhere on the lake.

Later, the fisherman is at his camp, tending a roaring fire. He pan-fries one of the trout he had caught and eats the entire fish, throwing the remaining bones into the flames. He cleans his frying pan thoroughly down at the lake and tidies up his camp before turning in. The night is long and quiet, uneventful, and it offers him nothing but a sound sleep.

In the morning, he decides he'll start his day on the opposite shore, to look for moose sign. He is unsatisfied with his observations from the day before and knows he will need to get closer to the land—on to the land—in order to find some good evidence. After a breakfast of freeze-dried eggs and sausage, he cleans his camp and then begins his recon by studying the opposite shore with his binoculars. He climbs in his boat, crosses the lake, gets out, and from here it doesn't take him long to find what he is looking for.

Around a nearby marsh he notices fresh tracks, and he moves slowly now, with the silence of a man who has experience in tracking such animals. He knows that the creature he is searching for has poor eyesight, but a strong sense of smell and hearing, both of which he carefully considers as he stalks through the forest. His intuition tells him he is close to the animal, but not dangerously so. On a southern sloping hillside, he notices several other tracks, one being from a large bear and many others from that of deer.

He looks around and studies the forest. It is a beautiful, bountiful habitat, with a richness he can smell in the air, an environment rife with shelter and foods for various critters. There are large granite slabs and boulders at the top of a small bluff. And in the distance he sees a berry patch and then an open area, a large meadow not unlike the one he has made his camp at.

For another hour he stalks along this side of the lake, making mental notes of his surroundings. He skirts along the edge of the meadow he had seen earlier and there he spots a cow—a female moose. It is an encouraging observation, and he knows that the animal is not the only one in the vicinity. Bryson decides, easily enough, that this spot, this lake, will make for a good hunt in the fall.

Later in the day, the fisherman sits idle in his boat, content with his newfound knowledge. He has paddled around most of the lake and has caught many fish, releasing all but one for dinner. As the day grows long and the sun sets close to the edge of a distant mountain range, he knows that the gloom of darkness will eventually fall over the lake. He paddles to the shore, steps out of his boat and looks toward his camp, cautiously searching and listening for a bear. Bryson knows it is easy, and dangerous, to startle such a creature, so he makes a loud hooting noise and slaps an oar onto the ground. Then he pulls his boat up on the shore and walks toward his camp.

In minutes, he has a roaring fire built and his trout cleaned and cooked. The evening is now approaching total darkness and a blood red sky streaks the western horizon. It has been a long day, Bryson thinks, as he finishes his meal. Then he stands from his spot near the fire, with intentions to clean his dinnerware before turning in. It is at this moment that he feels something watching him.

He turns toward the forest and thinks he sees a deepening within the land, something of a tall shadow slowly moving between two large trees. The fisherman blinks his eyes. He reaches down to his hip, gripping the can of bear spray attached to his belt. He listens to the night, searching for the sounds of danger, the signs of a predator. Then he sees it again—the tall shadow—as it comes out of the trees and toward the light of the fire.

It is a sight Bryson cannot fully comprehend. He blinks his eyes several times and then, instinctively, draws his bear spray. But then, against the backdrop of a roaring noise, the darkness falls heavily onto his shoulders. And with a sudden, painful thump somewhere on his head, the day at last comes to a close.

• • •

Hours later, a full moon looms high in the black sky. There is a soft, steady wind that breathes across the lake, sending ripples and small waves to the western shores. A grunt from a bull moose escapes a distant marsh, a sound which is quickly taken over by a pack of wolves howling somewhere in the forest. Then the surrounding wilderness of Earl Lake falls once again into its eerie silence, a silence that lasts for quite some time. And it is in this stillness of the night where another sound is suddenly born... as if the silence itself is the mother of such noise.

The sound is a single unseen scream of terror, a lengthy shriek of pain and fright that descends from high up a canyon, echoes down onto the lake and the surrounding shoreline, until it then fades away into the hollow darkness of the night.

PART 1

CHAPTER 1

Sam Nolan spent ten minutes eating a breakfast of jerked venison and black coffee before stamping out his fire and striking camp. He packed his sleeping bag, a few tools, utensils, and food into his rucksack. Then he strapped the pack onto his shoulders and headed out. Only five miles to go, but he was feeling anxious. He hoped to get to his mailbox in time to see the package delivered.

Sam knew the mail came early. And he rarely got to see who dropped it off—although he usually knew who did it. Most of the time there would be a note left on the outside of the box by one of the ranch hands who worked for his dad—Jim or Mason—with some wisecrack comment about Sam, comparing him to Grizzly Adams or whatnot. And often, beside the note, a can of chewing tobacco, which Sam understood to be a reminder of good times and pleasant conversations.

But as for today...

Well, today seemed different. There was a "somehow" or a "something" lingering in the air. A feeling Sam couldn't quite pin down. A notion somewhere in the back of his mind, or perhaps a vague whisper on the wind, pushing through the trees. Maybe it was his gut instinct. But something was speaking to Sam, telling him there would be an unexpected outcome to this day. Oddly, he suspected this had to do with seeing his mail get delivered.

It would be a novel moment for him. In the last four weeks, Sam had only seen three other people, all of whom he'd spotted in the far distance and through high-powered binoculars. More so, he hadn't spoken to another human in close to six months. Not that he didn't enjoy mixing with good company from time to time. But as it stood, Sam wasn't sure if he was ready for such challenges just yet.

He strode his way along a hillside dotted with mesquite and Douglas fir. The morning was bright and early, with the sun peeking over the crest of a distant mountain. He was somewhere deep in the Gila, America's first official wilderness and the state of New Mexico's largest, comprising over five hundred thousand acres of pristine backcountry. With the surrounding Gila National Forest, the place Sam presently called his home was a desolate area of well over two million acres.

It was a home he had learned to love, as a kid while growing up, and then later, as a young man, through various activities such as hunting, tracking, and exploring. It was a home he kept coming back to despite all the other places he'd lived throughout the world. To Sam, the Gila was his safest bet, the one place that had never failed him. The place he could always trust.

He followed along the hillside for a quarter of a mile, then descended into a canyon still shrouded by morning shadows. As always, the air was dry, crisp and clean, and it smelled almost as if rain was on the horizon. There were soft noises on the land, the sound of small critters moving, the diligent breakdown of wood. And in the distance, somewhere in the trees, the occasional fall of a dead branch.

When Sam reached the bottom of the canyon, he found a creek. He walked the water's edge for a few miles, stepping carefully across boulders and loose rock, knowing that a broken ankle was one of the many things that could end a person's existence out here. In the hour he spent picking his way down through the creek, he found evidence of several big animals, including a bobcat, deer, and elk. Later, he noticed the scratches of a large cinnamon bear on the bark of a pine tree—huge gashes that had torn clean through to the tree's phloem.

These tracks, markings, signs, and other features of the forest were natural sights for Sam. As a young man, he earned money honing his craft as a tracker, coming out here to find the various predators that had gotten too comfortable around people. Mountain lions, bears, gray wolves, and coyotes—Sam had tracked and hunted them all. Then, years later, as a United States Army sniper and Green Beret working overseas, he got paid for hunting a different animal...

Curiously, Sam wondered what would be in the mail. Other than the typical freeze-dried rations, sometimes his mom packed something from his childhood, such as a toy or a photograph. Undoubtedly, this was her attempt of trying to entice Sam to come down from the mountains and back home to the ranch.

Besides food, the mail usually consisted of practical items, such as ammunition, matches, the occasional book, and an assortment of first aid equipment. None of these were items Sam truly needed, considering his skills. But they were conveniences he appreciated. Also, the mail was a form of communication, which everyone appreciated. When a new package got delivered to replace the old one, which had invariably been picked up, the message stood plain and clear: Sam was doing okay. And if the previous care package was still in the "box," then that too was a message: Sam wasn't okay.

At the end of the canyon, red and orange sandstone and a scattering of ponderosa pine surrounded Sam. The smell of the forest floor, littered with pine needles, was refreshing. It was an odor that would grow stronger by the week as the drying months of summer made their way to fall.

He climbed up to the crest of the next ridge, a plateau overlooking a long valley of grama and bluestem grass, as well as the dirt road the mailman would travel on. It was a good five hundred foot increase in elevation, and when he reached the top, he stopped to catch his breath. The partially clouded sky loomed ominously above him, and in it was a red-tailed hawk, circling.

Sam took his pack off and hung it on the branch of a juniper tree. From his belt, he unclipped his binoculars and draped them over his neck. Then he drank water from a military canteen. The water was runoff he'd collected from a waterfall earlier, and it was still cold, and tasted pure.

He left his pack and walked twenty yards to the edge of the plateau, where he sat down and leaned against the flat side of a large boulder. It was a comfortable spot, a place he'd sat many times before, and immediately his mind pondered his much needed preparations for the months ahead.

Winter in the Gila Wilderness could be brutal, but Sam had endured it several times already. The acquisition of food and fuel for burning was his highest priority. When the nasty weather came, and it always did, more often than not, he would get shut in his cave for days, if not weeks, at a time. Without a stockpile of the essentials, his winter would be most uncomfortable. A bull elk would be more than enough for sustenance. Sam planned on taking one when the time got closer. But since cutting firewood was a never-ending chore, he'd get back to that as soon as possible.

A flicker in the distance caught Sam's attention. He looked through the binoculars and immediately recognized the red pickup truck from his family's ranch. He lowered the binoculars and retrieved a can of Skoal from his jacket pocket. Slowly, he opened the can, pinched off a wad of tobacco and tucked it under his lower lip. As the truck approached, with a trail of dust kicking up behind it, Sam looked again through the binoculars.

When the truck came to a stop, Denali, an Apache who'd been a friend of the Nolan family since long before Sam was born, stepped out from the passenger side. He was in his late sixties and crotchety as an old buffalo. But he was a dear friend.

It had been Denali who taught Sam and his brothers everything they needed to know about the land. He had taught them about the

Apaches, too, along with *their* ways of survival. Even the cave Sam presently called his home was a secret introduced to him by the old man. Denali claimed the shelter had once been the hideout for Geronimo and his band of Chiricahua warriors. Given the cave's natural concealment from wandering eyes, Sam believed it.

Located high up the side of a rocky outcrop, shrouded by a forest of ponderosa and mahogany, and obscured by a natural, flat slab of stone, the entrance to the cave was impossible to spot by accident. To reach it meant navigating through a maze of boulders and hollows and an all but hidden trail through a thicket of brush. Finally, upon reaching the cave's entrance, a person had to lie flat on their belly and crawl twenty feet through a small fissure in the mountain's side. It was the perfect hideout. And for as long as Sam had known about it, the cave had remained a secret.

Old Nali, out here dropping off the mail...

It was a surprise for Sam. But not as surprising as what came next.

He focused his binoculars on the person climbing out of the driver's side, who was the other influential man from Sam's life. And that man was his father, Thomas Wayne Nolan.

Sam watched as the two men meandered about, as if they weren't all that sure what to do. Then his dad pulled a small burlap bag from the back of the truck and carried it roughly twenty feet away, to a cluster of boulders surrounded by desert willows—which was, of course, Sam's mailbox.

There was a thick steel chain staked into a boulder, and connected to the chain, by a padlock, was a large metal container. Sam watched as his dad kneeled down and opened the container, then placed the burlap bag into it. Then he shut and locked the box once again. When he stood, he was slow to move, and there was a ripple of frustration on his face. The old man looked up into the hills and blinked his eyes, something Nali was doing as well, and Sam knew then that both men were looking for him.

He thought he should stand up and wave his arms, perhaps yell out, but they were several hundred yards away, and might not see or hear him. So he hesitated for a minute—a minute too long—and then watched as Tom and Nali climbed back into the truck, turned around, and drove away.

. . .

Twenty minutes later, Sam was at his mailbox. He was curious... damn curious. He should've stood and tried to get their attention. But they didn't wait very long, so maybe they were only out here for the drive. In any case, if there was anything of great importance Sam needed to know, there'd be something in the mail about it. He made a mental note to open the bag later that day, after he settled down for the night.

He dropped his rucksack on the ground and withdrew a key from a chain around his neck, which he used to open the padlock on the steel box. Carefully, he pulled the burlap bag out and studied it for a moment. The bag wasn't the most practical container for his mail, but it had become a tradition by now. His mother had made the bags out of larger, green chile sacks, which she'd procured from vendors in the area. She knew Sam loved green chilies, and not just because they tasted wonderful. He enjoyed the long days spent processing the spicy, southwestern fruit—from the roasting to the peeling, and then the canning. And more than once, he'd equated the smell of chilies with the smell of home...

Sam was no fool. He knew these bags his mother made were another one of her ploys to get him to come back to the ranch.

Feeling a twinge of guilt, he grunted, then stuffed the bag into his rucksack. A minute later, with his mailbox now secured, Sam was on the trail once again and heading back into the mountains.

Taking a different route this time, he walked for about a mile on level terrain, through sage grass and scattered piñon trees, before coming to the foothills he would need to climb. The sky was a mixture of shattered clouds and patches of blue. There was a warm breeze blowing in from the southwest, which Sam thought might bring with it rain later in the day. Or this evening.

Gila weather was something Sam had learned he should prepare for, as it was unpredictable, even in the summer months. And sudden, bad weather, while in the mountains with no protection from the elements except for what was on your back or in your head, could be a death sentence for an unprepared person.

The greatest danger was hypothermia. That was the elusive enemy, which, as Sam knew from his experience with Search and Rescue, happened to seasoned hikers as much in the warmer months of the year as in the dead of winter. Hypothermia was the assassin of the wilderness.

He reached the foothills leading up to the many canyons, then casually scanned the land for signs of elk, knowing he would need to take one soon. The big animals came down from the mountains to graze on the rich grassland, and they often did that in the evening or early morning.

Already, he had walked several miles. It was midday, and the wind had picked up, bringing with it more clouds. The terrain had changed, and he was now surrounded by a thick forest of pine trees peppered with enormous granite boulders. To his left was a running creek, and across from that, a wide meadow. It was in places like this where Sam found arrowheads while exploring as a young boy. He was reminiscing about that then, when he suddenly heard a loud *boom* off to his left.

There was no mistaking it; the sound was from the firing of a high-powered rifle. Sam froze in his tracks. Then, slowly, he moved forward, putting a tree between him and where the sound had come from. He waited, knowing that whoever had fired the shot might do so again, assuming they were simply target practicing.

Sam thought about that. He was way too far up in the hills to run across someone plinking cans. Also, the nearest access road was several miles away. He wondered if the shot had come from a lost hiker, perhaps up here scouting the area for a future hunt.

He walked further uphill and then spotted two tire tracks in the dirt, roughly three feet apart—tracks made by a quad-runner. Ten feet away was another set and, squatting down, Sam studied them. He quickly determined the direction in which the riders had traveled... which was the same area the gunshot had come from.

Sam wondered who was out here, driving quads. Quads that, oddly enough, he had not yet heard.

Again, he considered the possibility that some people were scouting the area for future hunting grounds. But then he heard more sounds, quite distant, yet distinct enough to decipher: a dull, animalistic growl, followed by laughter, and then... another loud boom.

Now Sam knew who he'd come across. And it made his blood boil.

He took a minute to think about what he should do—as he was *going* to do something. Deliberately, he scanned the area, observing the terrain, the topography, memorizing landmarks and peculiarities—things he would need to know should he have to find his way back here.

Spotting a cluster of pines near a fallen tree, he quietly walked over and set his rucksack down. He draped his binoculars around his neck, then retrieved a length of parachute cord from his rucksack and stuffed it into his pocket. Then he hung his rucksack on a tree and headed uphill, toward the direction of the sound.

He stalked through the forest for approximately a hundred yards before turning and going downhill. He heard more laughter, and it was closer now, so he moved toward an outcropping of large boulders. As he approached the outcropping, he crouched low and continued to keep his body in line with a tree. When he made it to the boulders, he got flat on the ground and slowly crawled up the short embankment, cresting the top of the highest rock.

His view was now complete. And with the binoculars, he saw every detail within the small meadow. Off to his left, and under the cover of the trees, were the quads. Sam studied the vehicles through the binoculars. Each was outfitted with stealth exhaust systems, devices that effectively muffled the mufflers. Then he observed the two men, both of whom were wearing a combination of denim and old issue, woodland camouflage clothing. They were hunched over an enormous bear—a *dead* bear—and one of them was working at the creature with a long knife.

Sam clenched his jaw. He surveyed the area, looking for points of concealment, points of access, as well as features he could take advantage of. Along with his jaw, he clenched his hands. He knew his time was limited.

Looking back at the quads, he estimated the vehicles were about thirty yards from the men. And he noticed that a cluster of shrubbery partially obscured them. Judging by the lay of the land, this would be Sam's best option.

Slowly, he crept away from the boulder, then retraced his footsteps back the way he'd come. He cut across the hillside, dropped into a deep arroyo, and followed it downhill for about a hundred yards. Then he cut back across the hillside once again.

In a low crouch, Sam crept toward the quads. Spotting a hand-sized rock on the ground, he picked it up as he moved forward. From beyond the cluster of trees and shrubbery, he could see the shoulders of the knife-wielding man, still working away at the bear. There was a foul odor on the wind, which Sam recognized as coming from the dead creature.

He gripped the rock firmly in his hand and stepped past the quads, toward the clump of shrubs. He looked through the leaves. Both men had their backs to him. They were now less than ten yards away—a quick sprint at best, but maybe not even that. He looked for the rifle, saw it leaning against a tree, out of reach of the other man, who was presently squatting down and holding open a plastic bag. Then, as the man with the knife tossed something into the bag and turned back toward the bear, that's when Sam made his move. He stalked out into the meadow, not once taking his stare off the two poachers.

The man with the knife was grunting as he worked while the other man sat motionless. They still had their backs to Sam. The sun was high and in front of him as he crept forward with the rock raised to his ear.

As Sam finished crossing the last yards through the meadow, the man with the knife stood straight and turned a shoulder, glanced to his left, then spotted Sam. The man's eyes sharpened with alarm. But he was out of time.

Sam was a tall, lean man, with broad shoulders and a back built strong from years of working on the ranch. His narrow face was deeply hidden under facial hair, but his eyes, intelligent and hawk-like, bore down on his prey.

In one quick, solid blow, Sam stepped forward and swung the rock across the man's jaw, dropping him fast, like a bag of sand. The other man stood and turned swiftly, caught by surprise. Sam reached out, grabbed him by the lapel, and smashed his forehead into the man's face. There was a dull, crunching sound, followed by a painful moan. Then the man was up and off his feet, high in the air, as Sam took him by a shoulder and below the knee, swept him up and over the back, and slammed his body roughly onto the ground, knocking both wind and consciousness right out of him.

Ten seconds of violence and it was all over. Quickly, Sam took the rifle that was leaning against the tree, then searched the two men for other weapons. He threw their knife into the plastic bag containing their trophies from the bear.

It was a sad scene, the results of which Sam was well familiar with. He had come across it in the past: a sprung bear trap containing a mutilated carcass, bereft of gallbladder, and sometimes paws and teeth. And often, for bait, as it was on this day, a few dozen donuts scattered across the ground. Sam had come across this type of evidence more than once, but never had he caught poachers in the act.

While looking for more weapons, he found a roll of Duct Tape inside a daypack, lying on the ground beside a tree. He used the tape to bind the men's hands behind their backs. Then he dragged their unconscious bodies over to the quads.

He used his parachute cord and secured each man to a quad, binding ankles and wrists together, and then their bodies to the vehicles. Then he took the plastic bag containing their bear trophies and placed it on the ground between the men. They had come around before he was done, and although groggy and confused, both men soon began to protest their situation.

"What are you gonna do, leave us out here? You're not gonna kill us, are you?"

Sam didn't reply. He took their gun, a .30-06, Bolt-Action Rifle, and relieved it of its ammo, which he put into one of his pockets. Then he searched the rest of their gear, and from another daypack strapped onto a quad, he found a Glock, 9mm handgun, with an extra magazine, fully loaded. He took all the rounds from that gun as well.

"So what's your plan, mister? You can't just leave us here?"

Again, Sam didn't respond. From the daypacks he found more rifle ammo (which he kept), a pair of two-way radios, car keys and water bottles, cell phones, two wallets containing driver's licenses, a bag of beef jerky (which he also kept), three marijuana joints, and a crinkled up map of the area. Finally—and best of all—he found a handheld, DeLorme Satellite Messenger unit, complete with GPS tracking system and personal emergency transponder.

Sam held the DeLorme in his hand and walked over to the men. He pressed the red SOS button on the unit, held it down until a distress beacon was activated, pinging their position to the nearest emergency responders. Then he hung the instrument high in a tree, within eyesight of the poachers.

"What the fuck, dude! You've got to be kidding!"

Sam took one last scan of the area before preparing to leave. Then he squatted in front of the men.

"You know," he said, "people go missing out here. And most times, they aren't ever found. Best keep that in mind if you think about poaching these woods again." He stood and walked away, but then hesitated. "And if it were me... which it wouldn't be... I'd be praying the law gets here before another one of them bears does."

They hollered for him to come back for a long while, but soon Sam was out of eyesight and out of earshot. He had his rucksack once again and was heading back up the canyon.

The wind had kicked up. And the sky had turned a dark, granite gray color. There would be rain tonight, and already Sam could smell it in the air. It would be a brief storm, he figured, as such storms often were during the summer months in the Gila. But the storm could be a strong one for the duration of its short temper and could bring with it a cold downpour.

He headed for a known shelter, a deep stony crevice in the side of a mountain, beside a stream. He'd camped there a few times in the past, the last being when he was a young man while working as a mantracker with the local Search and Rescue, and attempting to find a lost hiker. They had found that hiker the next day; but, and as it had often happened in the wilderness, they were too late. The elements had killed the man, who had been an experienced individual, but apparently not experienced enough to withstand the difficulties that came with being lost. The incident had happened in September and was something Sam had seen before, would see again. Something he knew all too well.

When he reached the rocky alcove, he was tired and hungry. He built a fire at the edge of his shelter, just out of reach of the storm's brunt, and the burning wood shed flames that were warm and comforting. From time to time, the fire released a loud *pop* or hissing sound, which was the pine sap being ignited. And that, too, was comforting to him.

He ate a dinner of rice and beans with strips of dried venison. Then he drank a cup of tea and climbed into his sleeping bag, studying the fire as it flickered, smelling the wood as it burned, and listening to the rain as it fell...

In less than ten minutes, Sam was out cold, and he never even opened his mail.

. . .

At daybreak, the forest reminded Sam of all that came with a brand new day. The sun had yet to rise above the mountains, but the sky was a glorious tapestry of indigo and orange. The forest floor spoke peacefully with its small sounds, typical after a hard rain. In the distance was the constant trickle of the stream, the sound of water tumbling over stone. The birds were alive, and their cheerful songs rang in every direction. Like all new days, the morning carried with it a promise of new beginnings, and Sam hardly missed the notion. He had put his thoughts from yesterday away, and was pondering now, with steadfast eagerness, his preparations for the coming winter—a winter that was still months away.

He rekindled the fire and made coffee, then cooked oatmeal with dried berries, and ate his breakfast slowly, observing the magical solitude of the forest. Since Sam was a kid, Nali had preached to him about the healing properties of the wilderness. The old man often said there was powerful medicine with being alone in the wild; and that, for all people, when they were in a place like this, they were in their rightful home. Sam had never known a time when he disagreed with those words of wisdom from the old Apache.

The morning was slow, and despite his eagerness, he wasn't in much of a hurry to get going. The cave was only a few hours away, and he would have the entire day to get there. He thought about his mail and, wondering, pulled the burlap bag out of his rucksack. The bag seemed to weigh over twenty pounds, a heavy load for the mail, yet not necessarily a bad sign. The more the weight, the more Sam had to look forward to.

With his knife, he cut the sack open at the top and dumped the contents gingerly onto his sleeping bag. Most of what poured out were various food items. There were several packages of freeze-dried meals, homemade, and undoubtedly by his mother. He counted a dozen of his favorite breakfasts as well—also freeze-dried, made by Mountain House, and of the scrambled egg and ham variety. In addition to the meals was a package of vacuum sealed cookies, a plastic bag of nuts and dried fruits, rice, pasta, two pounds of coffee, half that amount of sugar, a ration of salt and pepper, and four cans of SPAM. Combined, the bounty was easily enough food to keep something in his belly for at least a month, if not more.

Besides the provisions, Sam found a book of New Mexico poetry and two short story collections, each by authors he had not heard of. Sticking out from one collection was a long envelope addressed to him.

He pulled the envelope out and opened it. Inside was a single piece of paper with only a brief message, handwritten in large print...

Bryson is missing. Come home, Sam.

CHAPTER 2

Bryson woke into a darkness so complete he could not see his hand in front of his face. He woke to the sound of water dripping onto something hard, something like stone, with the sound coming from a short distance away, and from further into the darkness surrounding him. Bryson woke to the smell of a cold wetness, of earth and mildew, and the odors of a forest floor. He was in a cavern, perhaps a cave, and the air was stale and damp and still as the night.

He also woke to a blaring headache and a pain that shot down his spine and into his legs. He was wounded badly, of this he knew. He inspected his head with his hands, felt a warm swelling on his forehead and the caked remnants of blood on his face. Bryson took inventory of the rest of his body, noticing his boots and socks were missing, along with his coat. He was wearing only his long-sleeved flannel and a pair of pants. He had nothing else on him and certainly no tools of any kind. His pocketknife was gone and so was the bear spray and whatever else he might have had stored in his pockets.

He tried to remember what had happened to him, but thinking about that was like the stoking of a fire, as it reignited the pain inside his head. He remembered standing in his camp at night. And he remembered the noise of something moving in the forest, something beyond the firelight, a tall shadow creeping out from the blackened woods.

Bryson also remembered there was something dreadful about that shadow. Something menacing and... impalpable.

It seemed like a beast out of a nightmare. He couldn't quite figure it out. But then again, maybe he was wrong. Maybe the wound on his head had him imagining certain things.

Although, how did he get where he was now?

He was lying on a ground of sand and packed dirt. He felt around with his hands and found small pebbles and bits of wood, a few patches of wet earth, perhaps some clay. Lying still for a while, he listened to his surroundings. There were no sounds other than the constant dripping and trickling of water. Then he stood, albeit carefully, as he still couldn't see anything. The blackness was so deep and overpowering.

He moved slowly, searching the invisible space in front of him with his hands, taking small inspecting steps with his feet, walking like a blind man. Eventually, he found a stone wall, a part of which was wet and slimy, as if covered with black algae. He moved onward, using the wall as guidance, and he did this for quite some time, his feet finding nothing other than soft sand, his hands finding nothing other than hard rock.

Roughly thirty minutes later, Bryson came across the wet and slimy surface once again. He sank to the ground then, thoroughly confused, thoroughly in pain, and with his thoughts wracking endlessly over his situation. It seemed he was trapped inside a cavern with no way out.

CHAPTER 3

Hidden Creek Ranch was located a few miles northeast of Silver City, along the eastern foothills of Pinos Altos Mountain. Consisting of thirty thousand deeded acres, most of which was rangeland, the cattle ranch had been in the Nolan family for over one hundred years.

The business of ranching had spanned across several generations of Nolans, with the first rancher being that of Sam's great-great-grandfather, the audacious and enterprising Orrin James Nolan.

Orrin had settled in this part of New Mexico when two bigger ranches from the area were fighting over water and grazing rights. It was a move that put Orrin right in the middle of a deadly range war. But through shrewdness of the mind and a quick-firing gun, he had put so much hurt on those other ranchers that it forced them to come to the table and sign a compromise.

There would be little rest for Orrin, though. With the northern end of his ranch bordering on what is now the Gila Wilderness, the Apaches had been quick to bring him his next war. By his own hands, the rancher had hunted and killed many Chiricahua and Mimbreño warriors, for the sake of defending his life or that of his stock. Yet none of these deaths had ever sat right with Orrin. His opinion of the Native American was unusual for the time, because he understood what they were fighting for.

The Apache tribes respected courage and skill, and more than once, Orrin had demonstrated each of these talents in his war against his enemies. So when he traveled alone one day, high into the mountains, hoping to treat with the native warriors, his foolish bravery bought him more than he expected. Not only did he keep his scalp, but the Apaches had accepted his terms of peace—terms which included an annual allotment of beef for their people along with a host of other provisions. In exchange, the warriors would let bygones be bygones and honor a conditional ceasefire with the rancher. It was a deal both sides would find profit from.

Sam thought about the Apache in his life, Denali, as he walked the last stretch of his trip back to the ranch—a trip which he'd started immediately after finding the note regarding his brother. He was presently walking along a ridgeline, coming down from the north, and had less than a thousand yards to go before stepping through the front door of his family's hundred-year-old ranch-house.

A silver moon rode low in the night sky, like a bright eye gazing down upon the land. It cast a soft whiteness on the surrounding terrain, easing Sam's navigation through the hills. It was a pleasant evening, accentuated by his thoughts of spending time with his family and friends. Despite his preference for living a hermit's life, he looked forward to catching up on old times and continuing past conversations.

There was something peaceful and deliberate in the air. With each advancing step, Sam felt a touch closer to a world of familiarity. Less than a hundred yards now, and that's when he heard the dogs coming. The three mutts, each a mixture of Labrador, Collie, and Sheppard (the best ranch dogs money could buy) came barreling through the night, detecting Sam long before he would reach the house. Bixby, Charlie, and Lady were coming in fast, growling and barking at first, but then yipping and howling once they recognized Sam's scent.

He was delighted to see them. He realized they were, too. It had been three years since Sam had last been here, and he was surprised to find that they were all still alive. Ranching made for a hard life on the dogs, but damn if they didn't love every minute of it.

They howled and barked and ran in circles all the way to the house. And by the time Sam had crossed those last hundred yards, he knew somebody would be outside, shotgun in hand, checking on what all the commotion was about.

He approached the main driveway, a gravel road with a wide turnaround at the house, and saw that the front door was open. There was light spilling out into the night. He also saw a shadow cutting the light, and, judging by the outline, knew right away that it was from his older brother, Matt.

Crossing the last twenty yards, Sam was about to call out to his brother, but then saw a sudden movement off to his left, a distinct shadow stepping out from behind a small oak tree. Sam froze in his tracks.

"Known you'd come tonight."

Sam stared at the shadow. "Did you, now?" he said. The dogs were still howling and running about, and from the house, his brother shouted for them to calm down. "And why's that?" Sam added. "Why tonight?"

There was a pause and then the shadow replied, "The sky. It told me this."

Sam chuckled. "Get over here, old man." He threw an arm around Nali and gave the Apache a strong hug. "Why in the hell are you always speaking in riddles?"

They shared a laugh, then walked toward the house. As they approached the door, Matt stepped forward to greet Sam, and then the brothers clasped hands and hugged. Matt looked and acted every bit the same since Sam had seen him last, meaning he still had his cowboy hospitality and genuine smile.

"Damn hermit," Matt said. "It's about time you came down off that mountain."

"Well, I'd been missing Ma's cooking so much, thought I was beginning to smell it up there in the hills."

"Get in here, then. We've already eaten, but I'm sure there's something you can scrounge up."

They walked toward the house and Sam took a second to observe the family home, the place he'd spent most of his life. At one hundred years old, the ranch-house had seen its share of accommodations and add-ons. The original layout was a classic, Spanish style single story rambler with a low gable roof, modest kitchen, and two bedrooms. A bathroom had been the home's first addition and was added in the nineteen hundreds. Since then, the house has seen the addition of another bathroom, expansion of the kitchen, and four more bedrooms. Although the rambler remained a single story, the final layout was that of a U-shaped design. It had been and always would be a comfortable home for the family. A home Sam would never forget.

He walked into the house and was greeted with an immediate hug from his mom, Ruby Nolan, a small woman with a cheerful demeanor.

"I've missed you, my son," Ruby said. "Oh, how I've missed you."

"I know, Ma," he replied. "I've missed you too."

Tom hugged him next, and Sam noted the look on his dad's face. It seemed as if the man's happiness at seeing his son was being overshadowed by something much more serious. Sam knew exactly what that something was. He felt another twinge of guilt, this time for the pain and worry his family had clearly been going through.

"So what's this about Bryson missing?" he asked.

Ruby and Tom shared a look, a look Sam didn't miss.

"Come and eat some food, son," Tom said. "We'll tell you all about it. Just know this," he added, then hesitated, as if searching for the right words, "... it ain't... Well, I guess it ain't what you'd expect."

Sam set his rucksack on the floor of the main room, up against a wall and out of the way, then went to the bathroom to wash up.

When he came back into the dining area, there was a high level of commotion in the house, now coming from Matt's four children instead of the dogs. The kids were in their pajamas and excited, running from one room to another, all with electronic devices in their hands. It was a level of noise Sam hadn't heard in over three years. And one he knew would only get louder once more people showed up.

There was a guesthouse down the road which put up the two ranch hands, Mason and Jim. Sam figured those boys would arrive soon enough if they were around. It wasn't too late yet, and he heard his brother talking about Sam's arrival with one of them on the phone.

Sam took a seat at the long dining table and stretched his legs. He felt tired and sore, and was eager for a shower and some sleep. Seconds later, his mother brought him a bowl of beef stew and a slab of bread with butter, along with a warm piece of apple pie. She sat in the chair next to him and just smiled, her hand resting on his shoulder.

Sam ate his food while attempting to ignore the cacophony of noises surrounding him. He noticed the interior of the house, how it had changed very little over the years, except for the addition of various toys scattered here and there. Two of Matt's girls kept running over and hugging him while giggling obnoxiously, almost as if he was part of some game they were playing. It was hard for Sam to give the children the attention they were seeking, as he was busy eating and also trying to remember their names. The social blunder left him feeling guiltier than ever.

The main dining hall was the largest room in the house, but it seemed cramped with the ten-foot long teak table sitting in it. The piece of furniture was an antique, hand-crafted in 1861, the year the Civil War had ended. Similar pieces of furniture, all just as rustic, lay about the house, adding to the home's cozy bucolic appearance. To Sam's left was a massive stone hearth with a steady fire crackling away at the wood inside. Many times he had sat right there, next to the fire, drinking hot coffee while thinking the hours away. The last time, as he now remembered, Bryson had been sitting with him. Both on leave, they were debating the strengths and weaknesses of the Army and Marines, as well as their feelings about enlisting, which they had done shortly after 9/11. It had been a good conversation...

Sudden screaming coming from the children shattered Sam's fond memory. Apparently, there was an argument going on over who would get to show their uncle how to play a certain video game. Matt's wife, Cara, added to the ruckus by hollering back at the kids, scolding them for their unruly behavior.

Just then, Mason walked into the room with Jim not far behind. They came forward and shook Sam's hand, then started asking what felt like a hundred questions. They wanted to know how he was and what he was up to and if he had seen any trophy-sized elk while living up in the Gila.

Matt joined in the conversation by bringing up something he'd heard recently. "Ran into a park ranger last night. Told me about some poachers they found tied up in the woods against their quads." Matt's grin was a mile wide. "I don't suppose you know anything about that, little brother?"

Sam shrugged his shoulders, then took another bite of his stew, trying his best to block out all the noisy stimulation. He glanced at Nali and his father, both men now sitting across the table from him. They were quietly observing the inside of their cups. Then his mother, sitting to his side... she leaned her head on his shoulder and Sam felt she was holding back one long and painful cry.

That was the last straw.

"Alright, already!" Sam hollered, his deep voice at once silencing the chaos of the room. "Someone tell me what the hell happened to my brother."

• • •

The next morning, Sam, Matt, Tom, and Nali were sitting outside on the veranda, drinking coffee. The three ranch dogs accompanied them, and were each sprawled out on the wooden decking. It was less than an hour past daybreak and the western sky was layered in fiery bands of orange scarlet. Thick gray clouds sat heavy on the southern horizon, slowly rumbling forward like stone giants advancing across the land. Somewhere in the grass beyond the house, a quail chirped, and mourning doves were lamenting in a distant cottonwood. Two *ristras* hanging beside a nearby door kept the morning air ripe with the sweet smell of dried chilies.

"It doesn't make any sense," Sam said. "Not a damn word of it." The night before, he'd been briefed on the details of Bryson's disappearance and the subsequent search for the man. But it had gotten late, and Sam had a hard time wrapping his mind around the information. After a belly full of stew and his first hot shower in three years, it wasn't long before he'd fallen asleep. "And you talked to the officers on the case?" he added. "The Mounties?"

"We did," Tom replied. "We talked to them for a long while. And we even got a number and address for the Search and Rescue's lead man up there. A guy by the name of Andre McKinnon."

"What did he say?" Sam asked.

"Not much. Except for what we already told you. But it seemed to me..." Tom rubbed the whiskers on his chin, "it seemed there was something he *wanted* to say, but wouldn't."

"What do you mean by that?"

"Well," Tom replied, "I don't really know. If I had to speculate wildly, it seemed as if someone was with that man and pointing a gun to his head so he wouldn't say the wrong thing."

Sam clenched his jaw, then took a sip of coffee. He stared out at the horizon, contemplating. None of it made any sense to him. And because of this, naturally his mind was considering the prospect that his brother had become a victim of foul play.

"Did you ask if they had any escaped convicts up there?" Sam said. "Any wanted men in the area?"

"That's the thing," replied Matt, "there weren't *nobody* in the area. Not up there. From where Bryson went missing, the nearest spec of civilization is damn near thirty miles—and that's as the crow flies."

"What about gold miners?" Sam asked. "Any claims in the area?"

"Not sure," Matt replied. "But thinking about that, I don't really know what a miner would have against Bryson? He was just fishing the lake and scouting for moose, was all."

"And Jenny had no clue what happened to him?" Sam asked. "She wasn't aware of anything Bryson might have gotten mixed up in?"

"That's right," Matt said. "The girl was a broken wreck when I talked to her. I even invited her to come down to the ranch, but she said she couldn't take the time off from work or school. She swore Bryson hadn't been involved with anything illegal, though. That he had no enemies, for that matter. She didn't like it when I brought that up, I could tell. And neither did I. But I figured it was worth asking. I haven't seen Bryson in a while, so who knows what could have happened since then? That boy was always such a damn hothead. Maybe he did make him some enemies."

"I doubt it," Sam replied, considering the strength of his brother's character. He stood then, walked a few yards and leaned against a rail, his back to the sun. Bixby followed and then curled up on the deck next to his feet. "I wonder just how well they searched that area."

"I asked that Andre guy about that," Tom said. The old man's eyes squinted at the bright horizon. "I asked him if he searched it good—if he looked for sign, you know. I even asked him questions that only a good tracker could answer, just to see how much he did know... He did alright. But how could anyone really tell if they weren't up there himself?" Tom took a sip of coffee, then frowned. "And besides," he added, "they only searched for Bryson for three days. Three goddamn days. Hell, that wasn't but a fool's errand, if you ask me."

That might have been the most baffling detail of them all. It was definitely high on Sam's list of mysteries. He knew from his own experience that three days wasn't close to enough time to search for a missing person—in most cases, at least. Weather permitting, a SAR team, operating jointly with the local police, possibly Park Rangers if the incident occurred on public land, as well as volunteer personnel, could easily spend up to two weeks searching for a lost person. Two weeks or more.

So why then only three days?

Sam crouched and scratched Bixby's jaw, thinking hard on that detail. He looked up and caught Tom's stare. "Three days of searching... What did the SAR guy have to say about that?"

"Yeah," Tom said, "it was right about then when he started clamming up—like he was nervous about something. It seemed like he wanted to tell me more, but... well, he just wouldn't."

"Did you ask him if they had anybody else missing up there at the time?" Sam asked. "Someone with a high profile. A case like that would pull any search and rescue efforts away from Bryson."

Tom shook his head, then looked at his feet. "I'm afraid I didn't."

"No matter," Sam said. "I'll ask this Andre guy when I talk to him. And I'm going to find out why they only spent three days searching for my brother." He stood again, took a drink of his coffee, then rubbed his palm across the back of his neck. "Perhaps the weather was bad. But you asked about that, didn't you?"

"I did," Tom said, "and the guy told me it was alright. Nice weather, no storms of any kind."

"And there was no sign of an attack?" Sam said, confirming what he had been told the night before. "No sign of a struggle anywhere in the area?"

"That's what he said," Tom replied. "No bear or cougar tracks... No sign at all. Nothing, in fact. Not a *damn* thing..."

Sam pondered over the situation. Then he looked at Nali. The Apache was sitting in a rocking chair gazing up at the sky, his eyes focused on a distant cloud. The man's face was an atlas of weathered wrinkles, sun-baked and worn, a leathery map showing the passage of time and of life.

"Well, old man," Sam said loudly, "what the hell do you think about all of this?"

Nali stared at Sam, hesitated, then replied, "Same as you, *young man*. Everyone here knows that boy could never get lost up there, no matter how wild the land. And no bear or lion could get him, 'cause he was too good to let something like that happen. So what else is there?" He paused and looked back up at the sky. "But *something*..." he said, his voice now cryptic in tone. "Something supernatural, or... Something not right." Nali had everyone's attention then, as he looked back at Sam. "It is true: every man here knows that something *happened* to Bryson."

The old Apache was right. Sam knew his brother and of the skills he had. Like all the Nolan boys, Bryson had grown up on the ranch, which meant for a tough life. And like iron wrought by fire and anvil, the toughness that came from living in the Southwest had shaped their characters. The result was a hardening of mind and body, along with a vast world of knowledge. Adding to their upbringing, each had spent years learning how to live in the wilderness, which was right in their own backyard. The Gila Wilderness.

Nali had been instrumental in that part. He had taught the boys not only to survive in such a harsh landscape, but to *thrive*. They learned everything from the old Apache, from building shelters and making weapons to tracking and finding food. They learned how to stalk big game, and to hunt not just with a rifle, but with handmade bows, which they often crafted out of mulberry wood and elk sinew. The Nolan boys learned how to build animal snares, find potable water, and to identify which plants were good for eating and which ones to stay away from. And they learned how to read the wind and the sky for weather, and how to build a fire the old way, by rubbing two sticks together.

Sam smiled at that last thought. As a youngster, Bryson had the toughest time learning how to make a fire, and he would throw a fit and curse the ground whenever he failed at it. But eventually he got it down. And he got it down cold.

Sam suddenly looked up. "What chores need done around here?"

"*Chores?*" Matt replied, grinning. "Shit, you know how it is on the ranch. There ain't no end to our misery. But we'll be branding calves all day, since you asked."

"Has anybody ridden fence lately?" Sam asked. "I could use some time in the saddle."

"Mason did that a while back," Matt replied. "But that's a never-ending job, as you well know. You can ride it again, if you'd like. Might even check the northern perimeter where the bears come in at."

"Sounds like a good enough plan," Sam said.

"But why not take a quad?" Matt added. "It'll be quicker."

"No thanks," Sam replied, spitting over the deck rail and onto the dirt. "Those damn things make too much noise." He set his cup on a small table, then stepped off the porch. "Besides," he added, before walking to the barn, "riding horse gets a man thinking. And that's exactly what I need to do right now."

CHAPTER 4

Dee, a blue roan mare, was one of the best quarter-horses the ranch had. She was certainly Sam's favorite, as she liked to work hard and had a good temperament. She was also damn pretty, with a bluish-silver coat that shimmered in the daylight, as if a piece of moonlit night had escaped the dawn.

Sam was glad to see the horse. He was glad to be back on the ranch, despite his anxiety. He'd missed this place, along with the people and animals that ran it.

He saddled the mare and rode out, heading northeast along the creek, the sun in his eyes. In his saddlebags were fence tools and two roast beef sandwiches his mother had made earlier that morning. He also had a thermos of cold water and a fresh can of chewing tobacco in his pocket. If Sam rode fence until sundown, he would have no complaints whatsoever.

Two miles out, he passed the small cabin where Nali lived. Then he came across a deep hollow along the creek, with long green grass under a thicket of aspen trees. There were numerous coyote tracks peppering the mud near the water, and tufts of fur were strewn about, indicating that a raccoon or rabbit had met a violent end here. Sam got down from his horse and let the mare crop the fresh grass while he examined the area. He wasn't looking for anything in particular, just searching out of habit while his mind picked away at the details regarding his brother.

Too many things didn't add up. He thought about his brother's abilities and of the skills Bryson had honed throughout his life. Like Sam, after 9-11 Bryson had enlisted into the military. He'd joined the Marine Corps. and eventually served in the branch's elite unit, Force Recon. The man had spent years training in Special Forces, and he served two combat tours in the Middle East before entering back into the civilian world. But that was only the half of it.

After leaving the Marines, Bryson began a career as an independent tracker for wildlife organizations and hunting outfits throughout North America. He'd made a name for himself as one of the best grizzly trappers in the country, often stalking his prey for several days, as he gathered data regarding the animal's behavior before trapping it for researchers.

Knowing of his brother's skills, Sam couldn't believe that a large predator had gotten the drop on Bryson. Bears, cougars, wolves, and even moose were the most dangerous animals in the Yukon. Sam himself wouldn't think twice about sharing the wilderness with such creatures. But for Bryson, the time spent up there would have been just another stroll in the park. The man was too damn good to let a dangerous encounter occur, accidental or otherwise.

So what then had happened to him?

The weather had been decent, or so Sam was told. His brother had vanished less than three weeks ago, in the latter part of May—not a bad time of year up there. There might have been the occasional passing storm, but certainly nothing Bryson couldn't handle. He would've packed proper gear, no doubt about that. Moreover, if the weather had been a factor, Sam didn't see how this would have caused his brother to up and vanish. And to vanish without leaving a single trace of evidence?

It baffled Sam. In his mind, there were only two rational explanations for Bryson's disappearance. The first was that his brother had voluntarily left the area with plans never to come back. Other people had made similar journeys, stories of which Sam had read about. Free-spirited individuals such as Chris McCandless and

Everett Ruess, both of whom had gone into the wilderness hoping to escape the pressures of the civilized world... and where they spent their last breaths. Grimly, it occurred to Sam that he himself was not unlike these characters. Except that he, for the time being, was still breathing.

But what of Bryson? Did he, too, turn his back on society?

Sam didn't think so. That was something he would do—what he *did* do—but not his younger brother. Bryson was always full of life and vigor, always eager to be around his friends and family. He wasn't a loner and never had been. Even when life had beaten him down, as it does for everyone sooner or later, Bryson was quick to find healing amongst his loved ones. No... Sam was convinced there was nothing voluntary about his brother's disappearance. Nothing voluntary at all.

And that left the second explanation, which Nali had already pointed out. That something *happened* to Bryson. Something so inexplicable, so outrageous, and so effective, it made a human disappear without leaving a single shred of evidence.

Or did it?

Sam rode fence for most of the day, taking his time and thinking about his brother. He fixed one loose section where a small bear had obviously squeezed through. Then he checked the northeastern corner, along where a dirt road edged the property. He searched that area for signs of potential cattle rustling. Despite living in the twenty-first century, stealing cattle was still a common enough crime in the southwest. And it was a crime that was taken damn seriously in New Mexico.

By early evening, Sam was tired and so was Dee. He turned toward the ranch and rode easily on back. When he got there, he noticed the exhausted looks on the faces of Matt and the ranch hands. Sam knew they had had a tough day branding stock. The ranch used a contraption called a calf table, which required just a few men to operate, and was effective with the job of branding. But it was still tiring work. Calves are rarely cooperative with getting their hides burned.

"Sure could've used an extra hand today," Matt said. He was tossing rope and gear into the back of a truck, his body moving stiffly.

Sam gave his brother a big smile. "Yep," he replied, "I bet you could have."

"Well, did you fix anything while you were out there? Or did you just enjoy your ride?"

Sam chuckled, then climbed off Dee and walked her over to the barn. Coming from the house was the smell of dinner, beef and potatoes, or so he guessed. His mouth watered. But it would be some time yet before he ate. His first chore was to stall the mare, get her unsaddled and groomed, then check her feet for pebbles.

When he walked into the barn, Sam immediately understood he was not alone. He heard a woman talking to a horse, and she was using a soft, childlike voice. She was in a stall, her back turned to Sam. But as he approached, she turned around, and he recognized her.

It was Lolo-Tea (the Apache name for "Blessing of God") and she was looking as fine as ever. The woman's face betrayed her sudden surprise and elation at seeing Sam, but then she quickly composed herself.

"Hello, Sam," she said. "I heard you were around."

"Good evening, Lolo." Sam took off his hat and hung it on a wooden peg beside the door. Then he looked at her. "How've you been?"

She hesitated, then took a brush and started grooming Paul, a chestnut gelding. "I'm good. And you?"

"Well, things could be better," he said. "I'm sure you know about Bryson."

"Yes, I do." She looked away, putting her attention on Paul's coat. "I don't... I guess I don't really know what to say about that."

"What *is* there to say?" Sam said, leading Dee into the adjacent stall. "Although you could say it's strange—strange how Bryson, of all people, went missing."

"Well, I could also say that I'm sorry," she replied. "I'm sorry for what Ruby and Tom and the rest of you are going through."

Sam bit his lip, feeling suddenly guilty. He hadn't seen Lolo in three years, and this was hardly the way to rekindle old conversations or pleasant memories with the woman.

"So how's Flagstaff?" he asked, changing the subject. Then he smiled and said, "You married yet? A woman as fine as you wouldn't have any problems with that, I suppose."

She blushed, then feigned a reason to turn her back to him. "No, I'm not married, Sam. Not yet. But I do have a boyfriend... Sort of. Up in Flagstaff. Except... well, except that I'm not living there anymore."

"Is that so?" he said. "Any particular reason why?"

"I guess I just miss it here. I miss the ranch. And I miss my dad. He's getting old, you know. I'm not sure how much longer he has."

Her words sounded like excuses to Sam—excuses for something she was trying not to admit, even to herself.

"That old buzzard?" Sam said. "He's not going anywhere, Lolo. In fact, I wouldn't be surprised if Nali outlives us all."

Sam unsaddled Dee and groomed her, checking her back for dry spots or sores. Then he glanced at Lolo and smiled again. "I'm sure he'll at least wait around until he sees his only daughter tie the knot."

Lolo burst into laughter, and Sam knew it was out of embarrassment. She caught her breath and gave him a hug. "It sure is good to see you, Sam. It's real good."

"Likewise, Lolo," he said, pulling away and going back to grooming Dee. He hesitated, then added, "It's always good."

She put her hands in her back pockets and leaned forward, staring at him, smiling. "I will tell you one thing," she said, rather coolly. "The reason I'm not married yet is that I don't think I'm with the right man. Seems all the good ones are already taken... or living alone, up on some mountain."

Now it was Sam's turn to blush. He felt a ring of hotness around his neck and a weakness in his knees. His face grew serious, and he said, "You know there's a better man out there for you, Lolo."

She paused, as if letting the stretch of awkward silence burn a hole into his chest. "Alright then, stubborn cowboy. Be that way." Like Sam, she turned and went back to grooming her horse. And now she was the one who changed the subject. "So what's your plan, Sam Nolan? I mean... about your brother. Are you thinking of doing anything?"

The change in subject was a mild relief—until Sam thought more about Bryson. It was a hard case, his brother going missing. Like an arrow, the mystery struck Sam deep in his heart.

He knew the real reason his family had called him down from the mountains. It was a critical time of year for them, what with everyone busy tackling the demands of the ranch. And despite his personal reservations about... about people going missing and never returning home... Sam knew exactly what he was going to do. He knew what he had to do.

Sam set the grooming brush on a table and turned toward Lolo. "I sure am going to do something," he said.

"Oh? And what would that be?"

"I'm going up there, Lolo. I'm going up to the Yukon... And I'm going to find my brother."

CHAPTER 5

On the morning of his third day at the ranch, Sam was ready to leave. It was early, not yet daybreak, and he was sitting in a leather chair inside his father's study, drinking coffee and staring at all the volumes of books on the shelves. There were thousands of books in this room, some old and leather-bound, but many of which looked brand new. There were also many signed first-editions.

Tom Nolan was a major reader and a minor writer, and no matter what kind of lifestyle the ranch held for him, at the end of the day, he always had a book in his hands. He was also adamant about teaching his children the goodness found in such activity.

Sam appreciated this aspect of his father's character. Much about living on a ranch was a physical endeavor, with most duties being accomplished through hard labor. But his dad was aware of the importance of adding variety to his children's lives. One way he did this was by having them read books, knowing that many of life's problems demanded attention from the mind and less from the body.

Sam had been using his mind for three days now, and he was still using it when his dad walked in, a fresh cup of coffee in hand.

Tom sat in a chair next to Sam, put his cup on the desk, and retrieved an envelope from a drawer. Inside was a debit card, which he took out and gave to his son. "This will pull from ranch funds," he said, "so use it whenever you need to. And you use it, *goddamnit*. We've got no time for your petty pride."

"Thanks, Tom," Sam replied, taking the card. Normally, he would hold serious reservations about taking anything from anyone, but this was a special case. This was a family affair, so he'd use whatever resources the family offered in order to... well, to complete his mission.

"And take the Chevy, also," Tom said. "The camper shell will come in handy in case you get stuck sleeping on the side of the road."

"I appreciate it, dad."

There was an awkward pause as both men drank from their cups. Then Tom looked up and said, "Just make sure you come back, son. You hear me? Make sure you come back."

"Yes, sir," Sam replied.

"I'm serious. It would break my heart if something happened to you, too. And your mother... well, that would outright kill the woman."

"Don't you worry, Tom. I'll be coming back."

They talked more about Sam's plan and he told his dad that yesterday he'd called that SAR guy, Andre McKinnon.

"He didn't pick up," Sam said, "but I left a message telling him I'm coming up there. And that I've got his address, so he can expect me sometime next week. Don't know if he'll be around, but I'll wait a bit."

Tom nodded, then said, "You sure you don't want a cell phone? You can get yourself one of those burners along the way, if you want."

Sam grinned. "A burner phone?" he said, chuckling. "Look at you, old man... speaking high tech, and up with the times."

"Look around, boy," Tom replied, gesturing to the surrounding books. "Have I ever been behind?"

"I hear what you're saying," Sam said. "But I'll pass, anyway. Besides, where I'm going, I don't think a burner phone will do me any good. I might pick something else up, though. Something a little more practical."

Sam drank his coffee, then added, "I figure I'll stop by and see Jenny. It's a little out of the way, but there might be something there worth looking into. Something about Bryson. It's hard to get everything from a person by phone."

"Sounds like a good idea," Tom replied. "She's up there by herself, you know. School and all. You let her know she's welcome back here anytime."

"I certainly will."

"Do you have everything you need for supplies?" Tom said.

"Probably not. But I'll figure that out on the way up."

"What about a gun? Those grizzlies up there are mighty big."

"I've got that .44 Magnum, which I'll bring."

"Get some bear spray, also," Tom said. "How long do you think you'll stay in the bush?"

"Until I find him," Sam said, "or the weather kicks me out first. But I figure I got at least a few months before that happens. And who knows," he added, with a grin, "maybe I'll just like it up there, and find me a spot to settle into for a while."

They talked for another hour, about Bryson and about the ranch, then they ate breakfast with the family at the long table in the dining room. No one was happy to see Sam leave, especially his mother and Lolo. But they all understood.

After he ate a breakfast of bacon and eggs, pancakes, and drank two more cups of coffee, Sam was ready to go. He gathered what remained of his stuff, which wasn't much, and put them in the Chevy. His mother had packed an ice chest full of food for him. That was something he'd enjoy, since he was never fond of eating out.

He said his goodbyes, which he tried to keep short, then proceeded to leave. He got halfway to the truck before Lolo intercepted him.

"Make sure you come back, Sam Nolan," she said.

"You can count on it, woman."

"Can I? Can I, really?"

"Have you ever known me to lie?"

She stepped forward, paused, and Sam saw a tear in her eye. Then she reached out and gave him a powerful hug. "Good luck, Sam," she whispered into his ear.

He hated goodbyes, and this one ranked more difficult than many others.

Sam let Lolo hug him for a time, but then he kissed her on the forehead and pulled away. Moments later, he was driving down the dirt road and toward the main highway. Looking into his rearview mirror, he saw them all standing there, watching him leave. And running fast behind the truck, as if to follow him all the way to Canada, were the three dogs, Bixby, Charlie, and Lady.

CHAPTER 6

"Being a sniper is about eliminating some type of conflict. Your entire purpose is to resolve a difference, and the sooner you realize this, boys, the sooner you will achieve complete mastery over your job..."

Sam remembered the words as he drove the long hours to Seattle. It was one of many speeches from his old Army instructor, Master Sergeant Joe Paxton.

Hailing from the Deep South, Louisiana, Paxton was a large African American with a background of religious and academic origin. His mother had been a schoolteacher and his father a Baptist minister. Paxton used big words and big concepts that sometimes went right over the heads of most candidates. But not Sam's. He enjoyed listening to his instructor, gleaning much wisdom from what the man had to say.

"Understand this," the speech continued, "when you enter into an operation, it is *you* against another man, or *you* against Mother Nature, or *you* against a machine. Many times, it's you against your own damn self... But when the shit hits the fan, and believe me, it will, it just might be you against God."

That one lecture had stuck in Sam's head as if the Master Sergeant had opened his skull and planted it there. He had never forgotten those words, and had recounted them many times throughout his life, almost every time he was up against a conflict, in fact.

For certain, Sam was up against a conflict now. But of which type, he wasn't too sure.

He thought about his current situation. To some degree, he would face Mother Nature once he got into the far reaches of the Yukon. There would be unfamiliar terrain and a different climate. But Sam didn't think these details would pose a real problem for him. And honestly, deep down, it was something he looked forward to.

Being back in society, though... Now that was something Sam never quite looked forward to; nor was he enjoying. But he knew this would be a short-lived conflict. Once he got himself up into the wilds of the Yukon, it would be all over, as there would be no more civilization.

Thinking about the situation, Sam eventually figured out where his major conflict would come from. And that was himself.

He drove for two and a half days, stopping at hotels to sleep and also at a few outdoor stores along the way, picking up the essential items he would need.

It had been a long drive, and he was looking forward to finishing it for the time being. With any luck, his visit with Jenny would provide him with some important details and potential evidence. Sam hoped this would be the case. In the unlikely event he discovered his little brother had gotten involved with the criminal underground, or owed money to a loan shark, or had become a victim of a love triangle, any of which could lead to an explanation to his disappearance, well... As much as Sam would hate that, it would certainly bring him one step closer to resolving this conflict.

• • •

Jennifer and Bryson lived in a small house in the town of Bothell, a few miles northeast of Seattle proper. Sam had talked to Jenny before he left the ranch and they agreed to meet for coffee to discuss more about his brother. It was early Saturday morning when he'd finally arrived. Jenny appeared to be exhausted.

Jenny was in the kitchen cooking breakfast for the two of them. She was wearing flannel pajama pants and one of Bryson's long sleeved hunting shirts. On her feet were soft-soled slippers, and her hair was wrapped up in a halfhearted bun.

Sam noticed a wavering look in her eyes, and a subtle vagueness in the way she moved. The woman seemed completely out of sorts, as if she was having a hard time focusing on even the simplest of things.

"Can I help with anything?" Sam asked.

"No, thank you." Jenny replied. "I should at least be able to fix us some breakfast. I need to do something, for Christ's sake."

When she finished plating their food, they sat at a small table next to a window overlooking a gravel driveway and a detached one-car garage. Running alongside the driveway was a thin strip of green grass, and on it were two clay Buddha statues. Outside, the sky was piled thick with clouds, but the morning sun had somehow broken through, shedding its golden rays onto the moist land. It was a peaceful setting, Sam thought, despite being so close to the hustle of Seattle.

"I don't know what I'm going to do," Jenny said. She nibbled the end of a piece of toast, then set it back down on her plate. She was looking just outside the window, but Sam knew her eyes were focused on something much further away. Jenny had that thousand-yard stare on her face. He had seen the same thing on so many others while stationed in the Middle East.

"I just don't know, Sam. I don't know what I'm going to do."

"You can come back to New Mexico, Jenny," he replied. "Your family would love to have you come back home, you know that. And so would mine."

Jenny looked up at him. "You say that as if Bryson is never coming back."

Sam felt uncomfortable. "I don't know, Jenny. I don't want to admit anything, but at this point—three weeks or so—well, it's not looking too good."

"I just don't get it," she said. "Why would he do this? Why would he go missing up there?" She took a short sip of coffee, then looked back out the window. "I can't concentrate on anything, Sam. I can't sleep or eat. I've been skipping my classes and my shifts at work. Since Bryson had gone… it's like my whole world has crashed down on me."

She started to cry, and then Sam reached out and gripped her hand. "I know it hurts, Jenny," he said. "It hurts real bad."

"Since high school, Sam," she continued. "We've been together since high school. And we were supposed to get married soon. He promised me that."

"I know, girl."

A few minutes of silence passed. Jenny took another small bite of toast and stared out the window. "You know what the worst part is?" she said. "The worst part, Sam, is that it feels like I have to deal with this all by myself. It feels like nobody else out there could give one damn bit about any of this. It's as if nobody knows he's gone, or even cares… except me."

"You know that's not true, Jenny."

"I know. But it feels like it. Living up here, by myself… People all around me are going to work, going to the stores, driving here and there, living their fucking normal lives. Everybody but me. I'm all alone. And this is how it feels when the person I love the most has gone missing… Bryson's never coming back, and no one can tell me why. It's the worst feeling in the world, Sam."

They were powerful words. Sam knew exactly how she felt—and in more ways than one. He suddenly thought about Lolo. He pictured her in Jenny's shoes, crying over the loss of someone she loved dearly. Sam wondered if Lolo, to some degree, had already been in that position and the thought sent a shiver of guilt through him. He had been selfish for the last few years with his stubborn solitude. Damn selfish.

"I want you to help me out, Jenny," Sam said, pushing his thoughts away. "I want you to think about the time before Bryson left, and after. Was there anything unusual you noticed? Anything at all?"

Slowly, Jenny shook her head. "I've tried, Sam. I've tried to figure this shit out." Just then, a buzzer rang from down the hall. Jenny looked at the noise, then put her hand over her face. "The dryer. You see... that's the first load of clothes I've done since he's been gone. I'm a wreck, Sam."

"What about at Bryson's job?" Sam continued. "Was he still working at that woodworking place?"

"Only part time. He didn't really care for it that much. But he never complained about it, either. Or about anyone from the place. Bryson was biding his time, hoping to get another tracking job with some researchers up in Alaska."

Sam nodded, then took a few bites of his breakfast. "And what about his friends or acquaintances? Anybody weird he might have been hanging out with?"

"Nope. There was no one." She pushed her plate away and leaned her elbows on the table. "And besides," she added, "he went up there by himself, Sam. I can't think of anyone who would've followed him up there, if that's what you're getting at?"

"I'm not sure what I'm getting at, Jenny," Sam replied. "I'm just trying to piece things together. Not for a damn minute do I believe Bryson fell victim to the hazards of the wilderness." He hesitated, then said, "But I suppose I could be wrong."

"I wish I could help, Sam," she said. "God, I wish I could help."

"There's just nothing at all you can think of?" he asked.

"Nothing," Jenny replied, shaking her head.

Then she looked back out the window, her stare once again a thousand yards out while Sam continued to eat his breakfast. A few minutes of silence passed, and then suddenly, very softly, Jenny said, "Wait a second..."

Sam looked up, his fork halfway to his mouth.

"There was something..." Jenny said. "Something odd."

"What was that?" Sam asked.

Jenny blinked, then pulled her eyes away from the window. "I got a phone call... a little over a week ago."

"From who?"

"A voicemail, actually. And I don't know who it was from. It was weird. I figured it was just a wrong number, except for..."

"Except for what?"

"Well, there wasn't a person on the line. There was just a noise."

Sam set his fork down and picked up his coffee. "What kind of noise, Jenny?"

"It was like... like water, or something."

"Any chance you still got that message on your phone?"

"I don't think so, but I'll check." Jenny stood and walked to the bedroom, then came back with her cell phone. She scrolled through her messages for a minute and then slowly set the phone on the table. "I must have deleted it," she said. "But it wasn't really anything. At least I didn't think so. Just water dripping into... well, more water, I guess. Sounds from a pool or something."

"That is odd," Sam replied. "And when did you say you got this phone call?"

"It was about a week after Bryson had been reported missing."

"It might be nothing..." Sam said, then added, "but do you know if Bryson had a satellite phone?"

"Oh, God, I wouldn't know that. He kept all his gear in there." She pointed her cup at the garage. "I never paid attention to what he took with him, Sam. I know I probably should have. It's just that he had so much gear. You know how it is. So I suppose it's possible he had some kind of phone like that." Then Jenny looked at Sam, hope swimming in her eyes. "Do you think that could have been him, Sam?"

Sam shook his head. "I don't see how that call would've come from Bryson. You'd think he would've said something, at least." He finished his breakfast, then drank the last of his coffee. "I've got to be going, Jenny. But I want you to seriously consider going back home. Even if it's just for a couple of days."

"You're probably right," she said, looking at her hands. "I'm not doing anything around here except slowly dying." She looked up, a slight gleam in her eye. "Do you think you'll find him, Sam?"

"I'm going to try, Jenny." Sam set his cup on the table and stood. "I promise you that. I will certainly try."

• • •

Thirty minutes later, Sam was on the road again, heading north towards the border. And then, beyond that, to the great unknown, lying somewhere deep in the wilderness of Canada's Yukon Territory. He had sixteen hundred miles left to drive and every mile would be a gorgeous one. From the lush greenery of the Pacific Northwest, to the rolling hills of inner British Columbia. Every piece of land along his route would be something worth noticing.

But for Sam, he was going to miss most, if not all of it. For the next couple of days, the only thing his thoughts would be focusing on was the pain in Jenny's eyes.

It was the same pain shared amongst the rest of his family. And it was the same pain that lingered deep inside Sam's heart.

CHAPTER 7

Carmacks, a speck of a town, sat deep in Canada's Yukon Territory, and had a year round population of less than a thousand people. Along the confluence of the Nordenskiold and Yukon rivers, the town was known for salmon fishing and the hunting of caribou and other big game. Its history contained larger industries though, such as the mining of gold and coal, as well as logging. And being in the heart of the taiga, a world of scattered boreal forests and thousands of small lakes and streams, Carmacks was one of the few towns in the entire Yukon to offer an adventurer easy access to the great outdoors.

It was late afternoon when Sam pulled into the small town. He thought little of it, other than where he could find a place to sleep for the night. He'd been sleeping in the back of the truck for a few days, and would soon spend an indeterminable amount of time sleeping in the wilderness. With that in mind, he was more than willing to spend the next night or two in a warm bed.

Sam checked into the Hotel Carmacks—the only hotel in town—then settled into his room. He ate a dinner of steak and potatoes at a local restaurant, and afterwards, took a hot shower. When he finished cleaning up, he called Andre McKinnon, the team leader for the local Search and Rescue unit.

Andre didn't answer, so Sam left a message stating where he was staying and that he'd like to meet him in the morning—early, if possible. Five minutes later, the phone in Sam's room rang. It was Andre.

"I got your message, Sam," Andre said. "Sorry... but I was busy outside."

Right away, Sam could tell by the tone in the man's voice that something was slightly off. Immediately, his thoughts went to what his father had told him about how it seemed Andre was holding back with something he wanted to say.

"Can you meet me in the morning?" Sam asked. "Let me buy you breakfast."

"No," Andre replied, "I mean, yes..." he hesitated, then added, "why don't you come by my place in the morning. I guess, um... well, anytime would be fine. I get up early, so don't worry. You got my address, right?"

"I sure do."

"Alright, then. I'll make us breakfast if you'd like."

Sam paused, then said, "I'll be over around eight."

"Okay," Andre replied. "We'll see you then."

After he hung up the phone, Sam sat on the bed, thinking. Tom was right: there was something this SAR guy wanted to get out. But the reigning question was what?

• • •

Andre McKinnon lived five miles north of Carmacks, off a pothole-infested dirt road, and within a stone's throw away from the mighty Yukon River. His house was a log cabin structure with a detached sheet metal carport wide enough to park two vehicles in, but of which was presently storing an assortment of crates, fifty-five gallon drums, a Bobcat tractor, and a rat's nest of rope and chain.

Next to the house stood another building, an old workshop or mother-in-law unit, with rustic-red siding and gray trim, and a faded brown door presently swung open. There were two Shepherd-mix dogs standing in the yard when Sam drove up. Both were barking viciously.

The surrounding premises looked like a small junk yard. Heaps of scrapped metal, old refrigerators, washers and dryers, and a few beat-up cars were scattered about. Three snowmobiles sat near the carport, all of which looked suspicious as to their functionality. And beside them was a covered all-terrain vehicle, splattered almost completely in mud.

Sam saw what looked like a drift boat stored underneath a tarp, and in the middle of the yard sat an old Ford F-150, with raised suspension and knobby off-road tires. Inside the vehicle was a gun rack, holding a Winchester lever-action rifle (your standard ranch gun, as Sam recognized it) along with a shotgun. Both items were essential for living out here in the vast taiga.

He parked his Chevy next to the truck, grabbed a notepad and pen along with some maps he'd brought, then climbed out. The two dogs ran over to him, baring teeth, but Sam ignored them. He walked steadily forward, toward the cabin, and that was when Andre opened the front door.

"Sookie, Backa!" the man shouted, adding a sharp whistle. "Come!" The dogs turned and ran over to the cabin, where they promptly sat down near the door, licking their chops and looking apologetic.

"I'm guessing you're Sam," Andre said.

"You're guessing correct."

They shook hands, then Andre led the way into the house. He was a short, stocky man, about forty years old, with wide shoulders and massive hands. His demeanor was cordial, and he smiled when he talked, but there was a serious aura about him which Sam immediately picked up on.

"Those are some excellent dogs you have there," Sam said.

"Yes, they are," Andre replied. "I need nothing but the best out here. They're good at keeping the bears and varmints away."

They walked into the cabin's small kitchenette, and Andre gestured for Sam to have a seat at a table. "I've got hot coffee," he said, "and the eggs are in the pan, along with some caribou sausage I made myself. I hope you're hungry."

"Sounds real good," Sam said, sitting at the table.

"How do you like your coffee?" Andre asked.

"Black is fine," Sam said, observing the inside of the cabin, which appeared to be only a single bedroom home. There was a small television in one corner of the main room, sitting in front of a couch. Next to that was a large desk containing a laptop and a scattering of books and papers. Several mounted heads garnished the interior walls, with the largest being that of an American Bison, fixed above the fireplace.

"I've taken bigger animals," Andre said with a chuckle, noticing Sam's observation of his place. "But there's no room in here to mount them. Shot a moose last year, in fact, with a seventy inch spread."

"That's a big bull," Sam replied. "And good eating, I bet."

"The best."

They talked a little more about hunting while they ate, but eventually Sam got to the reason he was there.

"So you were the team leader," he asked, "while looking for my brother?"

"Yes I was," Andre replied. "I've been with the Yukon Search and Rescue for over ten years now. I was the first to get contacted once we got the call from the Mounties. A pilot called it in. He went up there to pick up Bryson, on schedule, but... well, that's when he noticed your brother wasn't around."

Sam opened his notepad and started writing. "Tell you what," he said. "I would like you to fill me in on everything you guys did up there. I've spent years volunteering for SAR myself, so I know the protocols. You can start with Point Last Seen. And also," he set the pen down and looked up, "I'm dying to know why you guys were only out there for three days."

Andre took two fast gulps from his cup, then stood and walked over to the coffeepot. "Need more?" he asked, refilling his cup.

"I'm good," Sam replied.

"Okay," Andre said, "but before I answer those questions of yours, let me ask you one myself: What's your plan, Sam?"

"Isn't it obvious?" Sam replied. "My brother hasn't been found, mister, and that's unacceptable to me or my family."

Andre shook his head, then came back and sat at the table. "I was afraid of that," he said. "Since that first message you left me a few days ago, I had the feeling."

Sam studied him, wondering what Andre was getting at. "Why don't you just come on out and say what's on your mind, mister," he said.

"Well, Sam, to begin, we stopped searching for your brother because the Mounties ordered us to."

"I beg your pardon?" Sam said. "And why in the hell would they do that?"

Andre shook his head. "Well, because… like most authorities, they're afraid."

"Afraid of what?"

"They're afraid of what we might find."

"Mister, I'm still not following you."

Andre stood, then picked up his coffee cup. "Come with me, Sam. There's something you need to see."

• • •

They walked outside and into the small building next to the house. The interior of the building was well lit, and Sam could tell it served as some type of workshop and a storage facility. There were long benches throughout the room and two wide tables in the middle. Fixed along the walls were at least a dozen cupboards and several shelves. Many more stuffed critters were present, hanging high. An entire corner of the room housed a bounty of fishing gear, ranging from various rods and tackle to a few old and weathered crab pots. Besides the plethora of gear and supplies within the room, Sam spotted a reloading station mounted on a workbench. The station looked as if it had recently been used, as the bench was littered with tools and materials, along with several canisters of what appeared to be 30.06 ammunition.

On the further end of the building, the far wall was decorated from floor to ceiling with power tools of all kinds. There was also a bench fitted with a miter saw. All throughout the building, on the walls and elsewhere, a cluttering of oddities, maps, and other miscellaneous knick-knacks were on display.

But it was the center of the room and straight to a table where Andre led Sam. And on the table was something covered with a brown sheet.

Andre looked at Sam. He held his stare, and it seemed as if he was going to say something, but then he slowly dragged the sheet away.

At first, Sam wasn't sure what to make of them. On the table were two cast footprints, both of which looked to be human, but were extremely large, easily twice the size of a normal man's. Even without a measuring tape, Sam guessed the prints to be at least sixteen-inches long and roughly seven-inches wide.

"Sam, I took these casts at Earl Lake," Andre said. "Less than a thousand yards from your brother's camp."

Sam looked at him. "Mister, if this is some kind of sick joke, I promise you—"

Andre raised his hands, palms up, and cut Sam off. "I swear to you, man, this is not a joke. I've been studying and tracking these creatures for almost twenty years now."

Sam took a step back. "These creatures?" he said, his tone incredulous.

"I can tell this isn't easy for you," Andre continued. "You might be a skeptic about this kind of thing, but if you give me a minute, I'll explain."

"Mister," Sam replied, "it seems to me you've got a whole lot of explaining to do. More than a minute's worth."

"I understand," Andre said, "and let me assure you, this is not a waste of your time, Sam. Around here, the wilderness is a lot different from what you might be used to in New Mexico."

"You've got that right," Sam said.

The table was a boxlike structure, similar to those found in science laboratories. It had several wide drawers, and reaching down, Andre opened up one of them. Inside were at least ten more similar casts, some as big as the two on the table, a few larger, but many of which were smaller.

"Sam," Andre said, "if I were joking about this, you'd have to ask yourself: Why? Why would I go through all this trouble to play a joke on someone I've never even met?"

Carefully, Andre started pulling the casts out of the drawer and lining them up onto the table. "This one here," he said, pointing to a print that looked to be at least fourteen inches long and six inches wide, "I took near a marsh south of Whitehorse while on a moose hunt. And this one," he picked up another of about the same size, "I found in British Columbia while fishing along a creek."

Sam clenched his jaw, then slowly sipped his coffee. He was glad he brought his cup with him from the house, as right now it was the only thing he could hold on to that made any sense to him.

Andre set the cast back down on the table, then looked at Sam. His face was deadpan and serious. "Your brother," he said, "Bryson Nolan, he was a well-known individual around here. Most trackers and outfitters had heard of him, if they didn't outright know the guy. We all knew of his talents, and of the work he did, tracking grizzlies up north... Shit, that man was insane, following them bears in the field for days, taking all his data before snaring them... And then the tigers in Siberia, trapping those for the Russians." Andre turned his whole body toward Sam and crossed his arms over his chest. "I'll tell you this right now," he added, "among everyone up here who knew of your brother, there isn't a soul alive who believes he got himself killed by a bear or wolves or even a mountain lion. And you know as well as I do the elements didn't get him."

Regarding his brother's skills, Sam could not deny Andre's words. More than anyone else, he knew of Bryson's capabilities. He'd long suspected something peculiar had happened to his brother, something beyond the normal expectations that would come from being alone in the wilderness. But to look at those casts on the table... Sam just couldn't shake the craziness of it all out of his head.

"Bigfoot. Sasquatch," Andre said, gesturing to the tracks. "And around here, we call him the Bushman. You can deny it all you want, Sam, but I'm of the opinion that this guy," he pointed now to the first tracks Sam had seen, the ones that were previously under the sheet, "he's responsible for what happened to your brother. This guy is the reason Bryson Nolan went missing."

CHAPTER 8

Sam needed a break. He left Andre with an abrupt, "I'll see you later," then got in his truck and drove back down the dirt road. But it was anyone's guess where he was going.

Mostly, he needed a minute to himself. He needed time to process a theory of which he initially took to be absolutely preposterous. Andre's assumption was way too much for Sam. He'd never been one to consider the possibilities of paranormal topics, including the existence of Bigfoot. In Sam's way of thinking, Sasquatch was up there with UFOs, both of which were nothing but headlines meant for a tabloid. But now, to consider his own brother might have been killed by such a creature?

The other reason Sam had to leave was because he was damn near at the end of his fuse with Andre. He wasn't sure if the guy was pulling his leg or was dead serious. And unfortunately, Sam still needed to work with the man long enough to ask a few questions about the area surrounding Earl Lake, as well as the SAR team's tracking efforts.

Sam drove to the main road leading toward town. At a fork, he turned left and headed north. He drove for almost thirty minutes, thinking about his circumstances and pondering over Andre's claim. Logic told him that the guy was nuts, a total loon. He'd been living out here in that cabin all by himself, and maybe there was a good reason for that. Some people, like Sam, needed to be alone. But others... others were forced into the situation because they were too crazy for anyone to be around.

In light of these thoughts, Sam considered a different explanation. Perhaps this Andre guy knew *exactly* what had happened to Bryson. Perhaps it was Andre himself who was responsible for Bryson's disappearance and now he was trying to put the blame on this local Bushman myth.

But then a doubt crept into Sam's mind. If Andre was the reason Bryson went missing, why then would he be so willing to meet with Sam? Why wouldn't he simply try to skirt the subject or not be available to talk? And also, why would he have gone so far to support his wild theory? The man had at least a dozen of those cast prints, all of which looked damn real to Sam.

And the casts weren't the only things supporting Andre's claim. Sam remembered now the various oddities and knick-knacks cluttering the building... all bits and pieces of the Bigfoot lore. There'd been numerous wooden statues of the creature, along with pictures and photographs. There was even a geographical map of North America on the back wall, with, in large print, the word "Sightings" stamped at the top of it. None of these details registered in Sam's mind at the time, but they certainly did now.

No, this Andre guy was serious about his Bigfoot theory. Dead serious. He might have been crazy in the head, but he wasn't kidding about how he'd been studying the creature. And this detail put a heavy doubt into Sam's mind, which, for the moment, pushed away his other suspicions regarding how his brother might have disappeared.

He pulled over to the side of the road, into a clearing of grass and wildflowers edged by a forest of stunted spruce. Off to his right loomed a grassy knoll spotted with clusters of small stones, giving the appearance of moose tracks crossing over the land.

Sam thought more about Andre's casts and wondered if they could have been some kind of mistake. He had known bears to make similar looking prints, after their back paw stamped down onto the track made by their front. It was certainly a plausible explanation for what Andre had. Sam also wondered if perhaps the casts were a hoax. Maybe someone from the SAR team got a little creative with a prank and fabricated prints near where Bryson disappeared, knowing Andre would eventually come across them.

But then again, there were all those other casts, the ones Andre claimed to have found from other parts of North America. Were they too from a bear? Possibly. Could they have also been hoaxes? Not likely.

Sam's head continued to hurt. He was thinking too hard about this topic—a topic that sat way outside of his comfort zone. He wondered what the Master Sergeant would do in this situation. Briefly, Sam smiled, picturing Joe Paxton looming over Andre McKinnon and claiming him as crazy as a shithouse rat.

Sam turned the Chevy around and drove back to Carmacks. He stopped at a gas station to fill up the tank and grabbed a donut and more coffee. Then he drove to the Carmacks Public Library, where he spent roughly two hours researching various topics of the area, including Earl Lake... a place that contained a curious history, as Sam discovered. A very curious history.

When he was finished at the library, Sam went back to his hotel room, reclined on the bed, and spent two more hours studying a topographical map of the area surrounding the lake in question. Sam had a natural born, unique talent for land navigation. He could look at a map and eventually memorize it, especially if the area contained features similar to what he'd grown up around, such as high mountain ranges with lakes and streams.

Over his many years as a woodsman, Sam learned that every terrain had a pattern to it, and once you became familiar with that pattern, it wasn't too difficult to find your way around. Combined with his infallible sense of direction, after studying a certain geographical area for a while, Sam would know the place almost as if it were his own backyard.

But in this case, he could only study a map for so long. At one point, Sam would have to get some more answers from Andre, and that meant having to go back out there to the man's house.

Very soon though, Sam would have his boots on the ground, prowling through the rugged terrain of the Yukon Territory and looking for clues to what really happened to Bryson. Sasquatch or not, tomorrow morning, Sam Nolan was going to be doing what he did best.

CHAPTER 9

"This is why you wanted me to come out here and meet you in person," Sam said, "and not in town, for breakfast."

They were standing once again in the workshop, overlooking the casts on the table. This time, they were drinking something stronger than coffee.

Before Sam arrived, Andre had produced a bottle of Maker's Mark bourbon and cooked a plate full of grilled moose loin. Sam rarely drank alcohol, but at the moment, he was enjoying the pairing of whiskey to the dry-rubbed, flavorful meat.

"This is the reason, isn't it?" Sam added, gesturing to the casts. "You wanted me to come look at these things in person before you hit me with your theory."

"Roger that," Andre replied. "It's hard to talk about this without seeing them firsthand."

"I bet it is," Sam said.

Out of curiosity, and perhaps the desire to discover evidence that the casts were a hoax, Sam picked one of them up and brought it over to a light. He looked at it closely under the lamp, expecting to see some type of clue, something to show that the cast was a fake. Interestingly enough, the surface was rough and had several blemishes, which resembled scarring.

But then Sam noticed something peculiar. "This thing..." he said, his eyes squinting for focus, "it's hard to see, but it looks like—"

"Here," Andre interrupted, handing Sam a magnifying glass. "Use this."

Sam took the glass and peered through it. He studied the footprint for several seconds, and then his heartbeat kicked up a notch.

"I'll be damned," he said. "This thing has dermal ridges on it." He set the cast back on the table, then picked up another one—the one Andre claimed he'd taken from Earl Lake. "Well, shit," Sam said, after a minute, "this one does too..." He glanced briefly at Andre, then looked back at the cast. "There's even a scar, right here on the heel."

Sam stretched the cast an arm's length away, studying the thing. Then he focused his attention on another peculiarity he'd discovered, near the middle of the cast. He set the cast down and made the same observation on a few of the others, scratching his chin as he did so. "There's something weird about these." he said. "Right about in the center. There's some type of fracture."

"It's called the midtarsal break," Andre said, picking up a cast and showing Sam. "And they all have it. It's the way the creature's foot is designed, unlike our own. While walking, their heel comes up first," Andre demonstrated the motion using his hand, "as the rest of the foot stays planted." He looked squarely at Sam. "This is a known feature for many primates... except humans."

Primates...

It was an interesting concept. Sam couldn't deny it. The prints looked human enough, other than their size, and he knew quite well what dermal ridges were. But to have a midtarsal break... that was especially odd. It was also one more detail to discredit the premise of the casts being part of a hoax. The very thought of that made Sam feel even more uncomfortable.

He glanced around the room, then looked back at Andre. "I don't suppose you've got any other evidence for this thing? I mean, have you ever seen one of them—assuming they're real?"

From another drawer, Andre retrieved a small cedar box. He placed it on the table and opened it. "Here are some photos I've taken over the years," he said, pulling out a dozen pictures. "Tracks, mostly. But these here, I believe they're nests, which I found down in Oregon."

"Nests?" Sam said, looking at one picture. He saw what appeared to be a large eagle's nest lying on the ground, although it seemed crushed and matted down. In the center of the frame was a backpack, obviously used as a scale for size.

"The interesting thing about these," Andre continued, "is that they're quite similar to the nests gorillas make."

Sam crossed his arms over his chest and rested a hand on his chin. "They look like a simple bird's nest to me. An eagle's... obviously blown down during a windstorm."

"Look at this picture," Andre said, showing Sam another photo. Taken in a forest, it was of a small sapling with a trunk that had been freshly snapped and twisted almost three hundred and sixty degrees horizontally.

"I've seen this about a dozen times already," Andre continued. "And there's nothing natural that can do this to a tree. Not that I know of. Machinery, sure, but what else? Certainly not human or even a bear. The trunk on this thing was as thick as a beer can."

"Well, maybe it *was* from a machine," Sam said.

Andre shook his head. "I checked the area... This was down in Washington, and miles deep into an Old Growth forest. There were no roads and no vehicle tracks of any kind. No machinery had been up there, I can promise you that.

"And check these out," Andre continued, showing Sam yet another set of photographs. "See how these poles are lined up?" He pointed to a picture containing several full-size logs that had been criss-crossed and woven against a larger, standing tree. The entire structure looked like the framing of a giant teepee. "Once again," Andre continued, "this was taken deep in the bush, miles from anywhere. Not the wind, not an animal. Nothing in nature that can make this, Sam, except for..."

"Except for what?" Sam asked.

"Again, this is a known behavior for larger primates, such as gorillas."

Sam chuckled, his tone nervous. "Well, maybe there's a gorilla running loose in North America."

"Look," Andre said, turning toward Sam, "I get it, you're a skeptic. I've run across plenty of your kind over the years, and believe me, I know how it feels—I used to be a skeptic myself. But to answer your first question: yes, I've seen one of these creatures, Sam. And it sure as hell was not a gorilla."

Sam felt a very small, very subtle shiver run down his neck. Andre's tone had changed. It'd become more serious and was almost conspiratorial, such that it had an influence on Sam, which he found to be most surprising.

"Twenty years ago," Andre continued, "I was backpacking with some friends down in Montana. The Kootenai National Forest—what a beautiful place. We had just spent the night, and it was early in the morning. I was the first one up and was messing around camp, getting breakfast going and whatnot, when I caught wind of a horrible odor. It was a god-awful smell, like shit and wet dog. So I started looking around to see where the smell was coming from, and that's when I saw it. About fifty yards out, staring at me from behind a tree. At first, I thought it was a bear—a huge bear—but then I started walking toward it and then it took off... Not too fast, though, just casually ran away.

"It walked on two legs, and I recognized it for what it was, plain as day: a hominid, covered in hair, and easily seven-feet tall, maybe more, with really wide shoulders... wide as this here table."

The shiver in Sam's neck traveled further down into his spine. Crossing both arms over his chest, he leaned his weight against the wall. He wasn't sure how to take Andre's story. But, as Sam noticed, the man had visibly changed. His hands were now shaking. His eyes were full and glistening with tears. His voice seemed on edge and his breathing had shortened. Sam recognized the signs, as would anybody else familiar with Post Traumatic Stress Syndrome. Andre McKinnon was reliving that moment in the forest and stressing out because of it.

"I wasn't sure how to feel," Andre continued. "I woke my friends up and told them what I'd seen, and of course they hassled the hell out of me. They didn't believe a damn word of it, and just figured I was pulling some kind of joke. I would've thought the same, of course. But it wasn't long into that morning that their feelings changed.

"About two hours later, while walking, we started hearing tree knocks in the forest, coming from both sides of the trail. And then came the rocks... which started landing near our feet. Something was throwing them at us—but not to hurt, just to warn, or so it seemed.

"We kept walking, maybe a little faster now, but every once in a while there'd be a rock thrown or a tree knock. Even after a mile, it was still happening, and my friend Mike was getting pissed. He still didn't believe what I'd seen earlier. He was convinced some guys were in the forest messing with us, so he pulled out his .44 and started shouting, cussing at whoever he thought was out there. Then he fired a few rounds, high into the trees, just to scare them off."

"What happened next?" Sam asked. He was curious, if not frustrated, over getting sucked into Andre's story.

"What happened next..." Andre said, and here he paused, as if he were reluctant to continue, "... what happened next, Sam, was by far the scariest thing I've experienced in my life."

CHAPTER 10

A cold fever gripped Bryson's body, plaguing him with a deep sense of dread. He was sick now, adding to his ravaging hunger, and the ever-present weakness lingering in his joints and muscles. Mostly, he just wanted to sleep. Sleep, until the darkness took him at last. But the fighter in him kept hanging on.

He had plenty to drink because of the consistent trickle of mountain water on the surface of the cavern walls. But he hadn't eaten in days, perhaps even weeks.

Trapped down in this black hole, he had lost track of time. He understood his demise would most likely come from starvation... unless he was killed before then. Depressingly enough, his entire world consisted of nothing but sand and stone, a few fragments of wood, a thin supply of water, and an assortment of human bones.

He had found the way out of the cavern and it was an impossible way out—an egress of which he had no hope of exiting through. Also, he'd learned what had captured him, and indeed, it *was* a monster. But not the monster he'd first imagined it to be.

Adding to his physical and mental pain, Bryson had to endure the occasional auditory displays of his captor, the horrid and primitive moans of anguish mixed with the bloodcurdling cries of a certain death. The sounds came and went intermittently, and were sometimes so loud that Bryson would push his face into the ground and force sand into his ears to keep from hearing the racket.

He thought always of Jenny. He wondered how she was doing. She must have been sick with his loss, and completely distraught. He would have given anything if he could let her know what had happened to him. The mystery of his disappearance and all the unanswered questions within must be a terror wracking the inside of her head. And Bryson wasn't even dead yet. For certain, he knew how the last chapters of his story would be written, how the final pages would be just as bleak and blank as the air before him, but after he died, Jenny would be none the wiser.

With his hand on his angry stomach, Bryson stared into the surrounding darkness and awaited his death. In however way it should decide to take him, he knew that the mystery of his disappearance would remain just that... forever a mystery.

CHAPTER 11

"I can't begin to explain the fear," Andre said. He picked up a piece of moose loin and took a bite out of it, chewed slowly, then swallowed. He helped the morsel down with a sip of bourbon. "I've tried, over the years, to equate the terror I had on that day with something else, Sam. Maybe if I had kids and their lives were in horrible danger… A fear like that, I guess."

"Well, what happened?" Sam asked impatiently.

"They started coming at us—that's what happened. After Mike fired those shots, we heard massive, and I mean *massive*, wood breaks. Like the surrounding forest was getting ripped apart by some terrible machinery or force of nature." Andre's eyes narrowed a little. "That alone was scary, for all of us, but then one of them rushed in. We couldn't see it, as it was concealed behind a thicket of brush. But it was coming, and it was coming in fast. I felt its thumping on the ground below my feet. And I could tell right off that it was running on two legs. Don't ask me how, but I just knew that it was."

Andre glanced over at one of the wooden statues of a Sasquatch, sitting on a shelf. Sam noticed the man's hands were shaking stronger now, and there was a thick tenseness in his voice.

"None of us did anything," Andre continued. "We didn't move; we were paralyzed with fear. I remember seeing Mike point his gun toward the bushes, but his arms, they were trembling something horrible.

"That thing ran up almost all the way, but then it stopped... I'd say not more than twenty feet away from us."

"Then what?" Sam asked.

"Then..." Andre shook his head. "Then it screamed. And my God, when it did that, I could have died because it was so loud. One long, low-pitched wail that damn near broke my eardrums and certainly broke my spirit." Andre stared directly into Sam's eyes. "I felt that scream throughout my entire body and it was fucking painful, man. And then the fear that came afterward, because of it..." He shook his head again. "There's nothing like it in the world, Sam... that fear. Nothing at all. It was *primal*."

"Did your friend shoot at it?"

"No," Andre said. "Fortunately, he did not. But the rest of that moment was kind of a blur. We all ran, ran for our lives as fast as we could go. And we didn't stop running until we were beat. And," here Andre chuckled, lightening the tension in the room, "we stuck together like glue—instinctively, you know. Safety in numbers and all. That's something I remember clearly. We couldn't stand to be more than three feet apart from one another, which had me thinking of cavemen on the run from a saber-tooth tiger.

"Eventually, we made it out, though. There were more rocks thrown and more wood knocks, along with more stomping in the bushes, although further away. But eventually, we got far enough out of there. And then things settled down. Things stopped, actually, as that was the end of it."

Sam took a deep breath and straightened his body. He ate some of the moose loin, then drank more whiskey. "That's quite a story," he finally said, not completely sure how he felt or what he thought about it. But there was one thing for damn certain: whether or not he was telling the truth, Andre McKinnon was one hell of a storyteller.

As if the topic was too uncomfortable to pursue any further, Sam changed the subject. Slowly, he pulled his topographical map out of his back pocket and set it on the table. Then he produced a highlighter, along with a notebook and pen.

"As much as I find your story interesting," he said, unfolding the map, "right now I need to consider some facts I *can* make sense out of. Regardless of what you've been telling me, I'm going out there tomorrow. And it would help if I knew where you boys did your searching."

"Of course," Andre replied. He took the highlighter and pen and started making notes on the map. He circled the exact location where they found Bryson's camp and labeled it "PLS" for Point Last Seen. Then he drew small squares over specific areas, showing where the different teams had searched. He explained to Sam that, for the time they were up there, the teams had searched using a grid-pattern method, which was a standard protocol for search and rescue operations.

"That's something I've never cared for," Sam said, shaking his head.

"I hear you on that," Andre replied. He gave Sam a look that showed he understood. "The search protocols are often stringent and confining, which is why I went back there a few days later."

"Is that when you found them tracks?" Sam asked, glancing uneasily at the drawer under the table.

"It sure is. Except, I didn't find them right away. I was out there for three days and it was late on the second day when I found them. After searching for two days and not finding anything, not a damn clue as to what happened to Bryson, then seeing those footprints in the mud, well... I got spooked." He lowered his head, as if suddenly feeling ashamed. "I left shortly after that."

"Hmm," Sam replied, stroking his beard. He pulled the map toward him and studied the notes Andre had written. "How big was the search party?"

"We averaged fifty people a day," Andre said. "And we had fifty-seven on that last day... the day the Mounties pulled the plug."

"That'll do it," Sam remarked distastefully. After fifty people had spent three days of tromping around out there, he knew there would be thousands of prints scattered about. Because of that, there would be no chance in hell for a decent tracker to find anything worth reading. Not in the general vicinity, at least.

Andre gave a nod of agreement. "Often times," he said, "—most times in fact—one excellent tracker is all a case needs. Too many boots on the ground will cause too much chaos, and that destroys all the evidence."

Sam looked suddenly at Andre, a curious stare in his eye. "Them Mounties," he said, "you mentioned they were afraid of what might get found out there."

"I did," Andre replied.

"And by that, I presume you mean this creature of yours."

"That's correct."

Perplexed, Sam thought more about that. It seemed like quite the stretch, considering that, as far as he knew, there was no proof Sasquatch even existed. So why then would the authorities discontinue a local search out of fear of finding evidence of the creature?

"It happens more often than you'd think," Andre added, as if reading Sam's mind. "Although this was the first time I experienced it, I've read about it all too many times..." He took a sip of whiskey while staring intently at Sam. "The national parks in the lower forty-eight... They're notorious for pulling the plug on searches."

"But why?" Then a thought suddenly popped into Sam's head. "Unless they don't want the rest of the world to know, for some reason..."

Andre smiled. "Think about it, Sam. There's a lot of money spent on the Great Outdoors, every single year. But how much of that cash flow would suddenly stop if the public found out there was an eight-hundred pound monster living out here? Even worse, a monster that *abducted* people..." He paused for a second to let that sink in. "Now, that's just the tip of the iceberg... Consider the financial restrictions that would be imposed upon big industries such as logging, which, as I'm sure you could guess, would occur immediately. This would be the second coming of Christ for environmentalists, and there would be no stopping them because they'd have the full weight of public's sympathy on their side. All across North America, *huge* swaths of land would be cordoned off from anyone and everyone, made as sanctuaries to preserve habitat for the rarest species known to man... The logging industry would get crushed... That would put a stranglehold on new businesses and housing developments... The chain reaction of indefinite, negative economic growth would be next, cutting drastically the river of taxes. And of course, it wouldn't be long after that the giant machine known as capitalism would come to a screeching halt..." Andre shook his head. "Listen, Sam. The official discovery of Bigfoot would be a financial disaster for a *whole* lot of people. But especially for the government."

Sam didn't want to believe any of it. In fact, he tried not to believe. Abruptly, he went back to the map, pen in hand. He was feeling uncomfortable, but not enough to leave, because also, he was feeling dissatisfied. It was as if all of Andre's stories and theories had put a bug into Sam's mind—a bug which he felt needed to be squashed.

Andre, apparently observing Sam's irritation, pushed his body away from the table, then walked over to the wall and opened a cabinet.

"What'd you guys do with Bryson's stuff?" Sam asked, looking up.

"I've got it over there, in the back," Andre replied, pointing toward a corner of the room. He explained that the search team had originally left Bryson's stuff at the site, in case the man somehow came back from wherever he was. But after Andre searched the area by himself, and after finding not a single clue as to what had happened to Bryson, other than those footprints, he brought Bryson's gear back. "Do you want me to get it all out for you?" he added.

Sam shook his head. "Not right now. I'll go through it before I leave."

He looked back at the map, and a few minutes later, Andre returned to the table with a notebook.

"I know it sounds crazy," Andre said, opening the notebook to a page, "about people getting abducted by this thing. It's hard to believe... sometimes even for me." He ran his finger across a list of notes, then stopped at a particular bullet point. "But in my research, I've recorded several incidents of people who've gone missing, and all under conditions similar to that of your brother's disappearance. And, well, the only rational explanation, Sam, is that something took them."

Andre pointed out several cases of missing persons across North America, people who had disappeared in the wilderness, and all of whom shared circumstances similar to Bryson's. Disappearances of skilled hunters and outdoorsmen, with no single shred of evidence found to explain what had happened to them.

"It just makes no sense," Andre added, "when you study these cases collectively. The only explanation—the one that makes sense, that is—is like I said. Something took these people."

"What about predators?" Sam asked.

Andre shook his head. "That's the thing. In each of these cases, there was absolutely no sign of predation. And you know as much as I do that when a bear or a mountain lion is involved, there's always a scene."

That much was true, Sam knew. With a bear or mountain lion attack, the amount of evidence left behind is abundant, and usually includes blood, torn clothing, and an obvious disturbance of the general area. It is a scene tracker dogs find almost immediately.

Andre referred to his list again. He started pointing out cases with even more peculiar circumstances. Cases involving missing children who were found days later, sometimes dead or sometimes alive.

"In a few of these cases," Andre continued, "they found a child of less than four years old, over ten miles from the point last seen. And we're talking about ten miles of rugged terrain. A terrain that is impossible for a toddler to navigate through, in my opinion. But here's the bigger mystery, Sam. In almost every case, these children were found naked. No shoes, no clothes... no nothing."

Sam had to admit, the cases were baffling. He knew how difficult it was to cross through ten miles of rugged wilderness. But for a toddler to do so? And at some point, without shoes? That seemed downright impossible.

The detail about people being found without shoes or clothing became a commonality amongst several of the cases, as Andre pointed out.

"It sounds like symptoms of hypothermia," Sam said in response. When people became hypothermic, they felt a burning sensation on their skin, which often resulted in the removal of clothing.

"Even so..." Andre replied. "Skilled outdoorsmen found dead in the wilderness... and their boots missing? And I mean, boots nowhere to be found... How does that even come close to making sense, Sam?"

It didn't make sense. Not any of it.

Looking again at the map, Sam asked Andre if he knew of any structures in the area, such as hunting cabins, ranger outposts, or fire lookouts.

"There's a fire tower roughly five miles east of the lake," Andre said. "Although it's not used anymore. Also," he added, using the pen to mark small points on the map, "there's abandoned mines all throughout the territory. I have no idea exactly where they're at, but most likely in the higher elevations, right about where I marked."

Sam pulled the map closer to him and studied the points Andre had made.

"But if you find one of them," Andre said dubiously, "be careful going in. They're old and dangerous."

There was little more talk. Sam studied the map for a few more minutes and asked Andre if there was anything else he knew about the area—anything at all. Sam was open to even the smallest of details, knowing that all it took was one spark to set off a forest fire of thought. If only he could identify something that would eventually start the blaze and then point him in the direction of solving his brother's disappearance...

Also, Sam was desperate to find something more useful to think about. Something other than skeptical theories involving kooky legends and unsolved cases.

But Andre had nothing more to add.

After a last look at the map, Sam folded it and tucked it in his back pocket, along with the pens. Then, with Andre's help, he went through Bryson's stuff. He actively searched the gear for notes or a journal. If his brother had meant to take his own life (something Sam didn't believe for a minute) then maybe Bryson had left a note indicating his intentions.

But there were no journals or notes. The only thing Sam found was exactly what he'd expected: your standard gear for camping.

"Well, I guess I better get going," Sam finally said.

"Before you do," Andre replied, walking toward a shelf on the wall containing a portable stereo, "I want you to hear something." He came back with the stereo and set it on the table in front of Sam. From a pocket, he pulled out a cassette tape, then placed it into the boom box. "Now, I assume you know just about every sound there is in the wilderness. I'm guessing you do, at least. In fact, without hesitation, you could probably identify the sounds from a bear, cougar, wolf, coyote, elk—shit, just about anything..." Andre paused as he pressed the play button. "But you just listen to this..."

Sam listened to grainy silence for a few seconds. Then, quietly at first, he heard the distinct sound of a *whoop*. This was returned by three more *whoops*, albeit much louder. And finally, suddenly, there came a long and continuous howl, ten seconds of a beastly roar which was deep and fierce, primal, and undoubtedly threatening...

It was a sound Sam had never heard before.

Andre stopped the tape. "I recorded that while camping one night in the bush, a few miles southwest of Whitehorse. And Sam," he added, looking up, "I hope this convinces you to reconsider your plan."

CHAPTER 12

In the end, Sam found he appreciated Andre McKinnon's concern for his wellbeing. They had talked a little more after listening to that recording, and Andre expressed his genuine apprehension about Sam heading off into the bush alone. Andre added that if that creature had killed Bryson, it was probably because of some territorial instinct, assuming it was unlikely Bryson would have wantonly provoked the animal. And if that were the case, if the creature had acted out in such a way, well, then... who's to say it wouldn't do so again?

Sam was grateful for Andre's sentiments. He was grateful for the man's initial and then subsequent attempts to find Bryson.

But in the end, he left the man with his worries and went back to his hotel room. There would be no convincing Sam to reconsider his plans. Regardless of Andre's concerns about what may lurk in the wilds of North America, nothing would change Sam's course of action now, because his brother was still out there. And like a never ending afterthought, so too was another person from Sam's past...

Then later, while lying on his bed, that old and dark and lonely thought crept back into Sam's mind. If he should succumb to what's out there, the same as what happened to Bryson as Andre feared, well then, wouldn't that just be for the best?

Sam entertained these and other thoughts well into the small hours of the night. Then the morning arrived, cold and quick, and it brought with it a gray lining on the horizon. In what seemed like only minutes after he had eaten breakfast and then checked out of his room, Sam was riding shotgun on a floatplane overlooking the immensely wide vastness of Canada's Yukon Territory.

• • •

"Are you sure about this?" The pilot asked, as he brought the plane to a slow and steady crawl on the surface of the lake.

Sam didn't reply. He was looking out the window, studying the various tree lines and hilltops, the distant mountain ranges, canyons and draws, every detail of the land his eyes could mop up.

Immediately, Sam sensed a forbidden quality about this lake, something he couldn't quite put his finger on at the moment. He'd first noticed this feeling when the pilot circled the area before bringing the plane down on the water. It was a feeling Sam suspected may have been summoned by all of Andre's hype about an eight-foot tall, thousand pound creature roaming the woods. That, and perhaps by the lake's own history as well.

"Do you know how this lake got its name?" Sam asked, still staring out the window.

The pilot glanced sideways at him. "No..." he said. Then added, "I don't believe so."

"It's named after a prospector," Sam replied, while observing a line of trees on the east end of the lake. "Earl Clemens was his name. He came here in 1890. Came here looking for gold. His wife stayed behind, back in Carmacks. She ran a bakery and she never saw her husband again. In fact, no one did." Sam had read about the lake's history when he stopped in at the Carmacks Public Library. It was a detail he'd kept to himself, refraining from sharing even with Andre, but for reasons he wasn't sure why.

There was a moment of silence, then the pilot coughed. "And, ah... you still want to go through with this?" he said, doubt lingering in his voice.

Again, Sam didn't answer the man's question. "Drop me off over there," he said, pointing to a small, isolated beach.

The pilot craned his neck, looking to see where Sam had indicated. "Over there?" he asked. "Are you sure about that?"

"I'm sure," Sam said.

"But that's the opposite end of the lake," the pilot said, steering the plane. "I dropped your brother off on the other side."

"I know you did. But this'll be fine."

The pilot ferried the plane over to the shoreline of Sam's choice, turning wide to avoid a large log lying in the water. Ahead was a narrow, sandy beach, laced with green moss and thin patches of grass. Lines of gray stones speckled the ground further up from the water, eventually fading away into a layer of dirt and forest floor. Pine and larch trees stood like sentries in the slender shadows of the morning, the pockets within their space kept forlorn and dull by the rising shoulders of a granite mountain in the immediate background.

"This will be just fine," Sam repeated, staring into the distant woods.

The pilot grunted his doubt as he brought the plane to a slow, lurching halt along the beach. Then he shut the engine off and Sam opened his door and climbed out of the cabin, stepping first onto the plane's pontoon, then knee deep, straight into the water.

Taking three long strides, Sam cleared the lake and walked up onto the beach. He stared meaningfully at the surrounding forest. It was a haunting sight, the shadows and the deep hollows of the hillside. The looming trees... And in the near distance, the scarred and blemished face of a granite wall.

Sam went back to the plane and retrieved his gear. He pulled three large duffel bags out from the back of the cabin and tossed two of them up onto the shore.

"Need any help, just say the word," the pilot said.

"I'm good," Sam replied, throwing the third bag over his shoulder.

He turned to walk back up to the beach when the pilot suddenly shouted, "Hey!"

Sam turned and looked at the man.

"Are you sure you don't want me to come back for you? Maybe in a week or two? It's no trouble at all."

"I'm sure," Sam replied. "And like I mentioned earlier," he added flatly, "I'd appreciate it if you didn't report this to the Mounties. This is a family matter, mister. Last I need is for them to come out here telling me what I can and cannot do."

The pilot gave an astounded look, but nodded his head. "Mum's the word." Then a gleam sparked in his eyes, and he added, "Good luck to you, Sam. I hope you find him. I hope you find your brother."

Sam nodded in reply. He turned away, then walked up the beach and set the duffel bag on the ground next to the others. He took a deep breath, noticing that the air smelled raw and sweet, damp and cool. Looking at his surroundings, Sam knew immediately he would have to make a shelter higher up, away from the waterline. And he would do that soon.

But first...

Sam turned and looked back at the plane. The engine was running once again, and the single prop propeller was beginning its mad spin needed for flight. The pilot gave a curt wave goodbye and then the plane was on its way, chugging slowly across the water, away from the shoreline and toward the opening of the lake.

Sam watched as it took off. And with a patient stare, he consciously observed the unfolding of his complete solitude, as if his day could not truly begin without the remedy brought on by silence.

The plane made a slow but steady ascent into the air. The sound of its engine eventually drifted off into the clouds until there was nothing but the whisper of a cool breeze and the lazy lap of waves on the beach.

The granite knoll loomed behind him in the background. Sam felt the weight of its presence. It was as if something great and mighty was looking down on him. He had had this feeling countless times in the past and it always made him feel both small yet special.

But right now...

Right now, Sam sensed there was something else behind that mighty stare.

The lake stretched out before him, ominous and blue, deep and cold, and with an unfathomable depth only the fewest of species had discovered. It was a peaceful body of water, calm and relaxing. The sound of its waves was a soft lull, inviting for rest. The lake even had a clean odor, one that Sam found refreshing.

But the lake was a dead end. Sam knew it wouldn't help him find his brother. There were no tracks of any kind, lying on top of all that cold water, and there was nothing in it that would help solve the fantastic riddle.

For now, the surrounding wilderness was a damn mystery. The trees had seen everything, but they would keep their silence.

And the earth, with its soil and rocks remaining forever quiet, quiet as the grave... like a wave crashing down on its back, the earth had felt and heard every sound made amongst this land.

These were facts Sam knew all too well, despite his general aversion toward anything supernatural. Nali had told him frequently that the wilderness was alive. Always, it was alive. And once a man learned to believe in this reality, and then how to connect with it, he would also learn its secret form of communication. Like all living creatures, the wilderness and its surrounding occupants, animate or otherwise, had their own language.

Sam had learned how to interpret this language long ago.

But right now...

Right now, things were different. Sam was a stranger to this land. And until that changed, the forest would be long in speaking to him. The forest would keep its silence.

Also, as he stared at the surrounding wilderness, the trees and the lake, the stones and the meadows, Sam felt it once again. That foreboding feeling he'd sensed earlier, from above, while on the plane. He shook his head, picturing what Nali would say right now if he were standing here feeling the same thing.

Looking out across the lake, the old Apache would probably claim this was an evil place. A place with bad medicine that one should only ever leave alone. A place not meant for a man's home, let alone his last breath.

Then, like an echo slapping across the surface of the water, Sam heard the entire jumble of Andre's theories and anecdotal evidence rattle inside his head. All the stories of sightings and missing persons... The enormous casts, two of which the tracker had claimed he'd taken on the shores of this very lake. The photographs of oddly twisted tree limbs and supposed nests. The harrowing account of him and his friends being chased out of the forest by numerous large creatures. And finally, the recording of those whoops and that dreadful howl—a howl that still kept Sam mystified about what could have made it. Other than, of course, what Andre claimed it to be.

Sam stared deep into the surrounding wilderness. With a dull sense of fear, he wondered if right now, this very moment, in fact, that creature was out there, lurking in the shadows.

It was a cold thought. And one that brought with it an even colder feeling and the rise of goose bumps all down his spine. He couldn't remember a time in his life when he felt like this.

There *was* something ominous about this place, he decided. Something very ominous.

Slowly, deliberately, Sam withdrew a can of Skoal from his pocket, opened it, pinched out a wad of tobacco and pressed it under his lip, not once taking his eyes off the lake.

"What happened to you out here, Bryson?" he said solemnly. "Just what the hell happened to you?"

PART 2

CHAPTER 13

At sixty-two years of age, Cora Dean feels like she is in the best shape of her life. She ran two marathons last year and will run another later in the fall, down in southern Florida—half a world away from where she is now.

She feels young, so young, and every day she finds this as a blessing in her life. Gratefully, she views the world around her with a content stare. She is even more blessed to share this perspective with her lovely husband, Ross Dean, her soul mate.

Currently, Ross is paddling his kayak ahead of her. He is always like that—the first at everything. But Cora doesn't mind. She believes this dominant aspect of his character is a demonstration of his protective nature. She's never viewed him as being oppressive.

Cora loves her husband, as he is the father of her children and the provider of their family. And she knows she will love him always, for many years to come, as they spend the last of what's left of their lives in full retirement.

Ross had done very well selling insurance and investments, which is another thing Cora is grateful for. She can't remember the last time she worried about finances. To the contrary, whatever luxury she desired, Ross had never denied her, nor did he complain about providing it. Plastic surgeries, her own Mercedes Maybach Sedan, vacations in Europe, the unlimited trips to Nordstrom. This is the life Cora has grown accustomed to. And it is a grateful, beautiful life.

If she had only one reservation presently on her mind, it is the decision of coming to where she is right now. Kayaking the Yukon River was her husband's idea, not hers. But Cora felt she owed her husband this indulgence.

Of course, she didn't have to come. And for a moment, she considered doing just that. But this was one of Ross's dreams, which he's had since he was a Boy Scout, an entire lifetime ago. He had always wanted to kayak the Yukon.

Together, they've kayaked many other places, mostly down in Florida, where they live. It is one of their favorite activities they do together. And feeling as young as Cora does, she thought a part of her was up to this challenge.

But Cora's one worry—her constant worry—is that of wild animals. She had never camped in a place so untamed, and, in her mind, so dangerous. The nights are the scariest for her. Sleeping in the tent, trapped behind paper-thin walls, and feeling so vulnerable to all that lurks outside. Even though she had already endured two nights out here, Cora still felt the onset of dread whenever the day crept closer toward darkness… as it was doing now.

"When are we going to stop?" she asks, her feelings a mixture of anxiety and potential relief.

Ross looks at her from over his shoulder, a reassuring smile strapped across his face. "Just a few more miles, darling," he says. "Isn't this nice?"

Cora nods her head and looks away. She wonders if he is growing impatient with her. Frankly, she wouldn't blame him. Only a fool wouldn't catch on to her constant nervousness. She feels a stab of guilt at the thought of being the one to ruin this vacation—ruining her husband's boyhood adventure. And the weight of this guilt convinces her to say no more. From now on, she will only speak words of excitement and words of encouragement. She will summon all the strength of her vitality—her young self—to support Ross's dream.

For the next two miles, the stretch of river is slow and winding. At one point, they see a moose standing in the distance with a string of wet grass hanging from its mouth like spaghetti. The creature reminds Cora of a cow. She wonders idly if it's just as docile.

Not long after the moose, they see a bird of prey, perched on top of a tall tree. She has no idea which type of bird it is, nor is she entirely convinced of her husband's identification (being that of a Golden Eagle). It looks smaller than what she thinks it should be, but then figures maybe it's just young.

These are the only creatures they have seen today, other than rodents and smaller birds. But in the back of her mind (only because she has forcibly placed it there) is Cora's curiosity as to where all the other animals are. Where are the bears and the wolves and the mountain lions...?

Their kayaks move through the river with little effort, and this reminds Cora of her morning jogs around Johnson Lake, back home in their neighborhood. In some ways, this passage of time is similar, and maybe it has something to do with the stillness of the area. There is a silence in this wilderness that Cora finds both peaceful and pleasing, and it is very much like what she encounters on her runs.

Nevertheless...

There is something unnerving about this place. It's probably just her worrying, along with her imagination. But it is a feeling she cannot let go, no matter how hard she tries.

Or could it be that *it* won't let *her* go?

What Cora thinks she feels is a nagging presence. Some *thing's* presence, to be precise, over there in the trees, or up there, on the other side of that cliff, or, perhaps down there, deep below the water.

It's just her imagination and nothing more. Once again, Cora tells herself to calm down. She tells herself to enjoy this day, this day of healthy life, and to enjoy this place, this place of wild beauty. And with that being her immediate thought, fragile as it might be, she paddles forward, cutting through the ripples of her husband's wake.

They finish their last mile and then Ross guides them to a small beach of pebbles and sand. It is a place Cora finds not entirely comforting, as a thick and dark forest crowds the tiny shore.

Her husband lands his kayak, climbs skillfully out, then pulls it up the shore a good three feet. He helps Cora climb out and pulls her craft up as well.

"Will you look at this place," Ross says, with a grand smile, gesturing sweepingly at their surroundings. His movements are full of energy. His voice teems with excitement. It is almost too much for Cora to bear. "Let's set our tent up over there," he says, pointing to a fallen tree, "next to that blowdown."

Blowdown.

There's another thing that has made Cora feel nervous. Not the tree itself, of course, or the cause of the tree's expiration, but, oddly enough, her husband's recent gratuitous use of such outdoor words. Words like "blowdown," "shelter," "cordage," and "survival gear." Words that she has never heard him speak before. It must be the long-lost Boy Scout in him, climbing up and out of fifty years of storage. She loves her husband all the more, seeing him act and talk this way, but it is still something unfamiliar to her. And anything unfamiliar reminds Cora of all the other things she does not know (or care to know) about this place.

"It looks fine to me," she says. She pulls her kayak further up the shore, then ties it to a nearby tree. Then she stretches her body widely and feigns a yawn, yet is not sure exactly why. She doesn't feel tired (she's not sleepy) and she certainly isn't looking forward to going to bed. "What should we have for dinner?" she says, attempting to change the subject in her mind.

"Oh, we'll get to that soon enough," Ross replies. He looks at her and smiles, his pearly teeth reminding her of her car. "I'd like to do some more fishing. And I've got to set up our shelter, as well. Here," he says, reaching to help her retrieve her waterproof gear bag, "let me get that for you." He has always been the perfect gentleman. Even out here, while "roughing it," he will not fail at lending his wife a hand.

"I have an idea," Cora says, suddenly feeling the need to return a favor. "How about I set the tent up while you go fishing?" She smiles, and she is proud to know that her smile is genuine.

Ross smiles back, but there is a twist in his eyebrows. "Are you sure? I mean, if you think that's something you can..." He stops himself short, then waves his hand in the air, as if to dismiss his words. "What am I saying? Alright, you do that, darling." Then he laughs as he reaches for his fly rod. "Maybe we'll have fish for dinner. How about that?"

Minutes later, Cora watches her husband leave. He is wearing his camouflage waders, and he heads upriver through a thicket of trees, where he disappears among the distance and foliage. She is alone now—not really alone, but alone enough. The feeling sinks into her gut like a stone and sets her nerves on end. As a result, she gets herself busy with setting up the tent.

She had never done it before. But she is surprised at how easy it was to put up. The tent is just big enough for the two of them, along with a few essential items. She thinks it looks almost befitting, sitting beside the "blowdown."

Curious, and having nothing else to do, she walks down to the water and looks for her husband. She doesn't see him, as there is a bend in the river which blocks her view. But then her heart lifts as she sees the line from his fishing pole whip back and forth from the shore. *Backing...* That's what he had called that part of the fishing line.

Cora finds a rock near the water and sits down on it, mechanically rubbing the joints in her knees, her hands. She checks the time on her watch, then looks at the sky. She considers for a moment to unpack the rest of their kayaks, or perhaps build a ring for the fire they would soon need, but then dismisses the ideas. She knows Ross prefers to do those things himself.

Cora stares at the passing water as the time slowly peels by. She checks her watch again. It has only been fifteen minutes since her last check, but it seems like an hour. She now feels the coldness of the rock through her clothes and into her bones, so she stands and stretches once again. Then she yawns, and this time it's a real one, but she is still not sleepy.

For the briefest of moments, Cora entertains the idea of going for a run—yes, a run, out here in the wilds of the Yukon. But then she shakes her head and laughs at herself for considering such a crazy notion. She would never make it back, having fallen prey to the first wild animal she came across. A mountain lion, probably. Or a bear…

She shivers the thought away, then jumps almost out of her skin, startled by her husband's sudden holler. He is standing in the river upstream, maybe a hundred feet away, or so, smiling, and holding up a large fish for her to see. He yells something to the effect of "dinner," and Cora smiles back, nodding her head.

Ross arrives back at camp several minutes later, carrying two large fish on a string. She thinks they're trout, but doesn't really know or care. She is relieved by his return, and her happiness puts a spark of energy into her body. "How does it look?" she says, pointing at the tent.

Ross beams proudly. "It looks great!" He hangs the fish on a nearby branch, then looks again at the tent. "I don't think I could've done any better." Then he laughs. "In fact, I know so."

"Hurry," Cora says. "Let's get a fire going. I'm hungry."

The day is long, as it normally is during the summer months in the Yukon. After eating their dinner and sitting at the fire for a few hours, Cora notices her husband yawn, and she knows he will soon be ready for sleep. She feels a pocket of fear burst inside her chest, knowing also that it is almost time to crawl inside the tent. She checks her watch and sees that it is well past nine PM. The sun is only now just edging toward the horizon, but there will still be light enough to see for a while yet. And if this night is anything like the previous two, Cora will find little comfort in it, despite the shortened length of darkness.

Slowly, Ross stands up and away from the fire. "Well, I guess I should go hang our food," he says. He grabs their food bag and a length of rope. "Shouldn't take long," he assures her. He turns and scans the area, then stops, as if he's found what he's looking for. "I'll hang it over there," he says, pointing to a small clearing through the trees. "It's not more than a hundred feet away. You can get yourself in the tent, if you'd like."

Cora smiles and looks away, unsure of what she'll do. She would like to stay by the fire, maybe even fall asleep right here, where she feels warm and somewhat secure. But seconds after Ross leaves, she follows her husband's suggestion and gets ready for bed.

Despite the buildup of her anxiety, she crawls inside the tent, leaving her shoes outside. Then she changes into her thermal underwear. Her clothes are soft and warm and when she slides into her sleeping bag, for a moment, she feels relaxed. She thinks that perhaps this night will be just like the previous two—both of which were ultimately uneventful. Cora thinks seriously about this possibility, and even speaks of it to herself, as if she could summon such an ordinary night into existence. "A good night's rest," she whispers softly, pale vapor lifting from her mouth.

She closes her eyes and feels it now... she is exhausted. A moment of time passes as Cora drifts off toward slumber, her mind retracing the steps of her day, thinking but not thinking, sleeping but not sleeping, the dull lull of semi-consciousness fogging her perception of the world...

Suddenly, a loud noise escapes from somewhere in the trees.

Cora opens her eyes in a flash, immediately awake. She sits up on her elbows, listening. *That was Ross, wasn't it?*

Then, a minute later, she hears it again—a cracking sound. Clearer now. And closer. The breaking of a large piece of wood, perhaps a branch, which is followed by a dull *thud*.

"Ross?" she hollers, her body frozen in fear. "Ross... is that you?"

What follows are long minutes of stillness, with the only sounds coming from the gentle flow of the river and the occasional crackling of the fire.

"Ross?" Cora calls out again. Her heart races. She feels it pumping inside her chest, pounding against her sternum, robbing her of her breath. This is the third time she has called for her husband and he has yet to reply. Will he reply?

Cora sits up, opens the tent fly. She pops her head out and looks around. She notices nothing, except that it has grown darker now. The land is harder to see.

"Ross?" she cries again, a fourth time. Then she crawls out of the tent and stands. She looks toward where her husband had gone and notices that the shadows in that area have grown gloomy. She can barely make out the small clearing where Ross had said he would hang their food. But as she focuses her eyes there, she thinks she sees her husband.

Cora takes a few steps toward the clearing. "Ross," she says, "is that you?" A few more steps into the surrounding forest and she sees that yes, it is her husband. A swell of relief swamps over her body, until she suddenly notices something odd.

Ross is standing next to a tree and like a statue, he is fixed in place, with his arms hanging low to his side...

Cora steps even closer. One of Ross's hands is moving awkwardly, waving to her, as if *shooing her away*. She keeps walking forward as she feels the rush of fear rise inside her chest. Then she runs to him, knowing something bad has happened.

She gets halfway to her husband before she sees him fall, dead-like, flat on his face. There is a long, gruesome piece of wood sticking out of his back. Cora halts in her tracks as a rictus of horror ripples across her face.

She then hears a distinct sound, a high-pitched growl mixed with some kind of siren. It comes from behind her husband, in the trees just beyond the clearing. She looks up, sees something terrible in there, a monster that is slowly approaching. It is a tall and menacing thing. Cora does not know what it is. She has seen nothing like it before, and yet, she knows it is coming for her.

She weeps loudly, turns and runs. She cries for her husband as she sprints toward the camp. And she cries for her life, her beautiful life, as she makes it back.

Quickly, she grabs her clothes from inside the tent, along with her shoes, and stashes them in her kayak. She reaches to untie the craft, but it—the creature—is still coming for her. She hears the thing crashing through the forest. Her body is in a state of panic, and she cannot get the kayak untied. She tries harder, her hands move faster, but the knot won't loosen. And the creature keeps coming. It's coming faster!

Suddenly, she feels it in the trees, almost upon her. Then Cora gives up.

Overwhelmed with dread, she doesn't even turn to look at the thing. She ditches the rope and vaults her body out and into the river, diving toward the bottom and toward the sweeping current and toward anything that will take her far away from here.

But the only thing Cora finds as she plunges into the mighty Yukon is the cold embracement of darkness.

CHAPTER 14

Sam had joined the Army for one specific reason: to become a sniper. The lure of hunting in the stealthiest manner possible had haunted him since he was a boy. Like the ancient Apache of his homeland, his preferred method was to sneak up on game, get as close as possible, then take them down using the bow and arrow. He had developed a mastery over many bows—the compound, recurve, even the crossbow—but his favorites were the ones he'd constructed under Nali's guidance. These were strong traditional bows crafted out of mulberry or hickory wood. Every time Sam shot an animal with one of them, he imagined what it was like to be an Apache warrior of long ago.

Eventually, rifles had become a second-place weapon for Sam. He would only hunt with them if he felt lazy, or was in the company of someone not fit enough to stalk through the bush to get within a hundred feet of their prey. But during his training in the Army, Sam had learned a greater appreciation for the advanced skills surrounding the usage of rifles, as well as their application in the field. Ranger and Green Beret schools taught him how to use firearms in ways he had never imagined. He would, of course, rely heavily on these skills during his tours in the Middle East and beyond. But he was also using them right now...

Sam had chosen his drop-off point at Earl Lake for a reason. Specifically, he was drawn to the granite promontory, the base of which sat just beyond his current location. Its pinnacle was the tallest point in the immediate area, and this geographical character had spoken to Sam while circling the lake, before the floatplane had landed.

Of course, any other sniper would have made the same decision. The structure's strategic bird's-eye view was ideal for identifying targets. But Sam also wanted access to the highest point in the area so he could look down on the land in a way the Apache would appreciate.

By studying the completeness of the land, Sam would gain not just a better understanding of the terrain he was working with, but of what he would live in. Also, such a view increased the chances of discovering something which could help solve the mystery of his brother's disappearance. This was something Sam understood all too well. And because of it, he wanted instant access to that view.

But access would have to wait. Sam's first priority was to create a shelter of some kind. That, and water, were the keys to a person's survival in the outdoors. Obviously, he had plenty to drink. But he needed a sturdy shelter, one that would last for quite some time, as he wasn't sure how long he'd be out here.

Considering this, Sam got busy. He left his bags on the beach and walked into the forest, toward the base of the granite crag. He was searching for a natural shelter of sorts, perhaps a cave or deep crevice somewhere along a rocky outcrop. Anything to make his job easier appealed to Sam, and that's not to say he was lazy. His mind was focused on absolute survival. Calories in the great outdoors were minimal, and because of this, every animal sought the most efficient path in whatever they did. Sam was no different.

The granite structure towered over him. There were small trees growing from various cracks along the side of the promontory. Thin slivers of grass and stunted shrubs added color to the otherwise massive wall of gray stone. Sam remembered how the thing looked from the air—like a big tooth rising from the land.

The rocky monolith could contain a natural refuge, but Sam wasn't holding his breath. He was thinking he may need to make a lean-to shelter, somewhere on a hillside, out of the wind and out of the path of any runoff, in case it rained.

His trek to the rocky base took him through a sparse forest of evergreens and scattered brush. The surrounding trees sat motionless. There was only a slight breeze and the smell of pine and spruce hung evenly in the air, an odor that was both sweet and bitter. Birds were chirping all around, likely warning their friends of his presence. Or celebrating the interesting sight of a newcomer.

Sam walked through the trees for a good twenty yards until he reached the base of the stony hill. Looking up, he estimated the top of the crag to be two hundred feet from where he stood. As he'd observed earlier, this was the tallest structure in the immediate area. The mountain range west of the lake was much taller, but it was at least three miles away, if not more. Sam would have a better idea once he climbed this rock, which he would do after he set up his camp.

He started walking around the stone's perimeter, scanning constantly for anything useful—small game trails where he could set up snares, signs of large predators in the area, or clues to the mystery of his primary mission. To most people, the wilderness was a simple tapestry of nature, showing them sights and sounds and smells that were mostly pleasant, yet starkly unfamiliar. But for Sam, this same tapestry was anything but simple. It was more like a motion picture, jam-packed with exciting action and countless dialogue.

As he walked the perimeter, the land took him on a slight incline. Soon he came to a spot where the base of the boulder lost its pitch through an extension of itself. Large rocks and stony nubs broke Sam's path, pushing away from the hillside and providing something for him to navigate over. He stepped and climbed between the obstacles, eventually making his way to the top of a ridge. On one side of a large rock, he spotted the partial skeleton of a small mammal. And behind him was the opening of a game trail, running up and into the trees.

Cautiously, Sam studied the area. He put his nose to the wind, knowing full-well the powerful odor that came from a cougar. Between the game trail, the skeleton, and the high rock looming before him, Sam suspected he was standing in the middle of something's hunting grounds. Or even worse—a den. And that "something" could be a two-hundred pound mountain lion.

Sam knew the behavior of these creatures. He wasn't fearful, just wary. Areas like this, a big cat would find itself a perch somewhere on the granite hill, perhaps a flat shelf sitting above a pathway towards the water. Prime time would be early morning or dusk, and such a cat would sit quietly in its hide, waiting to pounce onto anything coming down to the lake for a drink.

This was a detail Sam couldn't ignore, should he consider setting up camp somewhere against the rock. Out of respect for the creature, he was already feeling reluctant about doing so.

He walked around the circumference of the boulder, found nothing useful, then turned back and headed for his bags. He retraced his path and was about to continue down toward the lake when he suddenly stopped.

Sam was standing near the small skeleton he'd discovered minutes ago, and was looking off to his left, his stare following the trail of boulders leading up the hillside and into the forest. He was studying something that had caught his eye, and so he began walking toward it. He traveled about two hundred feet. Then his face lit up, after realizing what he'd found.

The trail of stones reaching away from the granite crag led to a grassy meadow devoid of any trees, and with a wide view of the sky. In the middle of the clearing stood an assortment of house-sized boulders, which, from afar, resembled the knuckles of a giant's fist.

Sam had found the making for a perfect shelter. He could see that the conglomeration of large boulders would offer him protection from the elements. The location was on a small rise, so storm puddles wouldn't collect in his camp. Access to the lake was less than a hundred yards. To make a lean-to, he could build up against a boulder and Sam was fine with that. Looking around, he saw plenty of wood to help with the chore.

He went back to the lake and got his gear, taking two trips to bring all three bags up. Afterward, he leaned against one of the immense boulders and caught his breath, thinking about his sniper instructor, Joe Paxton. The Master Sergeant was fond of saying "cardio is the king," which he gladly told candidates before and after a ten-mile run. Sam couldn't argue with the man's words. He was feeling a little regretful at the moment for not keeping his conditioning up to standards. Right now, it felt like the king had been replaced by a knight, or even a pawn.

After resting for a bit, Sam began the meticulous yet satisfying process of building his shelter. He found an agreeable spot against a boulder with a deep fissure between the rock and earth and with a prominent overhang above, to prevent rain from collecting on the ground. It would make an ideal spot to sleep in (which was all he really needed) and he expanded the crevice more by digging out some of the dirt and debris, using his collapsible shovel.

It was strenuous work, as the ground was hard-packed, but in time, it came loose. In less than an hour of digging, Sam had created a comfortable spot under the massive rock to rest his weary body.

Next, Sam got to work on his lean-to. He hated tents, which is why he never packed one, knowing the flimsy shelters to be inferior to something handcrafted. Sam also hated the vulnerable feeling that came with sleeping inside a tent, as he could not observe his surroundings at all times.

Thinking of being vulnerable, Sam's mind went to his conversations with Andre. Seconds later, he felt the rise of goose bumps on his arms. He took a moment away from his work and looked around, studying the environment, staring down at the lake, then off to his right at the massive granite hill. And finally, into the deep forest looming behind him.

"Get back to work, you dummy," he mumbled to himself, feeling foolish.

The loose boulders were perfect for a lean-to. For the shelter's frame, Sam took down several small trees with his hatchet and trimmed them clean to make poles. He leaned the poles against the massive boulder above the crevice he'd dug out earlier. Then he tied them together using cordage.

The resulting structure was only the half of it. Normally, Sam would tie a tarp over the shelter's frame to make it as watertight as possible. But after observing his surroundings, he would keep his tarp for other purposes.

On the ground in the forest behind him were thick patches of moss, quick and easy to harvest. Sam spent a good hour pulling up large chunks of the stuff, which he then packed onto, and into the seams, of his lean-to. The spongy plant matter would keep the weather out as good as any tarp.

When he finished sealing the cracks between the poles, Sam collected fresh spruce boughs, which he used as roofing shingles, over the top of his lean-to. He put more boughs on the ground inside the shelter for matting. After almost three hours of work, Sam's shelter was not just complete, it was impressive. He knew he would sleep well tonight.

It was only midday, and next on his list was to build a fire ring, then collect fuel for burning. He used local stones for the ring and set them up near the entrance to his lean-to. Then he built a reflection wall out of a piece of granite in the shape of a slab. Sam stood the slab on end at the outside perimeter of the fire ring. It was a large, heavy stone, and would work great for reflecting the fire's heat back toward him as he slept.

There was plenty of immediate fuel available. Deadfall and old, fallen timbers, which Sam trimmed with his hatchet, then dragged over to his shelter. And if he got desperate, there was driftwood down by the lake.

It took him roughly two hours to collect and prepare enough firewood and kindling to last him a few days. It was a good start, but as his experience told him, he may need a lot more. The maintenance behind keeping warm was an ongoing process, one of which he would attend to regularly. And so was the finding of food.

Sam sat on the ground next to his lean-to and contemplated his plans for provisions. If he stayed in the bush for several weeks, he would need more to eat. He only had two weeks' worth of rations, most of which were dehydrated meals—easy to cook and packed with calories. But his plan was to save most of that food for later, in case he got into a jam. In order to do this, he had to find another food source. And in the wilderness, this was a task that ranged from the comically easy to damn near impossible.

Most, if not all, of the next day, Sam would spend on the gathering of food. He would set up snares for small game, look for berry patches and a few edible plants he knew of, and would begin the process of actively hunting. He had plenty of essential gear in his duffel bags, including a carton of curing salt, should he need to preserve the meat from a larger animal. The necessity of such a kill ranked high on Sam's list, particularly if he stayed out here longer than a few weeks.

And as for his plans on how long he intended to stay... Well, Sam wasn't leaving until he found Bryson or the snow began, whichever came first. Since the winter was still months away, if he didn't find his brother after only a few days of searching, he would have to hunt for something big. In the meantime, he'd keep a sharp eye out for where such creatures were located.

For his first evening, he figured he'd try his hand at fishing. In one of the duffel bags was a carbon fiber, telescopic rod and reel, and an assortment of flies. Sam took the items out and fixed them up. He got the rod strung and ready to go, then leaned it against his shelter.

Dusk was on the rise, so Sam was now considering his personal safety. The evening was a prime time for predators to lurk about. He already had his .44 Magnum strapped to his side. But he had also brought a can of bear spray, which he dug out from a duffel bag. The last thing he wanted to do was kill an animal unless he absolutely needed to. And if he ran across an obstinate or hungry grizzly, the bear spray would help Sam maintain this goal.

He didn't think there would be too many hungry bears about, considering the time of year and that so far the area had had its share of rain. This was one detail Sam had collected from Andre, as it was important to know the current state of affairs for any local wildlife before heading out into the bush. Droughts caused poor vegetation growth, which in turn limited local prey populations, such as deer and elk. The effect of this was a lack of food for predators. Bears also relied heavily on the consumption of berries and grass, both of which were adversely affected by poor precipitation. If the water cycle had been disrupted by even a few inches, then the resulting domino effect could put a lone human in quite the danger from predators.

But the weather had been good, meaning that for now Sam's only concern regarding larger animals was running across a mother bear and her cubs.

Or so he told himself.

He paused and looked around, thinking more about Andre's crazy stories. What if they were all true? What if there really was an eight-hundred pound monster lurking in these woods, preying on humans? Would his bear spray be of any help? For that matter, would even his sidearm?

Feeling a chill run through his body, Sam secured the bear spray on his belt, next to his .44. Then he grabbed his waterproof bag containing all his food and hung it in a tree a few hundred feet south of his camp, and close to the lake's shoreline. He took this time to learn more about his surroundings and to look for signs from both animals and humans.

When he returned to his camp, he took his fishing pole and canteen along with his binoculars, then left again, this time heading for the upper end of the granite crag. He stopped at the base of the promontory and studied the boulder's incline. He set his canteen and pole down next to a tree, then began the ascent upward, all the way to the top, and at all times keeping his senses alert for a cougar.

It took him a little under ten minutes to finish his climb. The ascent was over five-hundred feet, most of which was angled at less than forty-five degrees. And the view at the top was stunning. It was just as Sam had expected.

He stood on the edge of the promontory. His view of the entire lake and the surrounding forests and valleys was now unhindered. It was the tallest point in the immediate area, dwarfed only by the chain of mountains in the near distance, and on the opposite side of the lake, three or four miles away. Those were true mountains, painted pine green with angled slopes, steep canyons, and craggy peaks that brushed the bellies of clouds.

There was a cool breeze coming off the water. The enormous yawning sky was a galaxy of blue and brass, forever deep, forever brilliant. The land itself was majestic and wild, void of anything that hinted the existence of man's presence.

Looking down, the surface of the lake was a straight drop. The granite peak had edged out beyond the shoreline a good fifty feet. A fall from here would make for a painful if not crippling landing in the water, and thinking of this, Sam took a step back. Then he put his binoculars to his eyes and studied the open landscape. His goal was to observe and absorb everything.

And also, to look at one thing. One thing in particular...

Regarding the land as a whole, Sam studied this environment through the lens of Nali's imparted wisdom, hoping to piece it all together. He scanned the valleys and ridgelines and then the canyons, with their crooked watercourses. And he studied the distant mountain range, wondering what secrets those peaks kept hidden. Sam looked on at the dark surface of the lake, guessing at its depth. He searched the lake's many shorelines, knowing that such places were the perfect spots for finding tracks, human or otherwise. And carefully, he studied the shadowy pockets of the many trees standing at the water's edge, looking for big game such as moose or elk, figuring he might have to hunt one of those creatures soon. Sam observed the land, the *entire* land, and he looked for anything he could use that would help him to not just survive, but to accomplish his ultimate goal.

And after he was finished, he lifted his binoculars and looked again. Only this time, he looked at that *one* thing—the spot directly across from him and on the other side of the lake.

It was a sandy shoreline with a small grassy meadow surrounded by trees. And by observing this spot, Sam felt a sudden punch to his gut.

He had seen this exact place many times before, in his younger years, while volunteering for the local Search and Rescue of southern New Mexico. In most cases, he worked in the Gila Wilderness, since that was where people often got lost. It was an exciting time for Sam. Working with the SAR had provided valuable experience, and it helped him learn more about the land and the wilderness. It taught him about the human mind, along with human behavior, while under the dire stress of being lost. Sam's SAR experience had perfected those tracking skills he'd learned years earlier, from Nali. And it exposed him to teamwork and coordinated efforts, both of which had prepared him for his future training in the military.

But the one thing Search and Rescue didn't prepare Sam for was how he was feeling right now.

Yes. He had seen this exact location many times in the past. And he had seen the looks on the faces of those loved ones involved, as they stared at this spot with such blind conviction or shaky resolve. And sometimes with a hopefulness that reached beyond logic.

Other times, they just looked on with a cruel and sad stare, one that always preceded their fall into emotional oblivion.

Sam had seen these people—the family members of the lost and stolen—and he had watched how they'd reacted. But he never imagined he would be one of them.

As he looked at the Point Last Seen, the last place his brother had stepped foot on, Sam wondered again about the mysteries of this land. He wondered how such a skilled and avid outdoorsman, a master survivor of the wilderness with all its splendors and hazards, how such a person could have simply vanished, leaving nothing behind other than his last unseen breath.

Slowly, Sam pulled his binoculars from his eyes and stepped back from the edge of the promontory. He felt a vague coldness take hold of his conscience. It was a dark and hopeless feeling, tainted with dread, and it reached up from the pit of his stomach and brought with it a confusing mixture of sadness and anger.

He still couldn't believe it. Like so many others from Sam's past, his own brother had joined the ranks of those who'd gone missing.

CHAPTER 15

That night, Sam ate a small trout he'd caught at the lake and he drank a few cups of tea, then promptly fell asleep. He slept soundly in his shelter throughout the night and was plenty warm. The evening had never gotten too cool. But by morning the chill had arrived and his fire had been dead for a while.

It was a brisk and quiet morning. He heard only a few birds singing somewhere in the far distance. The sky was overcast, just a thin blanket of moisture holding little promise of immediate rain.

Sam got up and relit his fire, then hung a small kettle of water over it. He was slow to wake and ready for coffee. He felt a steady heaviness in his bones. It was a normal feeling, the product of working a long day while exploring a new environment. He would be fully awake soon. A few cups of coffee and a calorie-packed breakfast would help him get there.

As he waited for the water to boil, Sam took a casual walk to retrieve his food bag. It was still hanging in the tree down by the lake.

Before he brought the bag down, he made a brief sweep of the area, searching for signs of anything that may have come snooping around, such as a curious grizzly.

But bear tracks weren't the only things Sam was looking for, as much as he didn't want to admit it. In the back of his mind were those other prints Andre had showed him. If Sam ran across something like that, an unexplainable track of a large humanoid creature, well then...

Well then, what? Just what would he do?

He retrieved his bag and headed back to camp. After he got there, he fixed himself a pot of instant coffee. He was very hungry, so he prepared and ate a breakfast of dehydrated eggs and ham, which seemed to only whet his appetite. Refusing the temptation to cook another package, Sam cleaned up and then hung his food back in the tree. He decided then to do a little fishing, mostly so he could get back to observing and thinking.

He stuck to the beaches and shorelines near his camp, and he took his time, splitting his attention between fishing the lake and studying the land. As usual, he was looking for anything out of the ordinary, knowing that sometimes clues were discovered when least expected—on a whim, perhaps, or a casual glance at just the right spot.

Sam thought about this... Then, to his surprise, his mind snuck back to his conversations with Andre. He remembered the man saying that the best time to see a Sasquatch was when you weren't looking for one. Andre had gone into detail about this theory, explaining how it was rare for people to witness the creature by "accident." According to him, the elusive beast had complete mastery over its environment, which is why it has remained undiscovered. But humans, on the other hand—even hunters, who often dressed in camouflage and stalked quietly through the bush—stood out like beacons to the animals of the forest. Because of this, it was impossible for a Sasquatch not to notice a person before they noticed it.

Sam pulled at the whiskers of his beard, thinking about that. Then he moved up the shore a few feet and cast his fly on the opposite side of a smooth boulder sticking out of the water. He figured if Sasquatch existed—and again, that was a huge "IF" in his mind—then another reason it was rarely seen was because it must be nocturnal. And humans were wary of the night. Also, Sam suspected the population of the species to be critically low, perhaps even on the verge of extinction.

Then another thought occurred to Sam: with his own skill set and in a place like this, it would certainly be easy for him to elude contact with other humans. He'd been successful at doing this exact thing while living in the Gila Wilderness. Even in broad daylight, Sam felt confident he could remain hidden from others for quite some time. The Chiricahua had done it, and while their own brothers, General George Crook's Apache Scouts, had hunted them.

Sam remembered his father's history lesson of long ago. Some of Crook's more notable scouts were Chief Chato, the Apache Kid, and the man who brought Geronimo in, Sergeant William Alchesay, otherwise known as "Little One." Although the combined efforts of these scouts had helped to end the Apache Wars, there were still bands of warriors that eluded even the best of trackers. These bands went south, deep into Mexico's Sierra Madre wilderness, where they continued to live their ways of life well into the twentieth century.

If both Sam and the Apaches could remain hidden, well then... why couldn't a nocturnal creature whose species was on the verge of extinction?

Sam felt a bite on his line. Seconds later, he had a fish on. He reeled it in, unhooked it, then secured it to a stringer. It was a decent sized trout, big enough for a meal, so there was no reason to let it go.

He started fishing again, whipping his fly out into the water, using the technique Bryson had taught him. His brother was a good angler. But he was an even better hunter.

Sam considered this characteristic for a while until an idea popped into his head. A really good idea. An idea Sam hoped he could follow up on by the end of the day.

He fished for a few more minutes with no luck, then cleaned his trout and went back to camp. He wanted to set up snares, and between finding suitable locations and preparing the traps, the job would take a good amount of time. But the need to find other food sources to supplement Sam's rations was crucial.

He placed his fish in a plastic bag and hung it in a tree, hoping nothing would find it before he came back. Then he cut himself approximately fifty-feet of parachute cord off the ample supply he kept inside one of the duffel bags. He rolled the cord up and stuck it in a side-pocket of his cargo pants, then headed off into the surrounding hills.

He scouted the land, searching for large thickets of brush or berry patches. These places were ideal for setting snares. They provided cover for small mammals and clear signs as to the paths critters took while traveling in and out of their shelters. Sam found several good thickets within a quarter-mile radius of his camp. After a few hours of work, he had half a dozen snares set and ready to go, and was back at his fire in time for lunch.

He cooked the trout over flames, rotisserie style, and supplemented the meal with a bowl of reconstituted black beans. When he finished eating, he cleaned up his dishes, then began the second half of his day...

Which was to search for Bryson.

Sam started by gathering up his essential tools for tracking: a broad brim hat, sunglasses, gloves, knife, gun, bear spray, notepad, caution tape, water bottle, binoculars, hand axe, and a cutting stick—a modified cane used for following tracks. Then he took one of the duffel bags and walked down to the lake.

Inside the bag was an Advanced Elements inflatable kayak. Sam unpacked the watercraft, then inflated it using a hand pump. It was well-designed, with a performance similar to that of a hard shell kayak, making it more than capable of navigating across the lake.

Satisfied with his preparations, Sam hung the duffel bag in a tree, then climbed into the kayak and paddled out. He decided to take his time and not cut straight across the lake, but to slowly cruise its perimeter. Intentionally, he stayed within twenty-feet of the shore, scrutinizing the land as he quietly moved along. Next to observing the land by air, a watercraft provided one of the best ways to collect information about the surrounding environment. And Sam knew exactly what to look for.

The lake was restless. There was now a slight breeze holding steady across the water, chopping small whitecaps onto the surface. The overcast sky had cleared. What remained was a brilliant blue amphitheater accented by small patches of high clouds.

The surrounding shores were a mixture of dense evergreen—white spruce and lodgepole pine—broken up by occasional hardwoods such as willow and aspen. There were several wide meadows brushed onto the terrain, their grassy fields freckled with wildflowers and berries. It was a peaceful landscape, and if the circumstances had been different, Sam would have enjoyed more of the scenery.

A small tributary fed into the north end of the lake. It dropped into a deep green pool accented with massive granite boulders. Sam made a mental note of the area, as it looked like a promising place to catch fish.

It took him a little over an hour to travel half the perimeter of the lake. He stopped almost directly opposite from where he'd dropped in at, and at a location approximately near where his brother had camped. Very slowly, he climbed out of the kayak and onto the shore, aware that any of his movements now could destroy evidence relating to what had happened to Bryson.

Sam thought more about that.

In this location, it was an absurd idea to be concerned about wrecking evidence. The Search and Rescue teams had already done that long ago, at least in the immediate area. And even though their search was ridiculously short, all those boots on the ground had likely made a mess of the terrain.

Sam pulled his kayak up onto the shore, shaking his head. He had never expected to find anything immediately, anyway. Not at the Point Last Seen. But he was prepared to dig deeper into the mystery. And he had a few ideas on how to go about doing that.

Before proceeding to where his brother had camped, he took his time searching up and down long stretches of the sandy shoreline. It was an ideal environment for track traps, a place that would capture and keep the prints of passing animals. More than once Sam had cut sign in areas such as this.

He kept his eyes open for anything of interest. In particular, he looked for those two prints Andre had made casts of, and which he claimed were from a Sasquatch. The SAR team leader had mentioned he discovered them within a thousand yards of Bryson's campsite. He even made a note of the spot on Sam's map.

But Sam didn't have to consult the map.

The dead giveaway was Andre's own tracks. Sam found those within minutes of searching. He followed them north for approximately five hundred yards, where they had suddenly stopped... upon discovering the two large prints in the mud.

Sam stooped down and stared at the colossal impressions. Their dimensions were larger than anything he'd seen before. The prints were old, crusted over with a layer of caked dirt. They resembled human tracks, with toes and a heel, but were much bigger. And they were deep. Real deep.

Slowly, Sam stood, the hair on his neck rising slightly.

He could tell Andre had cautiously searched the perimeter surrounding the large prints. The length of the man's stride had cut almost in half, indicating a slow and steady stalk across the immediate area.

Of course, that's exactly what Sam would have done. It's what he did right now, as he studied the surrounding terrain. He was responding to his inner voice, the one that commanded situational awareness. It was telling him that right now, at this very moment, he should observe *everything*.

Sam's heightened sense of awareness was common amongst military personnel. It was crucial for succeeding in a Special Forces unit. It was also crucial for law enforcement, air traffic controllers, and firefighters. Even driving a car took a certain amount of situational awareness. And so did growing up in the gang-infested streets of Los Angeles.

That last example came from Sam's friend and spotter, Ernie Valencia—whose fate still remained a mystery. Although Sam was surprised to learn gang members had a firm grip on situational awareness, it made sense to him afterward. Theirs was a stressful life. And stress was the key ingredient to knowing one's environment. In the end, it all came down to survival of the fittest.

More than once, Sam had seen Ernie's skills put into action—an action that saved both of their lives. Ernie was a fine soldier and Sam suspected his upbringing was responsible for the level at which the man had operated.

Sam stepped closer and studied the massive prints. They were less than ideal in the way of detail. That was because they had been cast and exposed to the elements for days. In their present condition, if he had run across them without knowing Andre's story, he would've assumed they were grizzly tracks.

What perplexed Sam the most, though, was that the large prints were the only ones to be found. He searched the area carefully, but couldn't find any more. Judging by the surrounding landscape—made up of muddy shoreline and a meadow of tall grass—there should have been something left behind.

Almost certainly, Andre had searched the area for more clues. Perhaps the man had inadvertently wiped away any less noticeable evidence. This was a common error made by inexperienced trackers. Their untrained eyes often overlooked the smaller details, such as compressed stones, bruised vegetation, transfers of terrain, and broken twigs and branches.

Sam spent several minutes looking around, observing the surrounding area and its features. Further up the beach, scattered driftwood broke the smooth sandy shoreline, their bony structures eerily reminiscent of broken corpses strewn over a battlefield. Roughly a hundred feet away, and off to Sam's left, a single, enormous cedar stood ominously over a ragged copse of birch trees.

Somewhere in the distance, two ravens were arguing over something.

Eventually, Sam came to the opinion that whatever had made those prints had come down from the forest to his left. He speculated the creature had then crossed through the thick meadow to reach the muddy shoreline, bending the lush grass down along the way. The healthy spring-grown vegetation would have sprung back to its original form within days, if not hours—another detail many trackers, such as Andre, might have overlooked. This route could explain why there were no more tracks to be found in the immediate area.

It made sense to Sam now. He guessed the creature had come down from the forest, walked over to the lake to get a drink, taking two steps in the mud as it did so, then turned around and went back the way it came.

Briefly, Sam searched the surrounding forest off to his left. He looked for the signs of something big that had passed through the area. But he found nothing. So he went back down to the shore and to his kayak. It was time for him to investigate the Point Last Seen. And for a moment, Sam felt a fleeting twinge of dread rush up into his chest.

He took a deep breath and continued onward, crossing the hundred feet of meadow before entering his brother's campsite. As expected, the area was a mess. It looked like a herd of buffalo had trampled the ground. There was no hope of finding anything left behind by Bryson, other than concrete clues, such as a pocketknife or food wrapper. And Sam doubted he'd be so lucky as to find something like that.

The campsite—what was left of it—was an area roughly thirty-feet in diameter. Sam could see where his brother had pitched his tent and where he made his fire. He also discovered the natural chair Bryson had used, made from the dead larch tree. There was, of course, nothing else to be found. There was no more evidence of any kind except for the rampant thrashing the land had sustained from the Search and Rescue teams. Sam suspected this would be the case. But he came to this spot prepared to look on with a fresh set of eyes. And he came with the idea his mind had conjured earlier that day, while fishing for trout.

Sam wondered if any of the searchers had considered Bryson's full intentions while they searched for the guy. Had any of them sought to see the forest among the trees? Or did they simply follow orders and scour the land, as they applied their grid search patterns?

Sam doubted any of the searchers had looked deeper into the mystery, except for Andre. But even then, there was one thing Andre didn't know, an insight which could have made all the difference in the world.

Andre didn't know Bryson the way Sam did.

Sam walked back to the beach and observed the distant shores on the other side of the lake. He put his binoculars to his eyes and he studied the terrain very carefully. He observed the deep hollows and thick tree lines, the muddy embankments and the rocky ground. He thought about why his brother had come out here. It certainly wasn't to fish. That was just a convenient, secondary adventure. Bryson had come to Earl Lake with one objective in mind. To reconnoiter the land for a moose hunt.

And this, as Sam knew, was the forest from the trees...

Within minutes, Sam discovered the location that his brother might have ventured into. He even imagined Bryson standing here, in this very spot, peering through his binoculars as he studied the green marsh on the opposite shore. It was possible Bryson had even seen or heard a moose before going over there to check it out.

Sam wasn't certain of anything, except for what his gut was telling him right now. And what his gut told him, as he looked on at the marshy terrain a few hundred yards away, was that somewhere over there, hiding on the other side of the lake, was his first real clue to the mystery of his brother's disappearance.

CHAPTER 16

The search of the marsh started late the next morning. After Sam had checked his snares and found one that contained a small woodchuck, he spent the first part of the morning preparing the animal to eat. He ate most of the critter for breakfast, salted and bagged the rest, then cleaned up his camp. Then he gathered his tracking gear and went down to the lake.

Sam was hopeful about the location he was heading to. He knew it was a long shot. But it was as good of a shot as any other.

He climbed into his kayak and paddled out, heading north. The lake was smooth as glass. But the sky carried with it the rough threat of rain. Heavy gray clouds drifted over the lake and treetops. From the mountain range in the far distance came a low roll of thunder. Sam looked up and cringed. He wasn't concerned about the weather for his own sake. It was plenty warm, and he knew how to stay dry. But with every spring storm came the likelihood of more crucial evidence being washed away.

Still, the cool mountain air had brought a calming effect with it. While paddling his kayak, for once, Sam felt comfortable about this place, as if that persistent sense of dread lurking somewhere in the forest had taken a temporary reprieve.

The low clouds reminded him of springtime in the Gila. With this memory came the assurance of being in a place Sam could easily call home. In part, he was feeling the effects of complete solitude, and that put him at ease. There wasn't a soul in sight. Possibly not even within a fifty-mile radius.

He paddled forward, and within a few minutes, came to the marshy area. It was a stretch of wetland that sat between the lake and a low rising hill. The lakeside of the hill held a sparse scattering of trees—not a thick forest, just a collection of tall cottonwoods and cedars.

The marshland was flat and looked like a mossy meadow freckled with an occasional water birch and a few thickets of berry bushes. There was a thin layer of fog sitting quietly over the area, as if biding its time before the onslaught of the inevitable afternoon breeze. Sam observed all of this from the comfort of his kayak, as he plotted a route he'd take up into the trees as soon as he came ashore.

He found a small gravelly spot south of the marsh, where he beached his kayak. He climbed out, and then the feeling of alarm came over Sam once again. It was the same feeling he felt the day before, when he stood on the beach of the opposite shore, near his brother's camp. He reminded himself that if he wasn't careful with how he traveled across the land, he could easily destroy valuable clues. Only, in this case, as opposed to yesterday, the possibility of evidence still existing was much greater.

He tied his kayak to the trunk of a nearby pine tree, grabbed his gear, then took three steps forward into a wooded area. Quietly, he scanned his surroundings—from the opening of the thin forest along the rising hill off to his right, the wide expanse of marsh stretching in front of him, and then finally, to the ground at his feet. Sam studied his entire environment as he took slow, calculating steps forward. For certain, his gut-feeling told him Bryson had been here.

Sam spent thirty minutes searching the first fifty-feet of shoreline. He looked for track traps, such as muddy flats or sandy shores. He found one area along the edge of the marsh that contained several tracks of both big and small animals, some of which were from a large bull moose.

But none of the tracks were Bryson's.

Sam crouched down and studied a moose track, thinking of his brother. Bryson would have carefully crossed this land so as not to leave too much of his scent behind. It was something Sam would have done if he was hoping to find a moose.

He went back to his kayak, stood on the beach, then surveyed the running shoreline in both directions. There weren't too many places to land a craft in the immediate area. The gravelly shore seemed to have been the easiest, most natural location. Supposing Bryson had come ashore at this very spot, there would be little evidence of his passing. The beach was too hard to catch a footprint, so Sam looked closer at the ground, searching for upturned stones or twigs. But it had been a few weeks since Bryson had gone missing, and the prospect of something that small showing itself to Sam seemed minimal.

Slowly, he walked the area again. This time he skirted further south, away from the wetland. Sam's hunch told him Bryson would have first traveled this way, in the opposite direction of the area of interest (being that of the marsh) before moving further into the trees. By heading outward, Bryson could quietly move up along the hillside, flank the land below, then gain a better view of the area without spooking any moose.

And as it turned out, Sam's hunch was correct.

He found the first of Bryson's tracks on the edge of a muddy seep. It was in a clearing south of the marsh and along a gentle slope of the reigning hillside. There were four boot prints pressed an inch deep into the mud, one of which had been muddled over by what looked like the passing of a beaver.

The strides between Bryson's tracks were shorter than average. That did not surprise Sam. Bryson had been scouting the land, paying attention to details and taking absolute care not to alarm any creatures. Again, it was what Sam would have done.

The tracks pointed east, toward the hillside. Sam followed in that direction for approximately fifty-feet before he found another print. This one was dry, but it had previously been pressed into a layer of mud that had collected water after a recent rain.

The direction of travel remained the same. And approximately thirty-feet from the print, Sam found a scuff mark on the bark of a fallen branch. He suspected the heel of Bryson's boot had made the impression.

Suddenly, Sam felt a rush of excitement; he was following the steps made by his brother. But also, he felt sadness and fear. With the time that had passed, he didn't believe for one minute his brother was still alive. Whatever had come across Bryson—an accident, the attack of a wild animal, or Andre's crazy theory—Sam knew from experience that the probability of his brother still breathing sat next to zero.

Sam had seen plenty of corpses in his life. More than his fair share. The worst had been his first. And not because of his lack of experience. But because it had been that of a very young girl.

Her name was Emily Parsons, a four-year-old who had gotten lost while camping with her family in the Gila Wilderness. The SAR team Sam was with had found her on the fifth day of searching. It was a sight he would never forget.

Cold and exhausted, little Emily had curled her small frame up against the trunk of a fallen tree and fell asleep for the last time. The tragedy had ruined Emily's parents. With empathy, Sam witnessed their devastation when he and the others brought the girl's body back to the base camp.

More bodies followed that. Missing hikers and hunters, each with a similar heartbreaking story. Then with the war came much, much more. Sam had observed those corpses with a different perspective. But the feeling of sadness had never been too far below the surface of his thoughts. To Sam, the sight of human tragedy was always a stark reminder of Emily Parsons.

With mounting fear, he thought of his brother. What would Bryson's corpse look like? At the very minimum, the sight would be just as bad as when Sam had found that little girl so many years before.

The hill sloped upward by about thirty degrees. Sam hugged its surface, looking for more signs of his brother's route. Not finding anything for a while, he went back to the last significant track, the boot scuff on the fallen branch, then prepared his cutting stick. He took two pieces of cord and tied them at a distance on the stick that measured roughly the same as Bryson's stride. Then he placed the stick on the ground, one end against the scuffed branch and the other end in the direction he thought Bryson had traveled.

After careful observation, Sam found brown coloring on a piece of green vegetation. The stain showed that the plant had been bruised in the past—and probably from Bryson's boot. Sam marked the spot and set the first end of the cutting stick down on it. Then he looked once again at where the next track should be.

It was painstaking work. And far from accurate. Sometimes Sam found evidence of Bryson's trail, and when he did not, he guessed his way forward until he discovered the next concrete sign. But this leap-frog method of searching kept Sam going. And little by little, he traced Bryson's pathway through the forest and up the hillside.

It took him several hours of tracking and reading sign before Sam felt he had a sound theory on how his brother had reconnoitered the land. After coming to shore, Bryson traveled south for approximately one hundred yards. Then he began a slow and steady climb halfway up the sloping hillside. He cut across the hill at its midpoint for three-hundred yards, where he then changed his course and began a gradual descent down toward the marsh. In the process, Bryson hugged a thin line of trees, keeping the trunks between his body and the wet meadow. He walked slowly now—very slowly—as he was undoubtedly conscious of a moose's keen hearing. When he reached the bottom, Bryson stood in place and studied the details of the marsh for quite some time. He'd obviously discovered plenty of moose sign, just the same as Sam had observed, and then, feeling content, Bryson must have decided to leave the area. Then he turned around and went back the way he came, to his boat.

This was the scenario Sam had pieced together—the complete breakdown of how his brother had navigated and studied this side of the lake. But unfortunately, it lacked any evidence that could help Sam right now. So what if his brother had been here? There was still no dead body or sign of an attack from a predator, such as a bear. And there was still the lingering mystery as to what had ultimately happened to Bryson. In the search for his brother, Sam was no better off now than when he first arrived on this side of the lake earlier in the day.

Feeling frustrated, Sam headed back toward his kayak. Then he paused, thinking more about the area. He turned and looked way up the hillside, above even where Bryson had been. He observed the trees up there and the open spots in between, and how they were covered in sparse brush and short grass. At the top of the hill was a granite spine, scaly and broken, and augmented here and there with stunted spruce.

Sam proceeded to climb to the top of the hill to see what kind of view it offered. He got more than halfway up and then stopped beside the trunk of a large alder to adjust the laces on one of his boots. Crouching down to deal with his boot, Sam suddenly froze in place...

On the ground behind the tree was a flat spot of dry mud. And in that spot were two distinct footprints set side-by-side. They were humanlike, but nearly twice the length of a grown man's foot and easily double the width. And they were, of course, identical to the tracks Andre had discovered down on the beach.

Sam stood up and took a step back to get a better perspective on what he was looking at. In his mind, he heard his memories replay themselves. *Some clues were found when least expected...*

It was an uncanny thought. And an eerie one.

Sam crouched down again and studied the prints with a sharp eye. And that's when the hair on the back of his neck stood tall.

He was a firm believer that even the smallest piece of evidence could tell a story. Observing those tracks in the mud, the story Sam read was a simple one. Something very big had stood here behind this tree. And whatever it was, it was looking in the direction of the marsh below and watching—with possible intent—something down there.

Or someone.

CHAPTER 17

Later that day, Sam stood at the perimeter of his camp chewing on a piece of woodchuck meat and scanning the distant tree trunks and shadowed pockets of the surrounding forest. He was feeling both nervous and foolish. He couldn't help wonder about Andre McKinnon, and what the man would have to say about those tracks Sam had just discovered.

He thought more about those footprints up on the hillside. Whatever made them had been overlooking the exact spot where Bryson had been standing. Sam considered the possibility that the prints were made either before or after Bryson had been there. But something in his gut told him that wasn't the case. Something in Sam's gut told him his brother had been stalked.

He considered the possibilities and wondered what, if anything, he could do about it. Sam had never taken Andre's stories seriously enough to fit them into any of his plans. But if his brother had become a victim of such a killer, as Andre had claimed... If that was true, well then, Sam just might have to hunt whatever was out here.

At the very least, he'd have to track it, hoping to find its shelter—assuming it had one. In his effort to discover what had happened to Bryson, finding that creature's den made the most sense to Sam. Wherever the thing slept, there was likely to be some kind of evidence of his brother—a piece of clothing, some hair or bone, anything. It was a grim thought, but a valid one.

Sam pulled a drink from his canteen and stared into the distance. If the creature truly existed, could it be out there right now, staring back at him?

Sam listened to the forest, suddenly noticing the dead silence within. In what he would normally accept as a peaceful lull, he wondered now if he was experiencing the "hush of fear"—a time when all the small critters stayed quiet while a predator passed on by. It was a phenomenon Sam had observed countless times before, and mostly when he himself was the hunter.

Sam shook his head at the thought. Maybe he was just being paranoid because he was spooked from finding those tracks up on the hill.

Still, there was one thing Sam knew: whatever had made those prints had also been overly cautious. Sam had scouted the area for more signs, hoping to determine a path the creature had taken either before or after it had stood behind the tree. But Sam had found nothing. Not even the smallest trace of evidence.

One reason for this had been the ground cover, which was made mostly of short grass and dense leaf matter. Such terrain inherently left behind little clues. And without knowing a direction of travel or even the creature's stride, there was little hope in tracking it.

Capping his canteen, Sam turned around and walked back to his fire, where he tried to relax. He spent the rest of his day close to camp, fixing things up, making it more livable. He crafted a comfortable place to sit near the fire ring, along with a table of sorts, by combining rocks with pieces of split timber. And he made another lean-to, to provide shelter for his gear and extra firewood.

When he was finished with the lean-to, Sam checked on his snares. He found one containing a strangled hare, which he field dressed down by the lake. Then he slow-cooked the critter and picked at it throughout the day. Later, he caught three good-sized trout, which he cleaned and salted, and then smoked over the fire.

In keeping busy, Sam thought mostly about what he was going to do. He felt he was at a stalemate of sorts after finding those tracks. That wasn't part of his plan. And in order to go forward, he had to consider his options and look at things from a different angle. Perhaps even from Andre's angle.

Also, assuming Sam's new plan was to track down a creature whose existence had yet to be proven—an incredible feat in itself—Sam now figured he would be out in the bush for much longer than a few weeks. And that meant he would need more food.

From one of his duffel bags, he retrieved a recurve bow with arrows, and then checked them for damages. Sam knew that in the next couple of days, he would have to kill something larger than lake trout or a small mammal.

Around dusk, Sam was feeling mentally tired and physically spent. He was cooking rice and beans together in a pot and heating one of the trout he'd caught on a flat rock set next to the fire when, incredibly, Sam suddenly heard a peculiar noise off in the distance.

He stood and took a few steps forward, listening carefully. After a minute, he knew what the sound was. And after another minute, Sam knew that whatever was making the sound was heading toward his camp.

CHAPTER 18

When the woman finally passed away, she did it lying next to her dead husband. Bryson felt a world of sadness for her. She had seemed so bewildered and beside herself with her unending terror. Because of the reigning darkness, Bryson never saw what she looked like. And to his saddest regret, he never got her name.

The couple had been thrown down there in such a rapidly violent manner that the incident had come and gone before Bryson could intervene or possibly escape. And then, just mere seconds later, the entire cavern was consumed by the woman's crying.

She lasted for maybe two days before she slipped away. Lying against the stone wall, Bryson heard her death unfold. He figured she had died from shock. Shock, from the brutal murder of her husband, the sudden collapse of everything she had known, and the horrifyingly hopeless reality of her future.

Bryson couldn't do anything for her, as he was too weak. And what could he have said to ease her pain or guide her through her mounting terror? There was no hope of escape or a rescue, so any words coming from Bryson's mouth conveying as much would only be a senseless lie.

In the end, he just let her be. Then the woman slowly slipped away, and he heard her breath become ever so shallow, until finally she vanished altogether into the gloom of her own making, dying at last from her shock.

That was a few days ago. And here Bryson was now, slipping away as well. He knew his own breath had become shallow and thin, as if it were hanging on by a thread. And his body felt light as air, seeming to weigh only that of a blanket. He had become a shell of a human being and he wondered how in the hell he was still alive. Bryson was sure his time would come soon, though. Maybe in a day, or two at the most. Certainly no more than that. And then he would find himself on the same path as that woman and her husband. Perhaps then he would finally learn what her name was...

CHAPTER 19

Sam stood quietly, listening with interest. With the evening sky now on the rise, the forest presented its darker shades of earth and pine. There was a buildup of clouds high above, a deep grayness that insulated the land like a heavy blanket. The subtle smell of rain lingered on a limp breeze, and from somewhere on the lake came the lonely call of a loon.

It turned out the sound Sam had heard was that of an old man walking through the forest, humming and whistling a tune. Following his lead was a smoky black mule with tiny sleigh bells attached to its harness, jingling with each step.

The duo had come down from the rising hill and woods behind Sam's camp. When they finally stopped in the clearing, with the old man looking around and smiling cheerfully and the mule eagerly bending down to crop at the grass, Sam felt a rush of mild curiosity. This was something he had never expected.

"Good evening, mate," the old man said cheerfully. He dropped the mule's reins and hobbled toward Sam. His gait appeared afflicted and labored, but he smiled easily and he quickly reached out his hand.

"Howdy," Sam replied, accepting the man's gesture. They shook hands and Sam noticed the rough, calloused skin behind the man's fingers, as well as the strength beneath his grip.

There was an ancient look in the old man's eyes and a vague frailness about his stature, as if he'd been broken somewhere on the inside and his wound had never properly healed. He had a slight hunch to his back. The whiskers covering most of his face were white as snow. He was wearing an assortment of clothing—Pacific Trail cargo pants, a long-sleeved shirt, and what looked like a handmade doeskin jerkin. The mule was loaded down with saddle bags and gear and its face mirrored the weariness of its owner's.

Sam immediately felt obliged to his guest. He quickly gestured for him to enter his camp. "Come on in," he said, leading the way toward the fire. "Name is Sam. Sam Nolan."

"Nice to meet you, Sam," replied the stranger. "And I'm Louis Pine." Then he chuckled. "Been a long time since I've introduced myself to another person. Surprised I remembered my own name. Just call me Lou, for short. And this here is Sally." He turned and gestured to the mule. "She's not big on conversation, except for when she's up for arguing. Thankfully, that's not too often. I guess she's a proper mule, if there ever was one." The man's voice carried with it a British accent, which Sam noticed immediately.

"Sounds like you're from across the pond," Sam said. He helped the old man unload Sally, then he tethered the mule to a sapling in the meadow. "I suppose you're a long way from home," Sam added.

Lou laughed. "Son, I've been in these mountains for so long that this is my home now." He straightened his body and scratched his beard. "But yes, you are correct. I was raised under the British Crown. Laverstoke, to be precise. That's near the River Test... Ever read the story *Watership Down*?"

"Can't say I have."

"Well, pick it up sometime. It's a mighty fine read. And it reminds me of my younger years."

They went over and sat by the fire. Sam insisted Lou sit in the more comfortable spot, the makeshift seat he'd crafted out of wooden timbers. It looked to him as if Lou had been on the trail for quite some time.

"I've got some fish here, if you're hungry." Sam dished some of the trout onto a plate and handed it to the old man. "Beans and rice are in the pot," he added, "and they're done enough."

Lou took the trout and smiled, the wrinkles in his eyes creasing deeply. "I guess I can eat a bit," he said. "And I've got plenty of dried rations over there in the pack, along with some jerked moose. There's even some canned fruit and a jar of honey!" He laughed out loud. "Why don't we have us a feast, Sam?"

Sam smiled at the man's candidness. "Sounds like a good plan," he said.

Lou reached inside his jerkin, fumbled for a minute, then pulled out a silver flask. "And to wash it down, here's a little whiskey I picked up a while back—if you got the thirst."

"Seems right for the occasion," Sam said. He paused, then added, "By the looks of it, mister, I'd say you're living out here."

Lou examined Sam's camp with interest. "You've got that right," he replied. "Like I said, these hills are my home. There's a place in Whitehorse I go to on occasion. A woman friend, if you know what I mean." Lou winked and grinned. "But I prefer to hang around here."

"Even in the winter?" Sam asked.

"Yep. Even in winter."

Sam thought curiously about that. Winters in the Yukon Territory were rough. To survive them, a man would need to have a good shelter of some kind. "Well then, I guess you do prefer living out here."

The old man settled back into his seat and started nibbling on the trout. He took his time, looking up at the sky, at the surrounding land, and then finally back at Sam. "You know, mate," he said, "I can't imagine living anywhere else. Out here, I have access to the biggest home on earth—and all to myself." He threw a smile at Sam. "Well, most of the time, that is. And this home of mine is brimming with luxuries you just cannot find within the confines of civilization. My home is a mansion, Sam..." He paused, stuck two fingers in his mouth, pulled out a fish bone, then flicked it into the fire. "I live in a *spectacular* mansion," he continued. "And it's better than the bloody Buckingham Palace." Lou wiped his mouth with his sleeve and took a drink from the flask. Then he offered the container to Sam. "Bourbon," he said. "Have some, if you'd like."

Sam accepted the flask and drank a small amount. The flavor was sweet and woody and it left a sharp bite on his tongue and a warm feeling in his gut. Tired as he was, his mind was now working overtime.

Sam was curious about Lou Pine and a little eager to hear more of the old man's history. Off the bat, he found Lou's personality infectious. And he guessed Lou to be intelligent, maybe even educated, based on the few words he had spoken. Lou had also mentioned he'd been living out here for quite some time... Sam suspected there was a reason for that. He wondered what had pushed Lou away from society.

Sam could only guess at a reason. Considering how he himself had been living the same life down in the Gila Wilderness, he wondered if some type of trauma had been the culprit to Lou's isolation—as it had been for Sam's.

But maybe Sam's inclination was wrong. It's possible the old man simply enjoyed living alone out here in his "mansion." He certainly wouldn't have been the first to venture off into the wilds in a quest for seclusion. Such people existed all throughout time and for reasons of which were many. Sam recalled reading an article once about these individuals, recluses known as "Perimeter Men." Men who, for various reasons, simply preferred a life of solitary confinement. Even if Sam hadn't been inflicted with PTSD, he could still see himself relating these individuals.

Whatever Lou's history was, Sam had more pressing concerns on his mind. Specifically, he was eager to find out if Lou had come across any evidence that could help him find Bryson. And also, if the old man knew anything about an eight-foot tall predator lurking in the Yukon Territory. Living out here for as long as he said he had, it reasoned to stand that Lou might know something about the creature—assuming such a creature existed. Sam was still unconvinced about that. And it was a topic he wasn't sure how to bring up.

"Well, Lou," Sam said, "you make a fine point. This place *is* a mansion of sorts." He capped the whiskey flask and handed it back to the old man. Then he slid on a glove and removed the lid from the cooking pot, which was sitting on a cluster of small stones inside the fire's perimeter.

Sam stirred the rice and beans with a spoon. "Pass your plate on over," he said, scooping up a heaping amount. He dished half the mixture onto Lou's plate and then set the pan down. From a waterproof bag, Sam retrieved a pouch containing spices, herbs, and condiments, each stored within small containers or miniature sauce bottles. "Here," he said, handing the pouch to Lou, "take whatever you want. There's salt and pepper, even a little hot sauce."

"Thanks, Sam," Lou replied, "don't mind if I do." The old man dug into the pouch and retrieved the hot sauce, then shook a few drops onto his food. He set the bottle down, took a bite, and smiled. The look of satisfaction crossed his face. "It's been a long while since I had hot sauce," he said. He ate some more, then looked curiously at Sam. "So then, what brings *you* out here?" he asked, almost as if he were privy to Sam's inner thoughts. The old man glanced around the camp. "Looks like you're planning on having something more than a brief holiday."

Sam looked up, then glanced off into the distance. He considered his answer. "I'll be honest, Lou. I'm out here looking for my brother. His name is Bryson, and he went missing a few weeks back." Sam gestured toward the lake with his fork. "Right over there, in fact. The other side of the lake was his camp. He came out here to fish… And to scout around… He was planning a moose hunt in the fall."

Lou stared in the direction Sam had pointed to, then stirred his body and gave a subtle grunt. "Gone missing," he said. He put his attention back on to his food. "And a few weeks ago? Is that what you said?"

"That's right," Sam replied.

Lou's face fell into a frown. "I hate to say it, but there are plenty of ways for a man to get into trouble out here. And if your brother was killed..." he cast a wary glance in Sam's direction, "well, chances are his body got dragged off by bears or coyotes by now. I don't mean to sound grim, Sam, but nothing dead lasts out here for very long. The wilderness is alive. And it's always hungry." Lou smiled down at his food. "Sure as you're sitting here with me right now, this wilderness will devour anything unlucky enough to stumble across its path."

Nodding, Sam picked up some of the trout from off the heated rock and deboned it. He dropped small chunks of meat into the pot of rice and beans now resting on his lap. "Mister Pine," he said, "I've been looking at this thing from every angle... even the one you just laid out. But the one thing I can't seem to come to terms with is the part about my brother getting killed out here. Bryson was as good a mountain man as anyone alive. He knew the ways of the wilderness better than most. Hell, a full-blooded Apache taught him how to thrive in a place like this." Sam took a bite of his food, chewed for a minute, then added, "My brother paid his bills trapping grizzlies and cougars. I just can't figure out how a man that good could go missing after being out here for a few days."

Lou smiled brazenly. "So your brother was a regular Davy Crockett, eh?"

Sam chuckled. "You can bet your mule on it, old man. My point is, I don't believe Bryson could have simply fallen victim to anything out here."

Lou took another drink of bourbon, then set the flask down on the ground. "What about his health?" he asked. "Could he have had a heart attack or a stroke? Maybe something like that took his life... Or incapacitated him."

"I suppose so," Sam replied, considering the possibilities. "But not likely." It seemed a stretch that a health-related tragedy would have fallen upon his brother. Bryson was young and healthy and he'd always taken good care of himself. Even so, such anomalies were known to happen.

But Sam's intuition was still speaking to him, just as it had on that first day he came down from the mountains to get his mail. "My suspicion," he said, "is that something *happened* to my brother. And my intentions are to find out what that was."

"Well, now," Lou said, "that is quite the noble sentiment. And I hope your intentions prove favorable. I am curious, though... how long do you intend to stay out here—looking for your brother, that is?"

"Until I find him," Sam replied. "Or the weather does me in."

They sat quietly for a while, eating their dinner and listening to the crackle of the fire. It wasn't fully dark yet and it wouldn't be for another few hours.

At one point, Lou got up and went over to check on Sally. When he came back, he had a can of peaches, along with a jar of honey and a small loaf of hard bread.

"So where're you from, Sam?" Lou asked. "You mentioned something about an Apache... I assume that would put you somewhere in the southwest. New Mexico or Arizona... Am I correct?"

"You guessed it," Sam replied. "Silver City, New Mexico. I grew up on a cattle ranch near the Gila. And I spent a lot of time up in that wilderness."

"I can see you're not kidding," Lou said. He gestured to Sam's lean-to, then added, "No weekend hiker would make something like that. They always bring those flimsy little tents with them. But a structure like yours... bloody hell, that'll last for quite some time."

"I've never liked tents myself," Sam said.

Lou nodded. He produced a pocketknife and used it to open the can of peaches. He dumped a few onto his plate and handed the can to Sam. Then he broke the loaf of bread in half and gave that to Sam as well, along with the jar of honey. "There's a unique feeling that comes with being alone out here," Lou said, "... or down there, I suppose, in your neck of the woods. Something that's hard to find while being surrounded by your fellow man. I call this feeling *timelessness*." Lou paused and looked up. "You ever feel that way, Sam? That feeling where, for once in your life, Time just slips away and leaves you in control."

Sam smiled. He knew exactly what the old man was alluding to. It was the feeling of being in complete control of your life and not subject to the interference of human stimuli.

"Still," Lou said with a smile, "it's nice to have good company once in a while."

They ate in silence for several minutes, listening to the fire and the occasional songs from distant loons out on the lake. Somewhere in the trees came the haunting screech of an owl. And then, from far away and in a lonely canyon, a pack of wolves began their evening chorus.

Sam added more fuel to the fire and took a few more sips of bourbon. His stomach was near full and he was feeling relaxed. He agreed with Lou, in that it was nice to have good company. And the old man seemed to fit the bill on that. After several more minutes of idle conversation, Sam was now feeling confident about bringing up the peculiar question lingering deep in his thoughts.

"Let me tell you something, Lou..." he began. "A few days ago, I met with a guy over in Carmacks. He was the team leader for the local Search and Rescue, so he'd been out here looking for my brother. The search teams didn't stay long, just a few days, if you can imagine that. But this guy came back later to do some searching of his own. And, well... crazy as this will sound, he told me something pretty darn weird. Something I've been having a hard time wrapping my head around."

"Oh yeah? And what was that?"

"Well," Sam continued, "it seems this guy thinks a Sasquatch took my brother." Sam chuckled and shook his head. "That just might be the craziest theory I've ever heard."

Lou looked down at his food. His face collapsed, losing all expression. He used the last of his bread to sponge honey off his plate, ate the piece, chewed for several seconds, then slowly looked up at Sam. "A crazy theory, eh?" he said. The old man paused and glanced over his shoulder, into the looming darkness, as if something in the woods had suddenly caught his attention. A few seconds later, he looked back at Sam. "And an interesting one... Because it's not the first time I've heard of that happening out here, Sam. Who knows? It just might be true."

• • •

When the night moved onto the land, it carried with it an eerie silence—a silence that seemed to seep down from the heavy clouds above and infiltrate the surrounding wilderness. The wolves had stopped their howling and the loons out on the lake sang no more. The fire still blazed and popped, and it seemed to be the only sound around, other than the few words spoken between Sam and Lou and the occasional breeze among the trees.

Both men were still awake, sitting at the fire and drinking tea. But there was a dull aura of quietude that had fallen upon them. An hour had passed since Lou shared his anecdotes regarding the "Elder Brother of the North," such being his term for Sasquatch. Lou said he'd learned of that name twenty years ago, from a Blackfoot Indian down near Crowsnest. The Native American explained how their "Elder Brother" would sometimes snatch people and take them up into the high country. The creature did this when he was angry with his younger "brothers" and "sisters". It was his way of reminding humans we should take better care of the land and of one another. It was also said that the Elder Brother was fond of taking children, but he was known to abduct adults from time to time. The one certainty regarding these abductions, though (and this, the Blackfoot had stressed) was that whoever the Elder Brother took, they were never seen or heard from again.

"I'm not so sure about that story I told you," Lou commented. "Sounds more like a silly legend mothers used for keeping their children close by. Especially at night—which was when the abductions were known to happen." The old man stared off into the darkness. "Besides," he added, "I've been out here for a long time, Sam, and I've been all over this territory. I've never seen any evidence for Sasquatch... And you'd think I would, wouldn't you?"

"I would expect so," Sam said reluctantly. Presently, his thoughts were being haunted by those tracks he'd found the day before. A part of him couldn't explain what had made them, other than a Bigfoot. And also, if Sam had come across those tracks in just the few days he'd been out here, then shouldn't Lou have found something in all his years?

But maybe Sam was wrong all along, and that he'd made a mistake with his previous observations. And that those tracks he'd seen had been made by something reasonable... Something that has already been proven to exist. And maybe Sam had made that mistake because Andre's stories were now too deep into his mind.

"However..." Lou said, holding a finger up, "I do make a lot of noise when I travel—as you've heard. I like to keep the bears and cougars up to date with my presence. And even though I've seen plenty of those critters around, despite my ruckus, with something as shy and reclusive as... Well, you get my drift. I've never seen a Sasquatch, Sam, but I won't say it doesn't exist."

"And you haven't seen anything that could be linked to my brother?" Sam asked.

Lou shook his head. "I'm afraid not. But I haven't been in this part of the country for a while. I'm usually on the other side of them mountains, over yonder."

Sam finished the last swallow of his tea, then dug out a can of Skoal from his pocket. He put a wad under his lip and offered the can to Lou, who raised a hand in rejection.

"No thanks," Lou said, retrieving a small leather pouch from his coat. "I've got my own." Within minutes, the old man had a pipe loaded with tobacco. He used a small stick from the fire to light it, then he puffed a large cloud of smoke into the air. He turned to Sam, smiling. "Nothing better to top a fine meal, proper jammy."

Sam nodded in agreement, then went back to thinking. He contemplated the tracks he'd seen up on that hill the day before. Perhaps they *had* been made by something else—such as a grizzly—and he'd just mistaken their identity. But he thought about that and wondered how a bear could have left such human-looking prints in the mud. It had been over twenty-four hours since he'd found those tracks. And even though time had slowly fogged the details of what he'd seen, he was sure the prints looked more human than bear.

They sat quietly for another twenty minutes. Then Lou set his cup down on the ground beside the fire and reached over and tamped his pipe gently on a rock, knocking the ashes loose. Slowly, he stood and stretched. "Well," he said, moving stiffly in his attempt to straighten his spine, "if you don't mind, Sam, I'd like to share your camp for the night."

Sam chuckled. "Of course," he replied. "I'd have it no other way." He watched as the old man moved about and Sam felt a little sorry for the guy. He realized old age, and possibly arthritis, had taken a toll on Lou's standard of living. "Let me help you get set up," he added, rising from the fire.

Lou held out a hand and shook his head. "No thanks, Sam. I can manage." He lifted his head and sniffed deliberately at the air. "There won't be any rain tonight. I think I'll just pull out my bag and blankets and curl up beside the fire."

"Sounds like a good enough plan," Sam said.

"Usually," Lou added, "I string up my hammock. That's a comfortable way to sleep out here. But I'm too bloody tired for that right now." He looked at Sam and winked. "I suppose that's what comes with fine meals and good company."

Sam sat quietly as Lou made his way over to Sally. Shortly later, the old man came back with a large wool blanket and sleeping bag. He kneeled down beside the fire and rolled everything out onto the ground. He gave an assortment of grunts and small curses before he finally seemed to settle in. And then he lay there on the ground, facing Sam with his eyes closed and a lazy smile strapped across his face.

"So tell me, Sam," Lou said after a while, "Have you ever served? You've got a military bearing about you."

Sam nodded. He was sitting on the ground and staring into the fire. "US Army," he replied softly.

"Figured as much." Lou's eyes were still closed, and he was still smiling. "Spent some time in the service myself, years ago." He chuckled. "Bloody hell—more like a lifetime ago. Her Majesty's Armed Forces. The Royal Marines. I even saw action in the Falklands War." Lou paused as his smile slipped into a look of dull concentration. "First time I killed a person was over there. That was something I'll never forget. A young bloke was all. Eighteen-years-old, I'm guessing. Maybe less. I shot him from three hundred yards away without a scope, if you can believe that. Got him right in the head. That was a lucky shot... or unlucky, depending on how you look at it." Lou paused, then added, "The kid never knew what hit him."

Sam focused his stare on the old man. He was wondering once again if there was something that had pushed Lou into the wilderness—something traumatic. Killing a young man in a war could certainly account for such trauma.

Sam also knew how it felt to take a man's life from afar. No matter the distance, to watch a body get destroyed through a high-powered scope has a way of bringing the war up close and personal to the man pulling the trigger. It was the grimmest of thoughts—and actions. And for Sam, it differed greatly from the killing of an animal for food.

In time, whenever Sam had shot a man with his sniper rifle, he thought hard about that person's life. He wondered if the man had a woman somewhere praying for his survival. For sure, there was a mother and a father, and Sam often wondered if they were sitting at home worrying about their son at the exact moment Sam's bullet tore a hole through the man's chest.

Sam's thoughts *were* grim. The instructors at the sniper course had warned the candidates about the dangers of such mind speak. Master Sergeant Joe Paxton often advised them to occupy their free time with thoughts of tan legs and sandy beaches, and to always have a plan for something to look forward to when they got home.

Sergeant Paxton also discussed the importance of keeping a technical mindset about the job. "We're no different from a mechanic, fellas," he would say. "Dispatching a target is the same as changing the oil in your car. Remember that when you're taking down numbers. And remember also, that for every tango who walks away, there's another one of our boys who might go home in a body bag."

In the first years of Sam's military career, the Sergeant's words had worked well. But after a while, something had changed for Sam. Every time he shot a person and every time he saw a dead body, he was reminded of little Emily Parsons, the four-year-old who'd perished in the Gila Wilderness, so many years ago. And finally, just as Sam thought he couldn't take it anymore, the unthinkable happened. He and Ernie got captured by the enemy.

"What am I doing," Lou said, "bringing up such a horrible topic before bed?"

Sam looked up, his mind suddenly pulled back to the present.

"I just thought you had that look, is all," Lou continued. "The look of discipline. That comes with being in the military. Anyway, to change the subject..." Lou opened his eyes and stared at Sam, smiling once again. "I just remembered something. A few years back, there was an incident out here. Something that I can't explain. I heard a noise one night. Actually, I was about ten miles away, and to the east. But anyway, that noise..." Lou paused, as he pulled his blanket closer in. "It was a loud scream. Very loud. Very long. It came from up a canyon behind me. One long howl running down the mountain and into the valley... It rolled like thunder. And I felt it in my bones. I've never heard anything like it, Sam. And I haven't heard it since. But I'll say this right now. It was bloody creepy." Lou snickered, then added, "Maybe there is something out here. An Elder Brother, as they say." Lou's smile faded. "And if it gets angry with its brothers and sisters—or perhaps just curious—well, then maybe it does take a person away."

Suddenly, Sam was wide awake. The slow approach of slumber had been halted as he thought about what Lou had just said.

A loud scream...

Sam thought about Andre's harrowing experiences. He, too, had heard a terrifying scream. And not from a wolf, cougar, bear, or a bird. But a scream from something much bigger.

"A loud scream, you say?" Sam asked.

"That's right. Very loud, and very long."

Sam grunted as he stood from the fire. "I'd sure like to hear that myself," he said. He remembered Andre's recording, the whoops followed by one long continuous howl. But a recording was just that—a recording. Audio samples were nothing compared to the real thing.

Slowly, he walked out toward the tree line and studied the night air. It was dark now. But there was a sheet of light from the fire that spread out among the trees, casting wavering shadows onto the land.

He wondered if something truly was out there. A creature that had yet to be discovered. It was an uncanny thought, and one that Sam still hesitated to think about. But it seemed every time he got it off of his mind, something came along to bring it back up.

The foot prints up on the hill... And now this old man, with his legends and folklore...

Sam observed the darkness, watching, listening, and even feeling the expanse of the night. His mind toiled with the unknown while reminding him it was time for sleep. He waited for a few more minutes, then slipped back into camp and got ready for bed.

The old man appeared to be dozing, so Sam moved about quietly. He added more fuel to the fire, then crawled under his lean-to and settled in. He focused his stare on the flickering orange flames before drifting off to sleep. And in this quiet time, Sam's mind conjured up an imaginary conversation between him and the Master Sergeant, Joe Paxton. The sergeant was telling Sam to be cautious and to be mindful, as he prepared for his big struggle ahead.

"Man versus man is one thing," Joe was saying in his southerly drawl. "But man versus beast? Now that's something entirely different."

CHAPTER 20

Sam was up the next morning before sunrise, stoking the fire and boiling water for coffee and for breakfast. Within minutes, he had a combination of dehydrated eggs, sausage, and pancakes ready to serve. The breakfast was much larger than Sam normally preferred, but he had his guest's appetite in mind.

The woods seemed to come back to life at the sounds of Sam's movements throughout the camp. From the nearby forest, there came the occasional rustle of a small critter and the sporadic dripping sounds of the night's moisture falling from the trees. Soon, the morning sky revealed itself. It was a gray curtain, hard and dense, and it carried with it the sure promise of rain. In the near distance, a woodpecker worked persistently at the trunk of a sugar pine. And down on the lake, the loons were singing their lonesome melodies once again.

Lou Pine woke up shortly after the food was ready. He tended to Sally, then sat at the fire across from Sam as they ate their breakfast. They made small talk for a while, discussing the weather, and of hunting, before revisiting the tranquility that came with spending time in the wilderness, and how that spared them the hassles of the civilized world. Sam disclosed to Lou that, like him, he too had been living off the grid.

"My home is in the hills of the Gila Wilderness," Sam said.

"Is it a lean-to like this one here?" Lou asked. "Or do you have a cabin down there?"

"Neither," Sam replied. "I live in a cave."

Lou chuckled. "A cave?" He set his empty plate on a rock and smoothed down his beard. Then he took out his pipe, loaded it with tobacco, and lit it. He took three short drags, laughed again, and said, "Well, I suppose it can't get no more primitive than that."

"It's a good place," Sam replied conversationally. "Known about it since I was a kid." He gestured to the old man's plate and added, "You want some more food?"

Lou shook his head. "No, thanks... I figure I've eaten plenty enough. Between last night and this morning, I may soon have some weight to get rid of."

Sam smiled, humored by the thought. Like him, the old man was tall, wiry, and lean. It appeared he had none of the padding common for a man of middle age or older.

"Besides," Lou said, "I've always been in favor of living a simple life. And less food in my diet is one way of keeping things that way."

Sam nodded in agreement. "I suppose I know what you mean."

They talked more about their simple lives as Lou cleaned out his pipe and put it away. He got up from the fire and stretched, then walked over to Sally and loaded the mule with the pack gear. He came back to the fire to get his sleeping equipment.

"Well, Sam," he said, "I guess I've taken up enough of your time."

Sam stood and helped Lou pack up his things. He didn't want to seem pushy, as he enjoyed visiting with the old man. But he was eager to get back to the business of searching for his brother. He rolled up Lou's sleeping bag and cinched it down tightly, compressing all the air out of it.

"Thanks kindly, Sam," Lou said, as the two of them walked over to Sally.

"So, what's your plan for today?" Sam asked, out of curiosity.

"There're a few spots on the other side of that mountain over there that I like." Lou gestured across the lake and to the west.

"Good for setting traps in the winter. Believe it or not, that's still a lucrative business out here... Well," he added with a laugh, "lucrative enough for me, that is. Anyway, I plan on scouting the area. Make sure things haven't changed much since last season."

"If you're not in a hurry, you can stay," Sam said. "There's rain on the horizon."

"Oh, no thank you. Like I said, I've taken up enough of your time. I'm sure you want to get back to searching for your brother." Lou looked at the ground, then added, "But if I find anything that might interest you, I'll be sure to come on back and let you know."

"I'd appreciate that," Sam replied. Then he stepped forward and set the sleeping bag onto the pack gear to secure it to the mule. One of the saddlebags was open, and inside was a roll of twine, some bundles of soft leather, and more cans of fruit. Sam smiled, remembering the peaches and honey they ate the night before.

Lou reached out calmly, intercepting him. "Let me do that, Sam," he said. "I'm particular about how I load her up." Then he smiled, looking embarrassed. "Well, to be more accurate, Sally's the particular one. If she's loaded up wrong, off-balance and what have you, she'll be giving me bloody grief every step of the way."

"Sure thing," Sam said, letting the old man take the sleeping bag. He looked up then and studied the sky. The grayness of the clouds had grown a shade darker. "It'll be raining soon," he said. "You sure you don't want to hunker down for a spell?"

Lou shook his head. "Oh, no thank you. I'll be alright. Just a little rain is all. Besides, it'll be warm enough. And in my book, warm rain makes for perfect traveling conditions."

"Suit yourself," Sam said.

Lou loaded up the last of his things, took Sally by the reins, then turned and shook Sam's hand. "It sure was nice being in your company," he said. "You're a good man, Sam, coming out here to look for your brother. I hope you find him. And who knows..." he added with a pause, as he turned and stared into the forest beyond, "maybe your brother's still alive... somewhere out there... Perhaps."

"I don't know about that," Sam replied. "To be honest, I'm not counting on it."

Lou glanced at Sam and smiled gently. Then he nickered at Sally and they both slowly ambled off.

The old man got thirty feet from the camp before stopping. He turned back around and said, "In case you run across that Elder Brother of the North, you tell him hello for me, alright?" He chuckled, then turned back around. "And tell him to leave this old man alone."

Sam laughed and waved goodbye. He watched the old man walk stiffly away, the arthritis pinching at his joints with each step. It was a good feeling having such pleasant company. A very good feeling. But even better was the feeling of getting back to work.

Sam looked up at the sky again. Maybe it *will* be a warm rain. And maybe the old man was right. That a warm rain would be good for traveling.

• • •

An hour later, Sam was thinking—thinking hard—about his plan. He came to a conclusion of what he had to do and of the process his plan would entail. Like a military mission from his past, he would go out into the field. And he would stay there for a long, long while.

Knowing this, Sam cleaned up his camp and took an extra few minutes to secure it down. He went out into the forest and checked on his snares, found that they were empty and disengaged them entirely. Then he went back to his camp and gathered the things he would need.

When he was done, Sam went down to the lake, undressed, then bathed in the cool water. He used an odorless bar of eco-friendly soap. And he cleansed his body, hoping to wipe away as much of his odor as possible, knowing that most wild animals can smell the stink of a man from far away.

After he finished washing, Sam went back to camp and dried off at the fire. He put on a clean pair of Under Armour clothes and a set of ScentLok waterproof outerwear. He headed back down to the lake again and brought with him his recurve bow, arrows, and his cutting stick. He knew he still needed to hunt for something larger than what he'd already taken. And if he ran across a deer, elk, or moose while searching for Bryson, well, with a bow in hand, Sam would be in the position to do something about that.

Along with his hunting gear, he brought his tracking equipment and a few items needed for staying out in the bush for multiple days. The plan was to recon the land by using his skills as a sniper. And if Sam ran across anything promising, such as more evidence suggesting the existence of Sasquatch, then he would consider finding a place to set up—a hide of some sort—and wait it out for a time.

When he got down to the lake and to his kayak, he felt the first raindrops splatter onto him. His clothing was waterproof, and he had on a wide-brimmed hat. As predicted, the rain was warm, and for now, Sam was still comfortable. He wondered how long that would last.

He secured his equipment on the kayak, then climbed in and slowly paddled out onto the lake. His thoughts were on finding Bryson. And he had a fresh idea of where to begin. In light of the evidence pointing at the existence of Sasquatch (Andre's tales, the prints Sam had found on the hillside, and then Lou's comments about hearing that scream), as much as Sam regretted to admit, he was now seriously considering that this creature was indeed the culprit to Bryson's disappearance. And if Sasquatch had abducted his brother, Sam figured it would have done so at night, while Bryson was in or near his camp.

But if it had taken his brother, then what did it do with him? That was the million dollar question Sam intended to answer.

He considered the many possibilities. He also considered the behaviors of other predators. If the creature acted like a bear, it would have attempted to consume Bryson while he was still alive, then bury the remains. If it acted like a mountain lion, it would have killed his brother on the spot, then taken his body up a tree or into higher ground. And in either scenario, there would have been a struggle, because Bryson would not have gone down so easily. And if such a struggle did occur, it would have had to happen a respectful distance away from the camp. In their conversations, Andre mentioned they had dogs out here looking for Bryson. Sam knew anytime a large predator attacked something in the wilderness, there was always a disturbance of the land containing sights and smells that no tracker dog would have difficulty in finding. There wasn't a scene like that anywhere near Bryson's camp.

Then Sam recalled another thing Andre had said. He remembered the fear the man had felt—the indescribable terror he'd experienced after coming across the creature. And that the only words he could use to describe the fear were powerful and primal.

Assuming Bryson had encountered the creature, what if that same feeling had come over him? Would there have even been a struggle? Maybe Bryson simply froze in his tracks as the beast stepped forward and snapped his neck.

Then another interesting thought popped into Sam's head. What if the creature didn't act at all like that of a bear or a mountain lion, but instead, it acted like a human predator?

The rain fell harder now, drumming down on Sam as he made his way further out onto the water. He was heading straight across the lake and to the general area of where those prints were, the ones Andre had made casts of.

It took a few minutes of paddling, but eventually, Sam found the spot. He beached his kayak, flipped it over, then secured it to a large piece of driftwood. The slight downpour muffled the small sounds he made while gathering his gear.

Ready to move on, he walked up and down the beach, scanning the ground for more signs of the creature. There may still be something he missed from earlier, or perhaps fresh tracks recently made. Mostly, Sam checked the sandy shoreline where such tracks would show up easily enough.

Not finding anything, he came back to the original prints, then headed for the nearby treeline. He'd previously guessed this was the direction the creature had taken, assuming it walked out to the shore, stood on the sand and faced Bryson's camp, then went back the way it came. Sam's plan was to backtrack the creature's presumed route and hopefully find something.

As he walked into the forest, the sound from the pouring rain quieted, as if he'd stepped out of the storm and into a building. The heavy clouds above kept the woods dark and eerie. There were pockets of blackness and gloomy hollows obscured by thick brush and tangled deadfall. Nothing stirred other than the wind and the trees.

Sam knew travel would be difficult in some places. As such, it would force him to compromise any planned heading he might consider. But he was thinking of the route a large creature would take through the denseness of this forest. Like any other animal, it too would have sought the path of least resistance. The land had a way of imposing this notion onto the lone traveler. Sam had learned of this phenomenon years ago while searching for missing hikers. People went around rivers, and around fallen logs, and around rocky formations. When lost, they almost always headed downhill, rarely uphill. And they never climbed through dense underbrush, as it was too difficult to navigate. Animals acted in much the same manner.

Sam applied this knowledge as he plodded his way through the forest. Carefully, he stepped over fallen branches or clumps of brush, keeping his movements as silent as possible. His body had instinctively gone into a slight crouch, despite the absence of any immediate danger or wary prey. Sam was in absolute hunting mode, stalking through the forest in the same way he'd been doing since he was a child.

He had yet to find any evidence showing the recent presence or passage of a large animal. But his gut told him that right now, that didn't matter. In the effort of finding something—whether it be a source of food or the source of his brother's disappearance—Sam would concentrate all his efforts on becoming one with his environment.

Slowly, he walked for fifty yards, moving between the trees and avoiding the noisy, brushy areas. He came to a small glade about half the size of a football field, but Sam refrained from walking into it. He paused and took a knee behind a tree. He watched and listened quietly as he studied the meadow. If the rain wasn't coming down so hard, it was an ideal place for an elk or moose to rest in. But the clearing was vacant at the moment, and Sam was hardly surprised. Again, like humans, most animals sought shelter from bad weather.

He moved on, heading again into the dense woods, but then he turned back. Meadows like this were popular throughways for large animals, as they provided a natural path of least resistance. They also provided easy food for herbivores. Sam decided he would skirt the entire perimeter of the meadow and check for signs of anything big which might have cut through it. At the very least, he expected to find a small game trail or two leading into the grassy field.

Sam's assumptions were correct. Walking up a low rise that gave him an overhead view of the clearing, he spotted half a dozen small paths cutting through the long grass within. He wasn't surprised, of course, but he was still hoping to find the tracks of something bigger which might have entered the meadow.

He continued with his search until he arrived at his starting point. Sam had navigated the circumference of the meadow and hadn't found a single track from an animal larger than a badger. He thought this to be odd. It was springtime, after all. Most animals were on the move in their efforts to gather up nature's abundant, precious calories. A large meadow like this, with its long lush grass and wooded perimeter, would be an irresistible destination for a large consumer such as a deer or an elk. Especially being so close to a water source. But there were no signs that such a creature had recently been here. No signs at all.

Curious, Sam moved deeper into the forest. The rain was coming down persistently. Its pattering drops created a rhythmic cacophony, drumming a path through the trees and to the forest floor. The air was ripe with odors. Sam caught the earthy smell of the damp undergrowth and loam mixed with the sweet scent of decaying evergreen needles. From the lake there came a subtle fishy aroma, which he knew was from the algae blooms in the water.

The land rose on a slight slope. He moved forward for another thirty minutes, making mental notes of the terrain and memorizing natural landmarks and the overall geography. This was what Sam did best. How he took in the land, studied it, learned from it, and then used this knowledge to weave himself into it. In the military, they called him "The Invisible Man," and for good reason.

Shortly after those thirty minutes, Sam spotted another meadow through the trees off to his right. He moved closer, eventually stopping ten feet from the tree line that overlooked the large clearing. And the clearing *was* large—being roughly four times the size of the last one.

But oddly, there was nothing in it. Nothing at all, other than tall grass and a few shrubs. Yet it was an ideal place to come across not just one large animal, but a herd of them. The meadow's vacancy only added to the many curiosities in Sam's mind.

He put a tree between him and the meadow and approached it cautiously. Sam stalked the last ten feet and stood behind a large hemlock, scanning the open field before him. It was a picturesque scene, wide and sparse, a green blanket of grass freckled with wild flowers, and the entire landscape hemmed in by a thick forest.

To his left, the slope he'd been climbing continued onward, rising gradually above the meadow. And to his right, a conglomeration of granite boulders interrupted the meadow's pine-laden perimeter. Sam noticed the rocky structure provided a fifty-foot high perch overlooking the grassy field, and that it was possibly accessible.

Looking back at the open piece of terrain, Sam considered the emptiness of the place. Most animals may be holed up somewhere, taking shelter from the downpour. But this was such a nice piece of real estate that he wouldn't have been surprised had he come across a herd of elk grazing in the middle of it.

The clearing would be stunning under the brightness of a sunlit sky. Sam thought it handsome enough right now while in the rain, as it was attractively peaceful and lonely. But it was empty of wildlife. Despite the downpour, something in his gut told him it should not be. And despite the meadow's striking beauty, Sam's inner voice was also telling him there was something wrong with this place. Something was not right, and that he should proceed with caution.

He decided to enter the clearing, anyway. But before he did, he used his binoculars and studied the meadow's perimeter. The tree line was vacant, so he walked out twenty feet and took a knee. He felt vulnerable and had a sense that at any minute now, something would come barreling out of the woods, heading straight for him. Sam felt foolish for thinking this, but still, he couldn't shake the notion that he was walking into some kind of ambush.

He surveyed his environment and studied the immediate landscape, expecting to see, hear, or smell something. Again, there was nothing.

He continued onward, walking further into the clearing. The meadow was currently empty of wildlife, but there should have been signs of recent activity within it. Where were the tracks, the scat, the game trails, matted down patches, and even the tufts of fur?

A place like this, there should have been something.

But there wasn't…

After twenty minutes of searching, the only thing Sam noticed was a single game trail, cut obviously by a small critter such as a porcupine or rabbit.

It baffled Sam. Maybe he was thinking too hard and expecting too much. But then again, maybe he wasn't.

"Why does this place seem so dead?" he muttered to himself.

He was almost in the middle of the clearing now, studying the rocky outcrop at the edge of the perimeter. Then he noticed something peculiar off to his right and near the tree line. It was a single sapling which had been snapped at the trunk and with its top half angled downward and facing south.

Sam approached the sapling and inspected the fracture. The tree's trunk had been broken at a spot roughly six feet off the ground. And it was a clean snap, having cracked through three inches of pine. Something damn powerful was responsible for the break.

At first, he figured the crack had come from a gust of wind while the tree was burdened down with snow. But then Sam spotted another sapling with the same breakage on the opposite side of the meadow. Like the first tree, something had snapped this one six feet from its base, and it, too, had its top half angled southward.

It was an uncanny find. Very uncanny.

Sam walked back to the middle of the clearing, paused, then looked again at the rocky promontory. He was thinking about his conversations with Andre and of the pictures the SAR leader had shown him. Then Sam remembered: Andre had pictures of saplings snapped exactly like the ones he'd just found.

Suddenly, Sam felt that forbidden feeling sweep over him once again. The same sense of foreboding he'd felt off and on since coming to Earl Lake.

Sam also had the feeling that something was now watching him...

He made an about face and stared at the opposite tree line, the one that sloped upward and into the forested hills.

There was something in there, deep in the woods.

Sam felt its presence. He sensed its hard stare. He thought he could even hear its breath on the wind.

Yes, Sam now knew. There was something up in those trees watching him. And not just watching… But studying.

CHAPTER 21

Thirty minutes later, Sam was a piece of earth lying halfway up the granite promontory. His body was wedged between two rocky fissures, and he had a complete, un-obscured view of the vacant meadow. Prior to this, he'd calmly walked into the forest, surveyed his surroundings, then slithered up the backside of the granite structure. He'd moved slow, slow as molasses, until he found the right spot in which he hunkered into. That was where he was now, waiting and watching.

His binoculars were at his eyes. He was studying the opposite tree line. There was still something in there, he could tell. What it was, he wasn't sure. But the cold tingle at the base of his neck told him it wasn't necessarily friendly. Was it perhaps a grizzly bear stalking him from inside the trees? Sam wondered...

A part of him didn't think so. He still had Sasquatch on his mind and was feeling a damned fool because of it. But Sam couldn't stop thinking about how the meadow was completely vacant of all signs from other animals, when there should have been something there. There were no tracks or droppings or anything. The place was dead.

Then a thought occurred to him: What animal hangs around a mountain lion's den?

The answer was simple. No animal.

But Sam knew a mountain lion wasn't in the immediate area.

He was also thinking about those broken saplings and considering them as being signs in their own right. Signs that warned other large predators just whose territory this was. Territorial markings made by the creature were another one of Andre's theories.

Sam waited for a long time, sitting as motionless as the rock beneath him. He felt his legs go numb. His body grew stiff and cold. Not dangerously so, just uncomfortably cold. The rain had idled to a soft drizzle and a slight breeze came across the land. The trees swayed sporadically against the wind and throughout the forest Sam heard the occasional branch or pine cone drop heavily to the wet ground.

He was curious as to what was out there. And he was still very certain of its presence. If it was a grizzly, he knew the animal would have come out into the open meadow by now, in search of Sam's scent.

So then, it wasn't a grizzly.

He waited for hours, so it seemed, his mind drifting never too far from the present, yet hovering once in a while along the fringes of his memories. Sam was deftly aware of how much this moment reminded him of his past and of the many operations he'd done while in the military. The coldness settling onto his back and coming up from underneath him, seeping into his body, brought out the aches and pains of half a dozen injuries, some of which he'd inherited from those military operations.

Sam caught a sudden whiff of something horrible. The stench came from across the meadow and on the breeze, wafting against the granite structure he was lying on. It was a foul, pungent odor, which nearly had him gagging.

He couldn't place the source of the smell, not from previous sights or experiences, but it was horrendous. His mind went to dead fish and wet dog mixed with feces and sour milk. Again, Sam's memories crept out from the back of his mind as he recalled from his conversations with Andre a description of the creature's odor. That description was very similar to what Sam now smelled.

Slowly, he scanned the opposite tree line with his binoculars, studying with a meticulous eye every branch, tree trunk, and bush. He imagined an invisible triangle set on the horizon, and he traced the corners and edges of the shape with his vision, knowing that this technique alone would help him detect discrepancies within a pattern.

And then that's when Sam spotted it.

The identity of the creature was hard to discern—it could have been a bear, for all he knew—but whatever it was, it had thick sable fur.

Or was that hair?

The exposure was minimal. Only a thin strip of the matted coat was visible on the edge of a clump of vegetation. The rest of the animal remained hidden behind trees and brush. But Sam had the feeling that it could see him somehow. And that it *was* seeing him, as it peered covertly through its cover.

Perhaps that last part was just Sam's imagination. But there was definitely something in there, a creature of some kind, which Sam now knew to be true.

It was difficult to tell what part of the animal he was looking at, whether it was a shoulder or a leg or the backside. But it was an animal, nonetheless. And, interestingly enough, whatever it was, it remained motionless, which reinforced Sam's notion that it was observing him. Or at least it was aware of his presence.

He guessed the distance between him and the creature to be a little over two hundred yards. Sam studied the thing for several long minutes, and he wanted to believe he was looking at a bear. But too many details didn't add up for that to be true.

If it was a bear, it had to be asleep or dead, considering its motionless disposition. Perhaps it was sleeping on a branch... But from Sam's view, there didn't seem to be a tree large enough to support the weight of an animal that size and at the height at which it must be laying. Judging from what he saw, Sam guessed the lowest point of the fur line to be roughly six feet from the ground.

Sam's mind ached, both from curiosity and uncertainty. If it wasn't a bear he was looking at, then what could it be?

And maybe the answer to that was something Sam didn't want to admit.

He decided to take action. Observing the surrounding geographical details of where he was looking, Sam memorized a few landmarks and key items, then slowly crawled backward and down from his hide.

When he reached the base of the granite rock and set foot on the forest floor, he cautiously inspected the surrounding area, suddenly wary of his position. The woods were gloomy and gray and dripping softly with the wetness of rain. Satisfied that his position was still secure, Sam slowly turned and stalked his way out of the tree line and into the meadow.

He headed for the landmarks he'd memorized as he carefully approached the spot containing the unknown creature. And he kept one hand on the bear spray at his side, ready to draw in case something charged at him.

As Sam came close to the end of the meadow, he spotted the location in the trees where he'd seen the creature. Seconds later, he heard a faint rustle in the bush ahead.

Instantly, Sam froze. He kept his position and maintained his eyesight on the trees. But he didn't move a muscle. For almost a minute he stood quietly and waited, his heart racing, his body gone rigid. He took a deep breath to help relax and then, very slowly, stepped forward.

Sam heard it again—the soft rustling in the bush—so he immediately halted. He waited for another minute, then crept forward again, until he heard the rustling sound once more, causing him to stop.

It became almost a game. With each step he took forward, it seemed as if whatever Sam was stalking took its own step backward.

It was uncanny, perplexing, and certainly not indicative of the behavior of any forest critter he knew of.

Slowly, he pushed onward, but this time not stopping when he heard the movement in the forest recommence. Sam followed the sound, one small step after another, with each step bringing him further into the tree line and away from the meadow. And each step bringing him closer to the spot where he'd seen the animal hiding.

The foul odor was still present. Only it was worse now, being thick and rank such that it invoked a nauseating feeling. Sam controlled the urge to gag as he followed the creature.

After a few minutes, he'd walked about twenty yards into the thick forest. He still couldn't see what it was he was pursuing, but he now knew for certain that the creature wasn't trying to evade him. Not entirely, at least. Any other large beast would have been long gone by now. But not this thing. It was moving away from Sam just slow enough to keep its distance—a distance Sam estimated to be of about fifty yards.

Also, the creature successfully kept itself completely concealed, never once letting Sam get a good look at it. But it was still there, lingering about in the forest. And it was obviously quite big and—as Sam regretfully admitted—apparently intelligent.

A sudden breeze crossed the land, causing the trees to rock violently. Water drops immediately fell from the branches above, cascading down to the forest floor. Sam was briefly relieved of the creature's scent as he caught a whiff of fresh rain and rotting plant matter. Then the breeze passed and once again the land fell quiet. The odor came back, strong as ever. And with it came the illusion that the forest was closing in on Sam.

"What are you, dammit?" he muttered. "And what the hell is your game?"

Twenty minutes passed, and nothing had changed. There was no variance in the cat-and-mouse game Sam was playing. He continued to follow the creature, maintaining the same steady pace but trying deliberately and unsuccessfully to get a good look at the thing.

Twenty minutes of a painstakingly slow pursuit went by until suddenly...

Sam heard a loud *whack* up ahead, as if someone had smacked a thick wooden branch against the trunk of a tree.

He stopped abruptly, listening. Then he heard it again. A single knock in the trees ahead—a wood knock—bringing to mind another one of Andre's theories. *It's how they communicate*, the SAR leader had told him.

Sam waited patiently for another minute before continuing forward. He took two steps, then heard a third knock.

Only this time, the knock came from behind him.

Quickly, Sam spun. His heart thumped and his breath took off. He scanned the forest all around, searching for something, anything. He'd been duped somehow, and he was keenly aware of it. Amazingly, he'd been lured into an ambush of sorts, pulled into a kill zone by his dumb curiosity, flanked now by the enemy, and stuck dead center in the middle of a brewing crossfire.

Sam closed his eyes and took a deep breath. At once, he felt foolish, as he allowed his past to catch up to him. This wasn't Afghanistan. And he wasn't surrounded by the enemy once again.

But he was surrounded by something.

Cautiously, Sam studied his environment. He was standing in a small open area in the middle of a cluster of willow and aspen trees. The canopy above was thick and crowded, but where he stood there was a wide swath of wet grass and a scattering of wildflowers.

Sam waited patiently as he looked around, observing, studying, feeling and sensing...

The wood knocks had stopped. But he knew that it—no, *they*—were still out there. And yes, as crazy as it seemed, Sam's inner voice told him they had been communicating.

But communicating with whom?

Sam snickered. *If that crazy fool were here right now*, he thought, thinking about Andre as he looked around, *he just might crap his—*

Sam's thought was suddenly cut short. His eyes stopped their scanning as his stare landed on an object on the ground not ten feet away from him.

Sam knew exactly what the object was. And more importantly, *whose* it was.

With a cold, eerie feeling rushing through him, Sam wondered just how intelligent these creatures really were.

Because they had led him straight to one of Bryson's boots.

CHAPTER 22

Sam found the other boot ten feet away, lodged between a piece of deadfall and a large rock. All of Andre's theories and stories suddenly flooded into Sam's mind. He remembered his and the SAR leader's conversations about specific people who'd gone missing, and how sometimes only their shoes were found. It was a mystery that had occurred to both experienced and inexperienced adventurers. Even hunters. And it was a mystery that continued to baffle Sam.

The only explanation he could think of as to why a lost person would ditch their shoes was the discomfort of frostbite. But for a hunter to do that, a person with experience in the field and who would have known better—well, to Sam, that just seemed downright implausible. And yet here he was now, staring at both of his brother's boots. It was hard for Sam to believe. Bryson would have had to be out of his mind to dump his boots.

Andre had a theory about this. The man claimed Sasquatch removed the shoes of those he abducted in order to prevent them from running off. Since most people lacked tough soles, they wouldn't get far in the wilderness without footwear, and, possibly, this was something the creature understood.

It was an interesting observation, Sam had to admit. And an eerie one.

With Bryson's boots in hand, he scanned the forest, not once forgetting that he'd been observed, lured, and followed by a creature of an unknown identity. Those things were still out there. And if they had taken Bryson for whatever reason, then who's to say Sam wouldn't be next? Cautiously observant of his surroundings, he made a concentrated sweep of the area, looking for more clues or evidence regarding his lost brother.

After a few minutes of searching and not coming up with a damn thing, Sam was stuck. He wasn't sure what to do at this point. Whatever was out there, it knew exactly where he was, so the element of surprise no longer existed for Sam. He could try to follow one of them, see where it took him. But he doubted anything worthwhile would come of that, not to mention the risk factor he would likely put himself in.

He kept thinking...

What if there was another motive behind getting lured out here? Sam looked again at Bryson's boots, his mind running in overdrive. The laces had been untied, which meant the boots hadn't been ripped off of Bryson's feet. They had been casually removed. Or maybe they weren't even on him at the time of his abduction. But then how did they get here?

Sam thought about the possibilities. Perhaps there was more to this incident of finding his brother's boots than he suspected. First, if Sam was truly in danger, then why hadn't something happened to him by now? Also, he realized those creatures out there—whatever they were—had led him straight to this spot. Why else, other than for him to find these boots? Without a doubt, that was a sign of higher intelligence. But was there also a malevolent motive behind the act?

Sam wasn't so sure.

He tied his brother's boots together by the laces and hung them over his shoulder. Then he stepped forward once again, as if to continue following the first creature. He heard a rustle in the bush up ahead and, once more, the cat-and-mouse game continued. Sam bit the hook and kept walking, with one hand on his cutting stick and the other hovering over the bear spray, just in case.

The rustling in the trees continued as he moved forward. He followed the noise for five minutes and not once did he hear the other one behind him. It was as if that creature had simply stayed put.

The terrain rose gently, and after another five minutes of slow pursuit, it angled sharply, giving way to a steady uphill climb. Owing to his impeccable sense of direction, Sam knew exactly where he was in relation to his brother's camp. He was approximately two miles due west, and at the base of the largest mountain in the area, the one he'd made note of when he first studied this land up close, while standing on the granite promontory overlooking the lake.

He continued walking. After fifty yards of climbing, the terrain grew less dense. Sam tried to glimpse the creature then, knowing that with less cover at its disposal, the chances of seeing it were greater.

Whatever it was, it was a master of its environment. Sam had yet to spot the thing, with his only sighting still being the thin outline of fur he'd observed through his binoculars. But the noise of its passage through the forest continued, and deliberately, so it seemed, as it was loud enough for Sam to follow.

After another fifty yards, he came to a reprieve on the mountain's slope. It was a leveled area that ran across the side of the mountain like a great scar across the land. The area was sparsely dotted with trees and clumps of grass and covered mostly with crumbled granite. It reminded Sam of a cross-country ski slope in the summer.

He caught his breath and looked around. From this vantage point, he could see Earl Lake once again. In the distance, the surface of the lake looked like a slab of black ice—cold and ominous under the heavy gray sky.

A chilled and persistent wind skimmed across the open face of the mountain with a steady ease. Sam listened carefully, took a few steps forward, then paused. He could no longer hear the creature's movement. Even when he crossed the leveled clearing and began once again to move uphill, he noticed that the game of cat-and-mouse had stopped entirely. It was as if the creature had vanished. Or slipped into the side of the mountain and into a deep cave, perhaps.

Sam walked back down to the leveled clearing and sat on a rock, setting his cutting stick and Bryson's boots on the ground. He took a brief break and ate a handful of dried fruit with nuts, then drank water from his canteen. It had only been a few hours since he left his camp, but the day already felt long and tiresome.

His thoughts centered on finding more evidence of his brother. Or his remains, at least. But Sam found himself once again at an impasse. He wasn't sure what else to do other than continue up the mountain, hoping to find something. He knew that animals, such as mountain lions, took their kills into the higher ground. So maybe Bryson was somewhere up there.

Sam was tired and, once again, he felt like a fool. He should have made a better search of the area where he'd found the boots. There could be more evidence down in there, perhaps even something definitive, such as a bone fragment. That's what happened when people died in the wilderness. Their bodies would swiftly decompose, and what was left got picked apart and dragged off into separate directions by various critters. This was how people "truly" went missing, Sam knew. And it's what he was telling himself right now, regarding his brother's disappearance.

But then his thoughts gave way once more to his instinct. The various scavengers of the forest might have done their deeds, but prior to that, something had happened to Bryson. And Sam's gut still told him that whatever that was, it was sinister.

Finished with his snack, he gathered his things and stood, his body facing the lake. He still needed to kill a large animal, knowing that his dried rations were limited. So Sam considered ditching his search for a bit of serious hunting.

But it pained him to come this far, to experience such a strange encounter and to find such a promising clue as that of his brother's boots, only to quit it all right now. Sam felt as if he were so close to something... yet still so far away. And all the while, the preciousness of his time was running its course to a determined end of one kind or another.

Undecided, Sam walked circles around the clearing, thinking, observing, and secretly hoping something would happen again. Hoping that he'd hear the creature up on the hill make another sound. He paced a slow zigzag course along the leveled face of the mountain, looking for anything of interest.

The ground was hard and rocky in most places, proving difficult for detecting sign. There were slender strips of grass and weeds growing out of cracks in the granite, but also a few wider patches layered with packed dirt or mud. Sam walked slowly, concentrating on those areas. Twice he came across wolf tracks. And lying on a rock near the slope of the mountain was some bear scat.

Methodically, Sam searched the softer areas of grass and dirt and mud. He plodded his way up the open terrain, with the view of the lake behind him remaining a striking scene.

Coming to another muddy flat, Sam suddenly stopped. Cutting straight through this section of muck was a definitive chain of tracks.

Stooping down, he studied the prints. They were fresh, only a few hours old, and for certain they had come from Lou Pine and his mule Sally. The direction of travel was west, along the face of the mountain, as if the old man had taken advantage of the leveled clearing for ease of travel. It's what Sam would've done.

Remembering Lou had mentioned he had trapping areas to check on, Sam wondered where this natural path went. He considered following it for a while, as he was still undecided about his plans for the rest of the day. Idly, he studied the old man's tracks through the muddy terrain.

Eventually, the mud gave way once again to hard granite. But Sam noticed the clumps of wet soil stretched out across the rocky ground. The observance of this terrain transfer was a tracking technique Sam had used both in the Gila Wilderness and beyond—worlds away, and in places he tried to forget about.

He followed the clumps of mud for approximately twenty feet until the granite gave way once again to a small patch of soft ground. It was another muddy flat sprinkled with weeds and thin grass.

Sam looked around, as he was mildly curious. The tracks failed to continue through the mud. He scanned the surrounding terrain, looking for a different pathway Lou had possibly taken, but came up empty. Just where had the old man and his mule gone?

Very curious now, Sam squatted down and examined the ground more carefully.

And then he saw it.

Where Lou and Sally's tracks should have been, Sam spotted several sections of compressed grass, as if someone had pressed something flat and featureless, such as a book, on the ground.

Sam followed the obscure impressions through the soft terrain until they gave way once again to granite. At this juncture, he noticed a lack of terrain transfer. Now there were no clumps of mud spread in precise intervals across the hard rock. The ground seemed wholly undisturbed, in fact, as if nothing had crossed it for quite some time.

It was a peculiar observation. Very peculiar.

Puzzled, Sam got down on his belly and put his face close to the ground. He examined the rocky terrain, looking for crush spots and overturned pebbles. Retrieving a flashlight from his pocket, he shined it across the surface of the ground, hoping to glimpse any recent disturbance. The manipulation of light and shadows was another tracking trick, but one used more so during the darker times of the day. Nevertheless, Sam employed the technique.

And sure enough, he found some sign.

Just past the muddy flat were two tiny stones which had been compressed and rotated. This minor disturbance resulted in granite flakes being crushed and pushed outward, beyond each stone's perimeter...

There was a broken twig, followed by an overturned rock...

And then more compressed stones and more disturbed pebbles, some showing minute signs of terrain transfer, as they were lightly coated with a thin layer of mud, hardly detectable.

It was a slow, agonizing process. But one in which Sam found most interesting.

Eventually, he determined the travelers' stride length. Then Sam used his cutting stick and followed the old man's passage for another twenty yards, before he paused out of curiosity. Just how had Lou covered his and the mules' tracks? And more to the point, why?

Thinking, Sam quickly realized how a person could obscure such tracks. He knew how he would've done it, at least. But as for the why, well now, that was still a mystery...

Sam's conscience told him he should turn around and go back down the hill to look for more evidence of his brother. Or perhaps ditch this part of the day entirely and attempt to find a moose or elk he could shoot. But his gut, nagging at him as always, convinced Sam to follow the old man's tracks.

Slightly frustrated with himself over this decision, Sam refused to put too much energy into the tracking process. He followed what he knew to be Lou's last known direction of travel and only dropped to the ground to search for sign when pressed by instinct or confused.

Sam trailed the nebulous tracks for approximately two hundred yards, which took the better half of an hour. He worked at a faster pace than normal, as he wasn't dead serious about whom he was tracking. He had better things to do and felt guilty for delaying his priorities. But the curiosity of the moment kept Sam invested, if only slightly so.

As for that other animal he'd been tracking, there wasn't so much as a hint of its presence. There were no more wood knocks or the sounds of rustling brush. And there was no more of that awful stink. But strangely enough, Sam felt as if the creature was still up there on the mountain, somewhere in the trees... and watching him.

"You've been a fool for too long," he muttered to himself.

Sam was about to turn back when he noticed scuff marks on the hillside off to his left. The tracks he'd been following had made an abrupt change in that direction, and now they turned upward. They were heading toward the top of the mountain, which appeared to be roughly a thousand feet in the distance and at a slope of less than thirty degrees.

"Alright," Sam mumbled. "To the top I go. But after that, I'm done."

The tracks going up the mountain were still undefined. But they were easy enough to spot, thanks to the weight of the climbing mule. Sam had no problem following the path in which Lou and Sally had traveled.

After twenty minutes of tracking, Sam was at the top of the mountain, which was a flat of rocky earth peering up into the sky, a scalp of bald granite capping the head of the world.

Clearing the last of the forest and walking out into the open, he looked around. A stiff wind whipped across the mountainside, ruffling his hat. He heard a familiar noise behind the breeze, then walked fifty yards across the top of the mountain and to the other side.

He came to a sheer drop-off, an escarpment that opened out to a dreadful plunge of several hundred feet, and ending at a flowing river below—thus being the source of the noise he'd heard.

Now what? Sam wondered.

The tracks he'd been following had vanished at the tree line, although Sam suspected the old man had come across the top of the mountain, just as he had. But where then did he go?

The view was impressive, encompassing a wide panorama of the great Yukon Territory. There was a buildup of heavy clouds to the south and an all but clear sky far to the east. The river below snaked its winding course southeast to west, through various stretches of timber and flatland, wide expanses of open muskeg, and then beyond, to only God knew where.

The sight of nature momentarily took Sam in. But then he noticed a different pathway, a thin trail running down the south side of the mountain and switch-backing downward, until it met the river below.

It was a clear, manmade trail. And undoubtedly an old one. Sam could see that it traveled from the river's shore and up to what appeared to be a cave entrance not more than three hundred feet below him and off to his right.

It wasn't a cave, though, he quickly decided. But an old mine. A very old mine, likely dating back to the eighteen hundreds.

Sam's curiosity was now duly peaked. He studied the old trail and what he could see of the mine's entrance.

Now what, indeed?

It took him fifteen minutes to get down there. When he reached the trail and then the entrance of the mine, Sam could see the area had been well traveled, perhaps even recently. Old iron beams stood outside the entrance, still propping up the mountain after years of weather and strain. To the side of the trail and on the ground lay various rusted components such as twisted pipes, drum fragments, steel sheeting... an abandoned foray of metal left to perish, long after someone had decided the death of this mine.

Sam wondered just how dead the mine really was. He approached its entrance and then went further on.

Six feet into the side of the mountain, the darkness closed in. But not before Sam came upon a door. Yes, a door. A heavy wooden door made from solid poles of timber. Aged, but not terribly so, and lashed closed by a thick thong of leather. It was an old-fashioned door, but still functional in design and possibly intent. Sam felt a little guilty as he opened the door and went in.

The darkness into the mountain was cold and terrible, but it shrank quickly from the onslaught of Sam's flashlight. He stepped forward into the mine, walked twenty paces, then blinked his eyes at what he eventually saw. His head and gut toiled instantly, battling with a mixture of emotions and thoughts.

As it turned out, the long day had become unlike anything Sam would have predicted it to be. Feeling mildly astounded, partially baffled, and, to some small degree, slightly misled, he shined his flashlight and looked on at what could only have been one small fragment of a greater ambiguity. Sam stared into the mine, understanding now that this day had led him from one enigmatic mystery to another.

CHAPTER 23

It was clear that the immediate interior of the mine had been organized as a storage space. There was a small alcove worked into the side of the mountain near the entrance, which obviously served as a mudroom of sorts. Sticking out from cracks on the alcove's rock wall were several wooden pegs, each holding gear such as rope, chain, leather tackle and leather bags. On the ground, just below the hanging gear, were various metal canisters, some of which Sam recognized as fuel cans and ammunition boxes.

The mudroom held various tools as well, including two shovels and a pickaxe. Hanging from a nearby beam were a pair of torn and weathered saddle bags along with what looked like the pelt of a coyote or small wolf.

Sam walked further into the mine. He followed a narrow tunnel that sloped downward by a few degrees, his footsteps echoing off the stone walls surrounding him. He was soon met with a dank odor—the smell of mildew and wet earth.

The tunnel would have been pitch-dark if Sam didn't have his flashlight with him. He observed the ground as he walked, searching for clues to who or what had recently passed this way. He moved slowly, and after a few minutes, he guessed he'd traveled roughly twenty yards. Then the tunnel opened up into a large cavern.

Sam stepped into the cavern, into a mouth of darkness, and then he shined his flashlight onto what appeared to be someone's living quarters. He spotted a military cot complete with pillow and blankets, which looked as if it had been slept in recently. On the ground below the cot was a green canteen, and next to that, a tobacco pipe resting in a wooden bowl. There was a small table near the cot containing a candle jar, two books, and a pair of reading glasses.

A more interesting detail of the cavern was what Sam noticed in the foreground, beyond the cot. Much to his surprise and curiosity, it was a study of sorts. Rustic and primitive, but a study all the same, with wooden shelves built onto the stone wall and a slipshod desk made of wrought iron and rough-cut wooden planks. Sitting beside the desk was a foldable stool with a leather cushion on it.

He spotted two kerosene lamps, one sitting on the desk and another hanging from a wooden beam above the study. Both were unlit. Sam moved closer and touched them, observing that they were also both frigid. It seemed neither had been lit for some time.

Pausing, Sam studied his environment further. He noticed the cavern smelled of rust and oil, aged leather and dampened earth. Slowly, he stepped forward and inspected the small study, scrutinizing both its construction and what it contained. He counted just a small sampling of the books on the various shelves and along the perimeter of the desk. He stopped when he got to a dozen, then estimated the total to be roughly ten times that number. Someone's study indeed.

Sam glanced at the titles. Most were non-fiction. There were books on the various sciences and mathematics and others on Roman architecture and Japanese gardening. A few in ancient history. But the vast majority dealt with global politics and philosophy.

In particular, he observed at least two dozen volumes regarding the German Philosopher, Friedrich Nietzsche. Sam had read a few works from that philosopher over the years, of which he'd considered as being both interesting and depressing.

Next to the books and on the desk itself sat a scattering of writing journals, along with a tin can filled with pencils and pens. Some journals were quite old, but others appeared to be rather new. And it was a curious find.

Sam shined his flashlight on the journals, then began leafing through one of them. Nothing caught his eye immediately. It was all just a bunch of pages with words and sentences scrawled onto them. But some sentences were written in a type of shorthand, which made no sense.

Then one page revealed a photograph taped to it. It was a small, faded picture of a group of men in combat uniform. The photo appeared to have been taken in what looked like a jungle environment. Sam studied it closely and saw the phrase "OO Pine" written on the margins of the photograph.

OO Pine...

He wondered about that.

The military uniform was noticeably British, and Sam suspected the "OO" stood for Operations Officer. Looking even closer, he spotted a particular insignia on some uniforms.

It was the dagger in flames emblem.

Sam knew what that symbol was about. And he knew who owned it.

Curious, he flipped through more pages in the notebook and found more pictures, all similar in content to the first one. He noticed the phrase "WHO DARES WINS" handwritten in capital letters in the margins of one photograph. And in the margins of another, once again, he saw the phrase "OO Pine". Only this time, there was an arrow pointing to a specific soldier.

Sam recognized the man.

Sure enough, it was Lou Pine. But a much younger Lou—by about thirty, perhaps forty years.

Sam scratched his beard, thinking. By the light of the fire, the old man had shared his military experiences with Sam. Lou said he had fought as a Royal Marine in the Falklands War. But he said nothing about working with the British Army's elite military unit, the Special Air Service.

Sam knew all about this famous Special Forces unit. The SAS were the equivalent of America's Delta Force, or the Naval Special Warfare Development Group, commonly known as Seal Team Six. They belonged to a distinctively tough unit which had been created and then led by the legendary David Stirling. The SAS had cut their teeth through the means of unconventional warfare, while stationed in North Africa during World War II. Their missions had been ruthless and devastating. Sam once read about how the specialized British soldiers led their first campaigns against German targets in Northern Africa. They would drive customized assault vehicles through enemy airfields in the middle of the night, shooting up parked planes and sleeping officers before the enemy knew what had hit them. Moments later, as the remaining German soldiers scurried about, putting out fires and regrouping their numbers, the SAS would be long gone, crawling back into the shadows of the desert night from which they had come. They specialized in classic, small-scale, direct action offensives, which the current world of Special Forces Operations now routinely exercised.

In the present day theater, the SAS were still making history in the Special Warfare community. They handled anti-terrorist operations, both in the United Kingdom and abroad. Sam had worked with the SAS many times on select missions in the Middle East. He respected the unit's skill sets and their integrity. But what impressed him the most was their attitude about warfare. It had seemed the unit's main objective was to gain experience through active conflict. And if there was no conflict presently existing somewhere in the world, well damn it, they would be happy to create one.

Looking at the pictures, Sam thought more about his current situation. Examining the geography in the photographs, he suspected they had been taken after the Falklands War, and probably while training in the jungles of Borneo or Malaysia—areas the SAS had been routinely involved with over the years.

Sam thought he heard a noise, so he turned away from the study and shined his flashlight into the surrounding darkness. He spotted a tunnel branching off to his right. It appeared to stretch down into the belly of the mountain. And to his left was another alcove containing old wooden crates and a sundry of weathered gear. The entire place reminded Sam of his cave back in the Gila Wilderness.

Thinking about this, he wondered if perhaps Lou *was* a lot like him, in that he preferred to live his life in secret, away from humanity, and all because of his past.

Feeling guilty, yet still curious, Sam looked down again and leafed through another notebook. This time he found pictures of Lou Pine dressed in a different uniform and surrounded by different looking men...

The French Foreign Legion.

The pictures were taken in a desert. And judging by the architecture of the buildings in some photographs, Sam guessed Northern Africa. The area was a well-known hot spot for the Legion, who had frequently sent men there to deal with fanatical Islamist terrorists such as Al Qaeda.

Sam noted Lou appeared older in these pictures, perhaps in his thirties. And he guessed the photos had been taken in the 1990s.

It was a curious and slightly unsettling observation. Lou had served in the SAS, and then later, in the French Foreign Legion. Sam wondered what else the old man had kept secret from him. Looking further into the notebook, he found a rather gruesome photo of several corpses lying in a row in the sand. To the side of the frame were three legionnaires posing with rifles and smiling, one of whom was Lou.

So the old man had seen more action than he'd originally admitted. Perhaps that's why he lived out here now, as a way of processing his experiences into something he could easily forget. It was an action Sam could relate to. And something he could not fault the former soldier for doing.

At last finished with his prying into the old man's personal life and feeling more than disgusted with himself for doing so, Sam closed the journal and turned to leave. It was then that he heard the noise again. And it came from down the dark mineshaft to his right.

The noise was an echo of sorts. One that Sam could not identify, but which stirred his curiosity all the same. He walked further into the darkness and listened until he heard what sounded like dripping water.

There was something about the sound that gripped Sam's thoughts. His mind struggled while listening to it, as if he was trying to recall something stored within his memory. For whatever reason, Sam thought it was an important sound.

And it compelled him to walk further into the black tunnel in search of its source.

PART 3

CHAPTER 24

Sam walks cautiously down a sloping tunnel, the walls of earth pressing closer into him. He comes to another alcove opening up off to his right, away from the descending mine. He hears the subtle flow of water coming from further down the tunnel. But he hesitates in going any further as he is inquisitive about this new alcove.

He turns and steps into the dark hollow. He shines his light into the blackness and then stares curiously at a sight he had not expected to find.

Looking forward, he notices a plethora of items that would seem natural to the previous environment—that of the Yukon, and on the outside, above and beyond the interior of this mountain. But taken out of context and here in this darkness, the items seem entirely out of place...

Sam shines his light into the blackness and sees backpacks, fishing poles, kayaks and paddles. He sees boots and jackets, hats and gloves, tent poles, snowshoes, tarps and lanterns. He sees purses, walking sticks, fishing nets, and brightly colored clothing.

He sees things that look old and things that look new. Things made from plastic and wood, metal and rubber. Valuable things, and things deemed altogether worthless.

Looking on and exploring further, Sam sees a host of items, all pertaining to an outdoor adventure of some sort. And all apparently left here to rot in this deep hole in the earth.

What Sam is really seeing—as he now realizes it—are the things that should not be. Things that had originally belonged to different individuals, *lots* of individuals, people who would have used these items in any other place other than down here in this cold and dark mine.

With an icy shiver, Sam also realizes that what he is looking at are the things that someone, somewhere, must have thought went missing...

He steps further into the cavern, sending the beam from his flashlight across the mounds of lost effects. He is searching now, not just out of curiosity, but out of necessity. Out of personal demand.

He is looking for items he might recognize, his thoughts bearing down on the mystery of his lost brother. Briefly, Sam considers the audacity of this find and wonders just how many mysteries he has uncovered. He wonders just how many cold cases there are before him, cases that were spread out across the wilds of the Yukon and over numerous years. Cases that had affected so many lives and that left so many unanswered questions.

Answers which could be lying right here, right now...

Sam is certain that some of this stuff he is looking at could solve many of those cases. He is sure of it, in fact. Feeling both angered and deceived, he thinks about Lou, along with the astounding implications of this hidden evidence.

Suddenly, Sam's feelings of guilt for prying into the old man's life washes away, leaving him with a new feeling.

The feeling of alarm.

Sam walks further into the cavern, moving items out of his way, checking for something familiar, something of Bryson's. In a far corner he sees what appears to be a hunter's backpack and resting beside it is what looks like an angler's bag, likely used to store fishing tackle. From this distance, the bag looks practically new.

Sam shines his light directly onto the bag and takes another step forward. But then he pauses, suddenly aware of something else within his proximity. Something not quite right.

A cold feeling washes over him. A cold thought enters his mind. And then both sensations are reduced by the sudden noise he hears coming from behind him.

Quickly, Sam turns, and the light of his flashlight splashes down onto something. It is a sight much more curious than the one he'd been staring at.

A tall, ghastly beast covered in hair or fur towers before Sam. The creature has a face resembling that of a bear, but a bear with elk antlers rising high above its head. And there are several smaller antlers dangling from its matted coat, which make a rattling noise as the thing steps forward.

Sam never figures out what the creature is. Not before his mind comes to a final resolution of impending danger. A danger followed too quickly by a pang of sound which erupts into the darkness and sends waves of blinding light and a deafening concussion through the mountain's belly.

As well as through Sam's head.

After the sound comes more darkness, a darkness that is total and uncompromising. A darkness that is black as an evil night. Black as the grave...

CHAPTER 25

When he woke, Sam's world had not changed. Darkness still surrounded him. It was as if his eyes had never opened, slow as they had been in doing so.

His head ached fiercely. A hot pounding emanated from his forehead and reverberated deep into his skull, spreading down his neck and down his spine. The pain was insurmountable, being akin to a force of nature. Uncompromising. Sam realized also that he couldn't move. Not that he felt like trying much, but when he did, the only part of his body he had control over was his head.

The horror of this detail washed over Sam, forcing him to wake himself further.

Seconds after coming to, Sam understood why he couldn't move. He was bound, bound tightly. Bound by rope or by leather. Bound by a professional with such fastening skills. There was no slack in Sam's bindings, and his muscles had been pulled taut, his arms stretched out to his sides, his legs spread wide. His whole body was suspended in a state of constant strain.

He had no idea how long he'd been hanging like that. A good measure, that's for sure. The muscles in his body ached from the pain of injury and fatigue. His throat was parched. His stomach felt like it had been empty for some time.

Sam felt at his bindings with his fingers and noted that they were made from leather. He probed for knots he could work free, but couldn't reach any. Then he strained against the bindings, despite his pain, as he attempted to break loose. He did this several times, to no effect. Sam was bound good and tight.

Over several minutes, he moved in and out of consciousness. At times, the pain in his head was too much to bear. He could taste caked iron on his lips, and he knew that the dull ache in his forehead was because of a terrible wound, a wound that had bled fiercely.

Something had hit him there, causing a wicked injury. At the very least, he had a concussion. As he moved between consciousness, whenever he came back to the living, Sam understood a little more of his situation. And with that understanding, the horror of his situation unfolded even more.

Sam had been captured. He remembered the alcove, seeing all those lost items, all that gear that had no business being crammed down into the gullet of a mountain. Items that had belonged to people who had gone missing.

Missing, just like Bryson.

And just like Sam was now...

Then he remembered hearing a noise and seeing that thing standing in the darkness. The hairy beast draped with an assortment of antlers. It was a confusing sight, one that Sam still couldn't figure out. He thought briefly about the Sasquatch myth and considered maybe that was the creature he'd seen. But that too confused him, as it made little sense—not with the way the creature appeared. And finally, there came that loud crack against the silence, and then the blackness of night had fallen over him.

Now here he was, captured. Something or someone's prisoner.

It was a horrible thought. And it brought with it not just the terror of the moment, but a terror from his past. Without mercy, Sam's mind slowly took him into his military years. He did not want to go there, into his dark memories, the memories he'd been keeping locked up for so long. But his current predicament would suggest no other way around it. Forget being tied up in a mineshaft in the vastness of Canada's Yukon Territory, and with a future as bleak as the darkness surrounding him; Sam's mind was heading into a world all its own. A world several thousand miles away and a few years in his past...

It was their thirteenth mission together, Sam and Ernie, and they were deep behind Taliban lines, conducting a mundane, if not hazardous, recon. They were looking for evidence of activity in a particular area. And more importantly, evidence of a particular Taliban field commander.

But the mundane quickly turned to the explosive. Sam and Ernie's position had been compromised. They were too far out and too few to fight back effectively, and in no time, they were wounded and overrun by the enemy. But as time would reveal, that would become the least of their problems.

Worse was what followed for Sam and his spotter: several months of torture. They were kept like dogs, crated in iron cages deep within a cave. Sometimes the men were tortured for information. Other times, out of pure entertainment. The worst was when they were tortured out of retribution. There would be an engagement of sorts, a battle somewhere, and the Taliban would lose men, lots of men. Then Sam and Ernie would pay for that loss with their own blood. It was a brutal time, which crafted brutal memories. Memories that would never leave Sam's heart and soul.

But the worst of the worst, worse than all his months of captivity and torture, was when Sam was finally released. He never learned the full details of his departure from the Taliban. He just remembered being tied and bagged, then driven to some compound on the outskirts of Kandahar, where he was left alone behind an alley. Yes, alone. And yes, that was the worst part. Sam was released, only him, and not Ernie, who, to this day, for all Sam knew, was still locked inside that metal cage deep in an Afghanistan mountain.

And because of this, for Sam, the torture never stopped.

Sam relaxed his body as much as he could. Then he tried to relax his mind. He let his memories run their course, painful as they were, then he let out a deep breath of air. There was nothing he could do about Ernie. And there was nothing Sam could do about his past, other than let it be. If his past hadn't yet killed him—something it kept trying to do, so it seemed—then that meant Sam was still alive. And if he was still alive, then that meant he could keep on fighting.

He blinked his eyes and observed his surroundings, searching for something, anything, that he could make use of in whatever way.

He was in complete darkness. The lifeless air smelled wet and stale. Sam hung silently, concentrating his attention on the black void, hoping to catch even the smallest of details—perhaps the slight breath of cool air or the faintest sliver of light. Anything at all that could show a way out of this mess.

He didn't feel a breeze or see any light. But he did notice something. And it instantly woke a haunting memory hiding in the back of his mind. Coming from a deeper darkness off to his right, Sam heard the echo of dripping water, a rhythm of drops falling into more water, as if falling into a pool.

It was the same sound described to him days earlier, by Jenny. The same sound she had heard over her voicemail.

"I'll be damned," Sam whispered, thinking of Bryson. His brother must have hung in this very spot. Of course, Sam wasn't surprised, as he'd put the pieces of the puzzle together.

Everything pointed back to Lou Pine. The man had undoubtedly captured Bryson, as he had now undoubtedly captured Sam. *It must be that old man*, Sam thought, *for all his elderly ways.*

Sam wondered about that as well. Obviously Lou wasn't as fragile as he'd originally made himself out to be. He had fooled Sam into thinking this—as well as other things. Sam wondered if anything about the man was true, other than what he'd observed in those journals. But to be sure, Lou was clearly a lunatic. He was clearly responsible for Sam's capture, most likely Bryson's disappearance, and probably many other horrific crimes. With a shivery feeling in the pit of his stomach, Sam remembered the photo of Lou as a Legionnaire, standing beside those dead bodies and smiling proudly.

But not everything became clear to Sam. He wondered about the creature he'd seen earlier. That thing with the antlers. That was still a mystery to him. And speaking of mysterious creatures, what about the one he'd been tracking through the forest and the other one that had crept up behind him? Those things had worked together to lead Sam straight to Bryson's boots. And as Sam thought more about this, hadn't he also been led to Lou's tracks? The same tracks that had suddenly disappeared—and in the mud, of all places.

Sam figured the old man had used some sort of moccasins to hide his and the mule's prints. It was a technique often employed by the Apache. And in current times, by human "mules" who hauled drugs into the United States for the cartel.

Then Sam remembered...

He had actually seen the moccasins that day in his camp, just before Lou had left. The bundles of soft leather in Sally's saddle bag, next to the twine and cans of fruit. Lou Pine was one clever old man.

Still, not all the pieces of the puzzle were clear to Sam. Except that he knew he was in deep trouble. There was nothing confusing about that. It was a fact that had constantly made itself painfully clear to him. Regardless of how he would solve the many riddles rattling through the walls of his head, at the present moment, he had to get himself out of his current mess.

Sam tried to break free from his bindings once again, pulling with as much strength as he could muster. But his struggling proved to be of no use. His only options were to think his way out.

And so Sam put his mind to the task. Thoughtfully, he wondered about Lou's intentions. He considered the key to escape may come from understanding Lou's motives and desires. Because Sam was still alive said something about what Lou wanted. The man was obviously a sociopath, and likely sought his pleasure out of causing harm to others. He probably enjoyed watching them suffer before he killed them. After all, why else was Sam still breathing?

Sam still wondered about the creature he'd seen in the alcove, though. That was certainly not Lou. And somehow, it seemed to cause Sam's sudden blackout and subsequent throbbing sensation in his skull. But did it tie him up also?

The unanswered questions and mysteries in the dark were too wicked and painful to think about for very long. Fortunately, for the sake of Sam's aching head, he didn't have to wait for some of those answers to reveal themselves...

As he hung in the black silence of his apparent doom, a flash of orange light suddenly bloomed not ten feet in front of him. Standing behind the light was the creature once again—the beast with antlers.

It held a sputtering lantern in one hand and a length of wood in the other. And it walked right toward Sam.

CHAPTER 26

The creature stopped within three feet of Sam. Then it hung the lantern on a metal hook anchored in a wooden support beam running just above Sam's arms.

The creature—or whatever it was—stood there, waiting in the light, waiting for God knows what as it stared back at Sam for many long seconds.

Sam heard it breathing. He looked up at the creature's bizarre face, with its bearish features that mingled grotesquely into a rack of elk antlers—antlers which loomed up and outward and were sharp and fearsome.

After what seemed like an entire minute of staring, the beast lifted its hands to its bizarre head, the black bear crowned with antlers. It grasped its antlers, and with a yanking motion, pushed upward.

Sam watched with unease as the thing pulled its head right off. The motion took not just the head, but the neck and shoulders as well. The creature's entire upper mass fell to the ground with a heavy thud.

Sam looked then at the smiling, cackling face of Lou Pine.

Shortened now to his original height, the old man was laughing hysterically. Then he caught his breath, wheezing as he drew in some air. "Just a trick, Sam," he said, still chuckling. "Nothing but a blimey trick, is all." He studied Sam, and his look was one of both humor and inquisitiveness. "It gets boring out here, living by myself. Can't blame me for wanting to have a little fun, now can you?"

Sam stared at the old man, his mind racing for clues about how he could escape this freakish hell. He glanced briefly at his surroundings, as much as what the lantern's light would afford him. He couldn't tell where he was. But he was somewhere in the abandoned mineshaft. He saw a lattice of support beams running haphazardly above him. And to his left was a chiseled stone wall, glistening with moisture.

Lou continued to smile as he paced circles around Sam. He was wearing what looked like fishing waders, festooned with thick patches of fur and deer antlers, completing his chilling disguise.

"Bet you thought I was that Sasquatch you've been hunting," Lou said. He spoke in a high, cheerful tone, but his eyes revealed a cruel malice Sam had not seen before in the man. "Well, sorry, Sam, but I must disappoint you. There's no such thing as Sasquatch. And I should know—I've been out here long enough. The creature's just a silly myth. An old Indian legend, is all." Lou hesitated, as if a thought suddenly struck him. "But me, on the other hand... I'm as real as it gets."

Lou was behind him now, and Sam had the inconspicuous feeling that a vicious strike from the old man was on its way.

"You're a sick man, Lou," Sam said. "You know that, don't you? You're sick in the head."

"Who, me?" Lou brought his face to Sam's ear. "What do you know about being sick, soldier boy?"

"I know enough," Sam replied. Then he felt a solid whack on the back of his knees, which shot a jolt of pain up his leg and into his hip. The strike wasn't damaging; but it hurt like hell. And it erased any slim notion that this might be a cruel joke Lou was playing. Not that Sam believed for a minute that it was. He'd been up against lunatics before and he knew damn well he was up against one now.

There was a pause as Lou strolled back in front of Sam, the length of wood bouncing on his hand. "Maybe you know something about being sick," he said. "Then again, maybe you don't."

Sam grimaced at the pain lingering throughout his body. "You're a sick old man, Lou. And you need help."

Lou laughed. "I need help, do I? And I suppose you're the bloke who's going to do that. Are you going to help me, Sam? Because it doesn't look like you can help anybody."

Sam held his words, knowing that talking was useless. Lou was clearly insane.

The old man continued, despite Sam's silence. "But you might be on to something, Sam... about being sick. At least the type of sickness that would plague me. I mean, you have that familiar look—the look of a man who's been running and hiding for so many years. Running because he knows he's contagious. And if he stops for one damn minute, he'll infect a whole bunch of people. Maybe that's what you can help me with, Sam. It's a proper sickness we share, don't you think?"

There was another pause and then Lou added, "Oh, and I bet you know what it's like to be a forgotten man. That's another thing we have in common, isn't it?" A look of anticipation stitched across Lou's face. "Well? Say something, mate. Your brother sure as hell wouldn't shut up. Why break the family pattern now?"

Fury and terror mixed into a white-hot passion, as Sam pulled against his restraints, pulled hard and angrily. If he could just break free, he would snap the old man's neck in less than two seconds. Then he'd be done with this nightmare.

Lou laughed again. "Go ahead. Fight, Sam. Keep on fighting. It'll only wear you out."

"What did you do to my brother?" Sam asked, anger welling out of him with his words. "I swear to God!"

Lou smiled then, a wide and knowing smile, full of contempt and conceit. "There it is!" he crowed, his body arching backward with triumphant glee as he pointed at Sam. "I had hoped your constitution was stronger than that. Damn, I had hoped. I sure as hell never took you for the religious type." Still smiling, Lou shook his head. "They always turn to God. Every bloody one of them. Even you. I guess people can't help to bring that bastard up. The all-knowing, all-seeing wanker—who never *says*, or *does*, a bloody thing. Go ahead, bring Him up, Sam. Call on your deity. *Pray* to Him. Then you might see just how bollocks it is to be a bloody human on this planet."

Then Lou's voice changed, dropping into a depraved, unholy sneer, as he said, "*Fuck God*, Sam." The old man hesitated, as if to let his words sink in. "Do you think you can teach me something I haven't already heard... but then realized to be false? Can you teach me something that is truly true—truer than the pain that comes with living on this fucking earth, only to end up a piece of rotting meat?"

Sam kept his mouth shut. The old man was baiting him once again, the same as he did with his comments about Bryson.

"I'll teach you all you need to know about God," Lou said. "Oh, yes, I will teach you all about Him. But first, I'm going to teach you a little about that other guy... Lucifer. Sounds like Lou, doesn't it? That's right. And Lucifer—the other wanker—well, Sam, he just might be me."

The old man reached into the darkness and dragged out an iron stool, which he then casually sat on with his body facing Sam. Nonchalantly, he drew a pipe from a hidden pocket inside his costume, along with a lighter, and lit up. Then he looked up at Sam and smiled.

"There are some people from this world—no longer alive, mind you—who would correctly refer to me as being the Devil. And you know, Sam, that's a right proper feeling, being the Devil. It's a *bloody proper feeling*." Lou spoke in a conversational tone as if the two of them were merely sitting down for a quaint visit.

"Why don't you just kill me and get this over with?" Sam said, not wanting to hear anymore of the old man's insane words.

"I've done a lot of things," Lou said, ignoring Sam. "I've killed a lot of people." He chuckled briefly. "A *lot* of people. And I have no regrets about any of that. At first, well... At first it was just all part of the job. Of course, you know how that goes. But then... Well, when they asked me to leave, Sam. When they asked me to *retire*... Now, can you imagine that? Them asking me to retire?" Lou looked down at his feet, his face rippling with guilt. "I have a confession to make, Sam. I lied to you. I was never with Her Majesty's Royal Marines. No, sir. I served with the Special Air Service—Her Majesty's bastard children. I did that for many years until I got bored with all their rules and regulations. That's when I went over to the fucking French—the Legionnaires, for bloody sake. And I served with those wankers for well over ten years. Hell, I was a bloody professional soldier for most of my life, Sam. And then, out of the blue, the sons-of-bitches asked me to... yes... retire."

Sam stared at the old man, trying to decode something out of his speech from which he could use to escape, however slim the probability. He didn't feel too hopeful at the moment.

Lou took a drag from his pipe, then continued. "How does one ask a professional killer to retire? How, Sam? I'm a fucking manmade devil. So how do you command a soldier like me to kill people for a living, all kinds of people, good, bad, young and old, and then let him go just because he's *supposedly* unfit for the job? I could never figure that one out, Sam."

"Maybe they just wanted to get rid of you." Sam's voice felt dry and it cracked as he spoke. It seemed there wasn't a part of his body that didn't hurt. Feeling a sudden stab of pain on his forehead just above his eye, he winced, then said, "Maybe they knew you were sick."

Lou smiled contemptuously. "Yes, you might be right, Sam." He gestured with his pipe to Sam's forehead, and added, "By the way, care to know how you got that little bugger there, above your eye?" He didn't wait for Sam to respond. From the darkness behind him, Lou produced a stout, homemade-looking gun with a pistol grip and a short and wide barrel end. It resembled a "7-11 special," a sawed-off shotgun frequently used in armed robberies, but Lou's was thoroughly painted in camouflage colors.

"I made it myself," Lou said, his voice beaming with pride. He opened the gun's breech and pulled out a single bullet that looked like a shotgun round. "Single shot only—but that's all I need." Lou stood and raised the bullet into the light, just a few feet from Sam's face. "See that there?" He gestured to the inside of the cartridge. "It's a dummy round, made from rubber. I carved it out of an old tire. And I loaded it myself. Works great for knocking people out without killing them... Well, most of the time." Lou chuckled, then winked at Sam. "But it leaves quite the fucking headache, now doesn't it?"

Sam blinked his eyes and looked away. He did not want to give this lunatic anymore satisfaction than what he already had. Thinking hard, he concentrated once again on a means of escape.

"So you think they retired me because I'm sick?" Lou said, reverting to the previous topic. "Maybe you're right, Sam. But let me tell you this: being sick, if that's what I am, it's really not all that bad. It's something a person like me gets used to when faced with the absence of a God. It's something the *Devil* learns to appreciate."

Lou chambered the round back into the gun and closed the breech. "But just because I might be sick doesn't mean I can't do my job. You know how many people I've shot with this, Sam?" He raised the gun in the light and smiled. "Thirty-three people. And of those thirty-three, I've killed twenty-seven of them. A few stragglers got away, but that's a different story, and beside the point. The point is *twenty-seven* people, Sam. And those bastards sent me into retirement."

"You think that's something worth bragging about?"

"Well, don't you?"

Sam shook his head. "It's sick and disgusting... Do the world a favor, old man. Put that gun in your mouth and pull the trigger."

Lou laughed. "Sadly, Sam, it's not time for me to leave this world just yet. I figure I got at least twenty-seven more people to kill. Maybe more, if I'm lucky. But that's my job, ain't it? I'm a *killer*."

"Whatever you say," Sam replied. "You're the crazy one here." He had all but given up on hope, and part of him was ready to be done with this. The old man had obviously killed Bryson and would certainly kill Sam in due time.

"Yes, I guess I *am* crazy. But maybe that's just another one of those hazards of the job." Lou's face turned pensive for a second as he glanced at his feet. "I'll tell you what I'm going to do, Sam. I'm going to make you a deal. You are a veteran, after all, which makes us... well, it makes us brothers, don't it?" A smug smile crossed his face. "And I like you, Sam. You're clearly a good guy. So what I'm going to do is I'm going to let you—"

Suddenly, Lou stopped talking. His arm holding the gun went limp, along with his smile, as his other hand went quickly to his chest, grasping and clenching at his shirt. His face broke into a look of fierce pain. He gasped, and his body convulsed. His eyes looked directly at Sam's, and in the old man's stare was both alarm and the request for immediate help.

It seemed Lou was having a heart attack.

Considering this, Sam was both relieved and anxious. If the old man died right here, right now, then Sam, along with any future victims, would be spared whatever the maniac had in store. But that also meant Sam would be left here hanging until he too died. It was a mixture of feelings he couldn't quite process. Nor did he have time to.

Suddenly, wickedly, deviously, Lou's frantic convulsion stopped, and was replaced by his calmly standing body and smiling face. "A trick, Sam," he said with a giggle. "Just another trick."

Then he raised his arm, leveled the gun at Sam's chest, winked, and fired.

CHAPTER 27

Sam woke once again in total darkness. He was no longer tied up and stretched out. Instead, he was lying on cold dirt and apparently free to move. But darkness still surrounded him. And it was a deathly darkness, an abysmal black world consisting of a dull aching pain which hung throughout his body, and a tomblike silence which emanated from the surrounding void.

Much worse than what he felt or what he could not see or hear was the cadaverous odor floating in the air. The smell of death, as Sam knew all too well, was thick and retching. For all he knew or believed, the very corporealness of Death itself was standing within arm's length from him.

Slowly, painfully, Sam stirred his body and his mind into working order. He assessed his situation, however dismal and unclear that it was. He still felt the agonizing wounds he'd remembered from earlier—the throbbing on his forehead, the constant aching of his muscles and bones. But now he also felt a sharp stabbing in his left side. He knew immediately that at least one of his ribs was broken. Sam felt it in his breathing—the jagged bite that came with the movement of air in and out of his lungs.

Remaining prone on the ground, he reached out with his hand and inspected the surrounding area. Nothing but dank soil and hard rock. Then he physically and mentally assessed his body, making sure he was still in one piece. He rolled over onto his back and then he felt a sudden jolt of pain in the back of his head. Reaching with his hand, he discovered a lump behind his ear the size of a ping-pong ball. And his fingers came away wet, wet with blood.

Sam thought about this. He vaguely remembered Lou's maniacal gag of having a heart attack. And he remembered that the old man fired his gun into Sam's body, which explained the pain in his ribs and his wind getting knocked out of him. But that's all Sam could remember. Oddly, he didn't think such a blast into his midsection would knock him out cold. Yet something had.

Maybe after the old man had shot him, he then hit Sam on the back of the head with something. Probably the wooden club or even his gun.

It didn't matter. None of it mattered, except for the fact that Sam was still alive and still suffering. But for how long?

He wondered about that also, knowing that people like Lou, crazy as they were, were unpredictable with their mental illness. For all Sam knew, his future was as indeterminable as life itself. He was fairly certain he would die at the hands of the old man. But when, or how, was yet to be determined.

Sam thought about what his dad had told him before he left, and about coming back alive. And that if he didn't, between Bryson's disappearance and then his, well, the double loss would downright kill their mother. Sam now knew that along with his and Bryson's fate, Ruby Nolan's was sealed as well.

None of the pain in his body compared to what Sam was now feeling in his heart. Adding to his dismal despair was that he also felt the fool. To think at one point, he actually entertained the notion that a legendary creature had been responsible for his brother's disappearance.

He thought about Andre McKinnon and all the evidence the man had shared with Sam, with his convictions about what he believed and his ludicrous theories and assumptions... Sam could have kicked himself for falling for it. In retrospect, he should have never listened to the man as long as he did. If he hadn't let the Bigfoot enthusiast put so much craziness into his head, Sam would have had a clear mind as he searched for Bryson. Then he would have been more aware and thus less likely to have become another one of Lou's victims.

Victims...

With sudden grimness, it dawned on Sam. The word "victim" and the smell of death lingering in the air... With a chilled heart, he wondered if what he presently smelled was the rotting corpse of his own brother.

Summoning his inner soldier, Sam steadily got up off the ground. He took a quick inventory of what he had on his person. He still had his clothes, but that seemed to be all. His watch was gone, and so were his knife and various tools. His canteen and his hat—those too were gone. And of course his shoes were missing. Sam's feet were bare. But that wasn't a problem. He had spent many of his youthful days running on the family ranch or through the Gila wilderness, all without footwear, toughening his feet in the same manner as the Apaches had. It was a tradition taught to him by Nali, and one that Sam had kept alive, even as an adult.

But his eyes were only as good as his human anatomy would let them be. The darkness surrounding him was total and the mere thought of walking into it put a shiver in Sam's gut.

Any step could be his last, sending him down a deep chasm or vertical shaft. Sam moved on hands and knees. He had no idea where to go, so he simply went straight, hoping he would soon find a wall from which he could navigate.

Carefully, he crawled for approximately twenty feet, until he found a wall of solid rock. It was wet and slimy, but he was able to use it to help him stand.

Once on his feet, Sam forced his eyelids open as wide as he could, hoping to expedite and increase his ability to see in the dark. He did not know how long he'd been lying down there in this hole in the earth. The wounds on the back of his head and in his ribs both felt fresh. But the darkness was so vast and unyielding that no matter how hard he tried or waited, his eyes wouldn't let him see.

He used the stone wall as a guide, placing his right palm against it and his left hand out in front of him, and then he slowly stepped forward. The injuries on his head ached with a sporadic bitterness, but the pain in his ribs was constant. With each step, he was reminded of the wound. And with each breath, Sam cursed at it.

He walked for roughly fifteen minutes, but was still unsure of his surroundings. By all accounts, he figured he was in some type of cavern, perhaps manmade and not unlike what he'd found earlier when he first ran across the old man in his monstrous disguise. But this definitely wasn't the same cavern. Not by a mile.

The smell of death hadn't let up, despite the distance Sam had walked. There seemed to be a mess of dead things down there with him, or else he'd only traveled the length of a simple perimeter.

Finding a rock on the ground, he threw it out in front of him and listened. In less than a second, he heard it strike stone, thus confirming his suspicions. Sam did this same maneuver several more times, throwing pebbles at different angles, and was able to determine that he was indeed trapped in a small cavern, with an area of perhaps that of a small house.

Sam thought about his situation and what he now had to do. The irony worked like a blow to the back of his knees. He rested his body against the stone wall and sank to the ground. *Once again*, he thought, *the darkness, the captivity, and losing a loved one...*

And now, of all things, once again he would put his tracking skills in effect and search the confines of this mountain's innards, hoping to find his brother's rotting cadaver.

Sam got up on his hands and knees and began to crawl, tracing a spiral pattern. He followed the cavern's perimeter and slogged his way toward what he thought was the center. It was slow going, and he'd made little ground as he paused for a break. He wasn't in much of a hurry, knowing that what he was about to find would be most unpleasant, if not traumatic. After all, the old man had confessed to abducting Bryson.

Sam remembered Lou's words, about how Bryson wouldn't stop talking. And he remembered the anger that swelled through him as a result. But knowing his brother's body was lying somewhere nearby was more than enough to keep Sam going.

He crawled for several more minutes until his hand struck something solid. Right away, Sam knew it was a human leg covered in pants. Slowly, he inspected the rest of the body with his hands, observing its frail, bony frame, the coldness of its fingers and then its shaggy and weathered face.

It was a complete body, but not much else. It seemed as if this person had died from starvation and the notion of that served as a grim preview to what could easily be Sam's own fate. But, oddly enough, the body did not smell dead. Certainly not enough to be the source of what Sam noticed in the cavern. And that meant there was more than one person, or thing, down there.

Sam was hardly surprised. *Twenty-seven people*, the lunatic had bragged.

Still, Sam was only searching for his brother. And because of the darkness and the state in which the body he'd found was in, he couldn't determine a damn thing about who was lying before him. But it was certainly a *he*. And he was dead. Or so it seemed...

Suddenly, Sam felt a thin wisp of air smooth across the back of his hand. Then he heard what sounded like a very faint, very subtle cough come from the body. He laid his ear down close to the man's face. Sure enough, he was breathing. Not much and not strong, but he was breathing.

Sam checked for a pulse, found a faint one, then gently slapped at the man's cheek. "Hey, mister," he said, "wake up. You're not dead yet. Come on back, now."

The man croaked out a single unidentifiable syllable, and then he groaned.

"Come on, let's go, mister." Sam grabbed the man's lapels and brought him to a seated position. Then he held him there, trying to convince him back into a state of consciousness. He could feel there was little left of the man, just a thin shell of skin wrapped around a skeleton, a vague beat of his heart and an even vaguer breath of air. This man was on the verge of death.

"Let's go," Sam said, hoping his voice would restore an ounce of life back into the man. "My name is Sam, mister, and you're not dead yet, so come on back."

"Sam," the voice cracked, albeit livelier now. "Sam... is that you?"

Sam's heart suddenly jolted.

"Sam Nolan?" the man repeated, and now Sam understood that this was Bryson. "You came for me... My big brother came for me."

Then Bryson's voice went silent, his body went limp, and he became nothing more than a twig in Sam's arms.

CHAPTER 28

Sam's world spun in a state of astounding relief... and grave panic. Amazingly, he had found his brother and his brother was alive, if barely.

But how much time did he have left? Sam wasn't sure. That there was little to nothing left of Bryson had Sam feeling sick to his stomach. It seemed as if his brother had undergone a few rounds of chemotherapy, he was that skinny. He still had his hair and whiskers, but they covered the face and head of a skeleton.

For certain, Bryson had only days, if not hours, left. This was a fact Sam had no doubts about, and it fanned the fire surrounding his panic all the more.

"Stay with me, Bryson," Sam said. He checked his brother for serious wounds or signs of bleeding. There didn't seem to be anything worth noting, other than the man was starving to death.

There was plenty of water trailing down some of the rock faces within the cavern. Sam had discovered this earlier, so he assumed his brother wasn't dying of dehydration. Just the lack of food.

"Don't give up now, Bryson. Just hang in there."

There has to be a way out, Sam thought to himself. Minutes ago, he was convinced, if not resigned, to the fact that there was no escape from this hole in the earth. But now, with his brother here with him, and still alive, Sam had no other choice but to find a way out for them.

He put his mind to the situation. If there was a way into this place, which there obviously was, then there also had to be a way out. Thoughtfully, he looked down at his brother in his arms, even though he couldn't see a damn thing. "Bryson?" he said. "Bryson, wake up."

His brother moaned in reply.

"Come on, think, Bryson," Sam said. "How did we get down here? How did that crazy old coot get us down here?"

There was a pause and then Bryson said, "Up there. A door."

Up where? Sam wondered. But a door... Now that was something to consider.

"Who else is down here?" Sam asked, thinking about the smell of death still lingering in the cavern.

"There's a couple," Bryson replied. It seemed as if he was coming more to his senses. His voice sounded stronger and his breathing had picked up a pace, both of which added to the brush fire now burning in Sam's heart. "An old man and wife. They're dead, though. Dead for a while."

"I figured as much," Sam said. But then he wondered if the dead couple may still be of use to his situation. "Hang on, Buddy. I'm gonna get you over to a wall." He reached down and picked Bryson up, and then stood. His brother was so light, it filled Sam with absolute dread.

He carried his brother in the dark, over to the cavern wall, then placed him gently on the ground. "Where's this door you mentioned?" he asked.

"It's up... I'm not sure... Up over there, I think."

"Over where?" Sam replied. "I can't see a damn thing. I'm not sure where you're pointing at—or if you're pointing."

"I, ah..." Bryson's voice stretched with the sound of confusion. "I don't know, really. It's up there, the bottom of it... Six, seven feet up."

"Okay," Sam replied. He stood over six-feet tall, and with his hands held high, seven feet was an easy reach for him. "I'll find it," he added.

Steadily, Sam raised an arm above his head and pressed his hand against the rock. Then he began tracing his steps from earlier, walking along the cavern's perimeter. It didn't take him long to find the shelf, which stood approximately six and a half feet from the ground. It was but a small alcove, just a few inches in depth. But concealed in it was the door Bryson had mentioned.

Sam probed with his fingers and found the bottom lip of the door. He studied it with his hands, feeling its features, concentrating and calculating. Despite the darkness, he was able to make a mental image of the door's construction. It was certainly heavy, made of solid wood, and perhaps two or three inches thick. And it was framed into the mountain by what felt like a patchwork of concrete and rebar. There were no steps leading up to it, and the shelf at the base of the door was only a few inches wide.

Getting up to, and standing at the edge of the door, would be difficult, if not impossible. Also, there was nothing about its features which Sam could capitalize upon, or find leverage against. He couldn't even kick his way out, let alone ram the thing with a running start. Nonetheless, he had to find a way out. Somehow, Sam had to get through that door.

Curiously, he thought about the couple Bryson had mentioned. Perhaps there was something on their body—a tool, a flashlight, anything—that he could use. Searching dead bodies was a grim prospect. But in his present situation, it was also something Sam couldn't ignore.

Worried about the state of his brother, Sam first went back to check on Bryson. He found he was still conscious. But his fear was that Bryson would die any minute now.

In its darkness, the cavern was cold and silent. Sam noticed that besides the smell of death, there were other odors as well. Dampness and mold... And the subtle hint of something that reminded him of pitch pine, such as the smell from a telephone pole. Curious about these other odors, Sam left Bryson and continued with his searching.

It was only a few minutes later that he found the dead bodies.

They were an older couple, a woman and a man, lying on the ground. The man was on his back and the woman was curled up against him, as if sleeping peacefully in a bed, with her arm resting over his chest.

Sam paused. Then, methodically, he inspected the bodies with as much respect as possible. It was a tragic scene, this man and his wife, who had been brought down here by that lunatic, probably tortured, and then left for dead. Sam felt a twinge of sorrow for the couple, followed by another surge of anger. It dawned on him then, with sudden surprise. Sam's task wasn't to just find a way out of this prison. He had to put an end to Lou Pine, as well.

Sam continued to search the bodies. Like him, they were both still clothed, yet missing their shoes. That seemed to be Lou's trademark—to remove his victim's footwear so they couldn't escape easily, if given the chance. The front of the dead man's shirt felt stiff and smelled of iron. Sam suspected this was because of dried blood. Then he discovered a large gash on the top of the man's head, a deep wound, which was likely the cause of his death.

The woman seemed unscathed. But she was dead all the same. Sam imagined sadly that she had lied down next to her husband and died from her combination of grief, terror, and overwhelming despair. The thought reminded him of his Army spotter, Ernie Valencia, and of the mystery behind that man's fate. More than once, Sam wondered if his friend had succumbed to a similar death.

But an even worse thought was the possibility that Ernie was still alive and still a prisoner. Still locked in a cage, somewhere deep in the earth. And still being tortured.

Sam brought his mind back to the present. His goal was to get out of this cavern, and he needed to do just that. He resumed his searching of the bodies, was about to give up, when he noticed something on one of the dead man's pant legs.

They were lightweight hiking slacks made from synthetic materials and with many pockets, one of which sat way below the knee, near the man's ankle. It was a small, discreet pocket, easily overlooked, and obviously missed by Lou.

Inside the pocket was a metal tin, roughly the size of a deck of cards. Sam unzipped the pocket and retrieved the box, which he promptly opened. The tin could have easily been filled with mints, such as Altoids, but he was thankful it wasn't.

Inspecting the contents of the tin gently with his fingers and careful not to drop anything, Sam discovered several items related to outdoor survival: a fishing kit comprising two hooks, a coiled leader and four lead sinkers; razor blade; small compass; sewing needle and thread; a small whistle; flexible wire saw; four chalky pills, which Sam suspected were water tablets; a round candle with a diameter no bigger than a quarter; and finally, amazingly, three wooden matches. And taped on the back of the box was a strip of sandpaper.

Sam couldn't have been any luckier. He'd found the old man's survival tin, and Sam hardly missed the irony of this discovery. As far as he knew, carrying a tin such as this was a survival strategy first endorsed by members of the Special Air Service—Lou Pine's former attachment. In time, this strategy was adopted by wilderness enthusiasts outside of the British military, people like this old man lying dead on the ground, no doubt.

But now this little piece of wilderness preparation sat in the palm of Sam's hand. And he knew exactly what to do with it.

"Bryson," Sam called, "you still conscious?"

"Yeah... I hear you."

"I found something we can use." Sam closed the tin and stuffed it in his pocket, then carefully made his way back to his brother. He crouched with his back against the stone wall, retrieved the tin, opened it, then took out the candle and one of the matches. "Get ready for some light," he said, gripping the match tightly at the neck. He struck the sandpaper on the box just once and then the darkness surrounding them fled instantly into the shadows.

Quickly, Sam lit the candle and then looked at his brother. His gut clenched at the sight of the man, who was hardly recognizable.

Bryson's face was covered in whiskers, but Sam had no problem identifying the thin curves and tight angles behind his brother's cranium. Beyond the hair and grime, Sam spotted sallow, ill-colored skin. And Bryson's eyes seemed weak and hollow, having nothing left to bleed now, except sorrow.

It was a sickening spectacle, one that sent trepidation, sympathy, and blood-boiling anger coursing through Sam's veins.

"You hang in there, Bryson," Sam said. "I have a plan."

"He's crazy," Bryson replied. He coughed then, a long hack, and Sam heard the wetness inside his brother's lungs. "That bastard is crazy," Bryson continued after recovering his breath. "He'll kill us for sure."

"Not if I can help it." Sam stood then, shielding the candle's tiny flame with his hand. "You wait here. I'm gonna look around some, see if I can't find something else we can use."

"Be careful," Bryson said. "Don't let that flame go out."

Sam walked carefully throughout the cavern, inspecting it from top to bottom. On the ground, he discovered dozens of bones, which he suspected were human and most certainly the remains of Lou's past victims.

Near where the dead couple lay, he found several small lengths of old timber, half-buried in sand. The pieces of wood seemed to be splinters of an old support beam or brace of some sort. Something used during the construction of this mine. The wood had been treated with chemicals to prevent rot, which explained the telephone pole odor Sam had detected earlier. And this was a good discovery, one that fit evenly into the plan he'd been developing since finding the survival tin.

Carefully, Sam gathered the wood fragments together into a pile next to the dead couple, sat the candle on the ground, then dug out the tin and retrieved the razor blade. He used the blade on the dead man's pant leg, cutting away a strip of material. Then he wrapped the material around one length of wood, creating a small torch, which he placed gently into the candle's flame.

The torch went up in seconds. And it cast the darkness further into the shadows, revealing much more of the cavern.

Sam picked up the candle and blew it out, deciding to save the wax for as long as possible. He placed it in his pocket, then walked around some more, inspecting the rest of his stone prison. He found more ancient mining debris, such as two rusted out, fifty-five gallon drums, and several scraps of thin metal. The entire lot was more or less junk. But lying on the ground next to the drums was a solid wooden beam, about six inches square and roughly five-feet long. Like the pieces of wood, it too was an excellent find, fitting nicely into Sam's plan.

It didn't take long to search the entire cavern. When he was finished, he walked over and stopped five feet from the door, raised his torch up to it, then studied its construction. For sure, it had been made from solid wood. And the door was wrapped in what appeared to be an iron frame, with little to no space between its margins and wooden slats.

"Strong," Sam muttered, pulling at the whiskers of his chin. "But maybe... Just, maybe."

Considering his possibilities, he went back to his brother and sat down on the ground. He re-lit the small candle with the torch, then jammed the torch into the sand, snuffing it out. Like a hand from hell, the darkness came creeping back, reducing the perimeter of light surrounding the men.

"What did you do that for?" Bryson asked. His voice was wet and frail, cracking between syllables.

"Don't worry, little brother. I got a plan."

"I hope your plan is good... Because that old man is a piece of work." Bryson put an elbow to his mouth and coughed again, which ended in a wet, wheezing noise. He sounded bad, real bad.

After his coughing fit, Bryson sighed, and then both men sat silent for a minute. Somewhere in the distance was the echo of trickling water, which, if put into different circumstances, Sam would find highly relaxing. The sound reminded him, in fact, of his cave back in the Gila Wilderness. On quiet nights in that cave, he could hear the creek flowing steadily nearby, and it was a sound always worth falling asleep to.

"A piece of work," Bryson repeated, his voice grim. "Like nothing I've seen before... Shit, the guy's out of a movie."

As if on cue, from high up and in the darkness came a sudden, electrical crackling noise, breaking violently the quaint sounds within the cavern.

"Testing, one, two. Testing..." There was a clearing of a throat, followed by, "Hello, Sam. So how's the family reunion going?"

It was Lou's voice, coming from a speaker somewhere above them. And it sent an immediate chill down Sam's spine.

"Is that little bugger still alive? He wasn't looking so good the last time I checked on him." The old man cackled then, and his laugh echoed throughout the cavern, adding gooseflesh to Sam's arms.

"Can he hear us?" Sam whispered.

"I don't think so," Bryson replied. "He does this, though. He gets on that thing and talks to us, sometimes for hours at a time. He's nuts, Sam. Fucking certifiable." Bryson paused to catch his breath. "Sometimes, the asshole reads poetry and short stories. Weird shit, like horror. Even worse is when he reads philosophy."

"When you say 'us', do you mean you and the older couple? Or were there others down here?" Sam was thinking of the possibility of finding more useful items.

"No, just me and the woman. Her husband was dead when they came in. But she was still alive. She didn't last long, though. Only a few days." Bryson sounded weaker, his voice thin and cracking. "But there *were* others. I know that. Lots of others."

Sam rubbed his hand across his face, thinking. "What about surveillance?" he asked. "Can he see us?"

"I don't think so," Bryson said. "But I don't really know. I don't know much at all..." His voice trailed off, and it seemed to Sam his brother was fading once again, slipping out of consciousness.

Just then, Lou continued talking. "You're a worldly man, aren't you, Sam? I know you are. You're educated, at least. You aren't the typical cowboy wanker or military grunt that most people would take you for. And I bet you like to read, don't you?" He chuckled, then added, "Sure you do. You're a big reader, Sam. That's how you got so damn smart. Smart enough to track me down, you little bugger. That was bloody good, by the way. You trailed me all the way to this mine."

Sam stood and listened carefully, trying to distinguish more details from Lou's rambling. Perhaps there was a chamber nearby, a hollowed out room of sorts, in which the old man was camped out in. Maybe he was even watching Sam through a night vision camera, hiding in some alcove. If that were the case, it could prove disastrous to what Sam was planning.

"Well, I like to read," Lou continued. "It's really all I got, living by myself up here in this lonely wilderness. Reading keeps me sane, Sam. It keeps me from going crazy... as you can plainly see." He laughed again, and then Sam heard what sounded like pages turning in a book. "I read all kinds of stuff, really, but I do prefer the philosophers. My favorite quotes are from Nietzsche. They're short and simple, but quite proper. Posh, even. In fact, here's one right now: In Heaven, all the interesting people are missing." Lou laughed riotously then, as if the sound of his own voice humored him. There was a brief pause and then the old man added, "Doesn't that just have to be the bloody truth, Sam? I believe it is. Yes, I do... But you already know how I feel about God and all that jazz. Even so, that quote kills me every time."

Slowly, quietly, Sam walked the cavern's perimeter, his ear cocked to the stone wall. He was hoping to find another way out, but also hoping to see if Lou could somehow detect his movements.

"But let's not get too much into that right now," Lou said. "I don't want to interrupt your time with your brother. I just wanted to see how you've settled into your new home. Yes, it's a little dark down there, and perhaps a bit creepy... But you'll make the best of it, Sam. You're good at that. Just remember: darkness is nothing more than a lack of light. And light, as we all know, is overrated. Unless, of course, you're dying to do some reading...

"So get yourself settled in, Sam. There's plenty to drink... As for something to eat, well, ah... Times have been bloody rough up here, as you can imagine. Lean winter and all. However, if you're desperate enough, I suppose you could always chew on those old folks... Even better, you could dine on your brother. That's assuming he's dead. But then again, maybe that doesn't really matter. I'm not sure it does, actually. Anyway, meat is meat. And you, Sam, being a worldly man, you would surely understand that.

"On that note, I'll leave you with another one of my favorites... Hope, in reality, is the worst of all evils, because it prolongs the torment of man... Well, goodnight, Sam. And God bless!" The old man laughed one last time and then Sam heard the speaker turn off. Then the cavern filled once again with silence.

"A piece of work indeed," Sam said, walking back to his brother. "You weren't kidding." He questioned Bryson some more, asking if he knew anything else about Lou or the cavern, hoping to find some minor detail he could use to help make their escape. In particular, Sam was interested in patterns. How often did that lunatic contact his victims, either by speakerphone or in person?

Bryson mentioned there were long stretches of "silent time," in which he wouldn't hear from Lou—maybe for days, or so it seemed. Other than that, there was nothing else Bryson offered.

As far as audio and video surveillance within the cavern, that was still a risk Sam would have to take. The light from his torch hadn't been strong enough to illuminate the complete depths of the cavern, so it was still possible that the old man had both eyes and ears constantly on his prisoners, via a hidden camera or microphone. But the notion of Lou being absent for long periods of time was promising in itself.

It made sense, really. Living out here in the bush, it was unlikely for Lou to have a stringent daily routine. Sam knew first-hand that wilderness survival entailed being flexible to the shifts of one's environment, pursuant to the most basic needs of hunting and gathering resources. Sure, it made for a busy life, but the routines of that business were not always rigid. And they were also in constant motion, as one had to be prepared for worst-case scenarios. Undoubtedly, Lou understood this necessity of being flexible. Sam figured that this explained, in part, at least, the lulls between the old man's visits.

Other explanations for these lulls could be Lou's trapping endeavors and then, of course, the searching for and capturing of future victims.

The key to Sam's escape would be to act out his plan during one of these lulls, in which the old man was hopefully outside and beyond the mine somewhere. But there was no way for Sam to know when that time would be, so success would only come from sheer luck.

Suddenly, Bryson coughed again and there was a ragged sound deep in the man's chest, as if his lungs were tearing. Frowning, Sam sat down and put his arm over his brother. Luck or no luck, Bryson's last breath was now critically close. And if Sam didn't break them out of there within the next several hours, he would have plenty of time to execute his plan for escape.

He would have all the time he needed, in fact.

Because Bryson would be dead.

CHAPTER 29

"Don't you die, little brother. I need you to stay with me." Carefully, Sam used a finger to encourage Bryson to open his mouth. "Here, drink some of this," he said, wringing water into his brother's mouth. Earlier, Sam had torn the bottom half of his shirt away, then laid it at the base of a wet stone wall, allowing it to soak up the water.

Bryson looked and sounded terrible. Sam wasn't sure how much time the man had, but he was certain it wasn't much. One thing was for sure; his brother was in no condition to help with implementing their escape. That task lay solely on Sam's shoulders. And its probability of success was something even he considered being low.

But he had to try. No matter what, Sam had to try.

"I'll get you some more," he said, standing up and walking over to the wet wall. The movements of Sam's body were a constant reminder of his own aches and pains. His cracked ribs hurt like hell and his head continued to throb. Although his deep headache was gone for now, which Sam was grateful for, he was sure he had a mild concussion. And his many old scars, wounds from his past, were taking advantage of the situation to make sure he didn't forget about them.

While letting the torn cloth soak, an idea struck Sam. He took off the rest of his shirt and laid that too on the wet rock. The coolness of the cavern brushed across his back and shoulders, giving him a slight chill. Gathering up the smaller strip of cloth, he went back and sat next to Bryson.

"I've got a plan," Sam said, helping his brother drink some more. "A plan to get us the hell out of here. But I'm gonna need you to stay put, Bryson. For a little bit, at least."

His brother glanced at him and in the vague candlelight, Sam saw the trepidation in Bryson's eyes.

"You're not strong enough to walk out of here on your own," Sam added. "And I've got to deal with that lunatic... or at least know that he's not around, before I risk taking you out of here."

At first, Bryson said nothing in reply. He just nodded and turned away. But then he looked back at Sam and said, "Still trying to prove your Army is better than my Marines, huh?"

Despite his situation, Sam grinned at his brother's words. "I'll come back for you, Bryson," he said. "That's a damn promise."

"I know you will," Bryson said. "It's just that... well..."

"Well, what?"

"Sometimes that freak plays more than words on that speaker. Sometimes he plays recordings... Recordings of people screaming... Of people dying. He plays recordings he's made of people begging him to stop, begging him to kill them already. I don't know who they are or when it all happened. But they're real, that's for sure."

"Calm down, Bryson," Sam said, noticing his brother's breathing going shallow. "Just calm down and relax."

"Thing is," Bryson continued, "I can't hear a recording of you screaming like that, Sam. Promise me that won't happen." He closed his eyes then and rested his head back against the stone wall.

Sam understood how his brother felt and what he feared. One of the worst tortures ever was to hear a brother cry in pain. And that was something Sam knew all too well.

He figured it had been roughly two hours since he last heard Lou on the speaker. God only knew where the old man was now, but Sam was hoping he'd gone to sleep. Or better yet, that he had left the mine. One problem was that there was no way to distinguish what time of day it was; something which, if Sam knew, he could take a guess at the current activities of their captor and then capitalize on this.

Bryson had completely lost his sense of time. And even Sam couldn't determine if it was closer to morning or night. He tried to assess his own exhaustion, to figure out whether his body was lacking sleep or just downright beaten up. It had been late in the day when he discovered this mine, but that could've been hours ago. He had no idea how long he'd been knocked out, for both the first time, when Lou was wearing his hideous monster outfit, and then the second, just after the old man shot him in the ribs with that homemade shotgun. But regardless of the time of day, Sam would need to make his move soon, if only for his brother's sake.

The candle was on the verge of going out. Sam debated whether he should relight his improvised torch and get to work or just stay put for a little while longer. Bryson seemed to slip in and out of consciousness, but Sam wanted him to be fully awake and coherent when he made his move. He only had two matches left, so he had to be careful with how he used them.

He was debating his options when the speaker above suddenly crackled to life. Apparently Lou was coming back on the wire, and Sam just couldn't wait to hear what the old man had in store for them now.

"Hello..." Lou said. "Hello... Is anybody out there?" There was a panicked tone in the man's voice, which Sam rightfully took as facetiousness. "I can't find my way out of here. Lord, it's so bloody dark. I can't see a GOD DAMN FUCKING thing... Is anyone there?"

There was a long pause, and then the old man continued. "Oh, there it is. Yes. Now I see... *Beyond* the darkness. Pictures. I can see them now, because they're in my mind. I can see them in my mind, Sam. Such beautiful pictures, stained crimson and white, the colors of *blood* and *bone*. And I can *hear* them, too. Have you ever heard the sound pictures make, Sam? Little pictures. Big pictures. Warm and fuzzy pictures... Cold pictures, sitting right there in your mind, resting behind your closed eyes. *God's* pictures, Sam. Fucking GOD..."

Sam retrieved his torch from out of the sand, then brushed it off with his fingers. He had decided that, at the very least, he would get things ready. And by doing so, he might learn if Lou could see or hear him as he put together the means of his escape.

"Let me play some of those sounds for you, Sam," Lou continued, "the sounds of such beautiful pictures." There was a "clicking" noise then, the act of a recorder being turned on, and then Sam heard a medley of industrial sounds coming out of the speaker. It was a musical recording of sorts, a melodic pattern containing what sounded like the hammering of steel and the strikes of deep, resonating drums.

Clang... thoom, thoom, thoom... Clang... thoom, thoom, thoom...

Sam's environment had transformed into a concert of bizarre industrial grunge music.

"Ah... the glory," Lou said. The smile behind his voice glared over the cacophonous recording. "A most gorgeous sound, the sound of man, and all his lovely endeavors. What was it old Freddy said about music? Oh, yes. I remember... Without music, life would be a mistake... Isn't that the bloody truth, Sam?"

Clang... thoom, thoom, thoom... continued the recording.

Sam did his best to ignore the old man's ravings and his chaotic orchestra as he placed his torch against the weak flame of the candle. Seconds later, the torch was burning fervently and Sam was up on his feet, moving throughout the cavern.

The first thing he did was gather up all the wood he could find, which he placed in a pile roughly in the middle of the cavern. Then he inspected the rusted out fifty-five gallon drums he'd seen earlier and found a loose sliver of metal hanging off the side of one of them. He pulled the metal shard off the drum and pocketed it. Then Sam checked on his brother, to make sure he was still breathing, and found Bryson wide awake, staring back at him.

"Here he goes," Bryson said weakly. "His damn recordings."

"Just ignore it," Sam replied. "We'll be out of here before you know it."

"So what's the plan?" Bryson asked.

"Oh, you'll see. Hang tight until I tell you it's time."

The industrial sounds from the speaker droned on, echoing off the walls of the cavern.

Clang...thoom, thoom, thoom... Clang...thoom, thoom...

Lou continued. "Over the years, I have come to the opinion that every sound made from humanity is, well... quite beautiful, Sam. You really have to admit. Even the most repulsive sounds have a strikingly stunning aspect about them."

The recording transformed itself then, as the blood-curdling cries of a young woman were overlaid against the metallic grunge noise. Her screams were brutally long and bleeding with hopelessness.

Lou spoke again, his voice rising above all the other sounds. "Number sixteen, Sam," he said with a giggle. "That cry you hear there. She was number sixteen—sixteen out of twenty-seven, mind you. And the irony, the *beautiful* irony, was that she was also sixteen-years-old. How's that for synchronicity?"

Ignoring Lou, Sam kept moving. He found and retrieved the solid wooden beam. Five-feet long and six-inches square, it was a heavy piece of wood, weighing between forty and fifty pounds.

Sam dragged the beam toward his pile of gathered wood, then stopped and listened. With patience, he ignored the old man's crazed cacophony and focused instead on determining if he could hear anything beyond the stone cavern. He decided now might be the time for his attempted escape, even though Lou was undoubtedly close by, because the old man didn't seem to know what Sam was up to. And that meant there were likely no microphones or cameras in the cavern. Just that damned speaker.

The absence of any surveillance was something Sam certainly hoped for, as his plan would have a better chance of succeeding if the element of surprise was on his side.

"Not long now, Sam," Lou said. "Not long, and that number will most certainly rise. Twenty-eight—or twenty-nine, if that brother of yours is already dead... Then thirty, thirty-one, thirty-two, and so on and so forth!"

Clang... thoom, thoom... Cla-clang... thoom, thoom.

Sam worked quickly. He wedged his torch into the ground, freeing up both of his hands. Then he retrieved the sliver of metal he'd pocketed and used it to shave thin pieces of wood off the beam. It was slow going, as his improvised tool was less sharp than it was heavy. But eventually, Sam had a handful of wood shavings. And that was more than enough to get a good fire started.

Carefully, he took the shavings and transported them to the stone ledge, then placed them at the base of the door. Using his torch, he studied the construction of the door further and noticed a small gap at its bottom—a gap of about an inch wide, maybe a little more. It was a good find. A damn good find!

Sam went back and gathered up his pile of wood, then brought it to the ledge, where he sorted them into sizes. Using his iron strip, he whittled away at some of the bigger pieces, creating smaller splinters—the perfect size for kindling—and wedged some of these pieces into the gap of the door. Then he assembled the rest of the wood into a tinder bundle at the door's base and placed it all on top of the kindling.

Clang, clang... thoom, thoom... Clang, clang... thoom, thoom...

Lou's music was a constant deep ramble, interspersed with frequent howls of terror. Worse yet, was that the racket seemed to be increasing in volume.

It took less than five minutes before Sam was ready. He was confident his plan would work. The wood was bone dry, including the door, and some of the wood had been treated for rot prevention, which would no doubt expedite the burning process.

But would it burn fast enough? Or would it burn *too* fast? Either case would certainly limit Sam's chances of success.

Sam thought about what his alternatives were, should any of these undesirable results present itself. One thing was for certain: the longer it took him to escape, the less his chance would be to catch Lou by surprise.

As if on cue, the old man chimed in again.

"Thoughts are the shadows of our feelings, Sam. Always darker, always emptier, and always simpler."

Cla-clang . . . thoom, thoom . . . Clang, clang . . . thoom, thoom . . .

It was another quote from Nietzsche, and its relevance was hard for Sam not to contemplate. Those words were a direct account of what had become of Lou's character. Or maybe this was the wrong assumption. Perhaps the old man had always been like this. Perhaps he was born a sociopath, rather than made into one.

"I've been watching you, Sam," Lou continued. The words sent a gust of anxious dread into Sam's gut, until the old man added, "Watching you in the forest, doing what you do best. How you made that blimey camp of yours in no time flat. And how you went about with your reconnaissance, scouting the land, and all that wonderful tracking you did. You *are* good, I'll give you that.

"But what I appreciated most, Sam, was when I watched you *contemplate*. Standing silently in the forest, just thinking. Or when you were on that rock overlooking the lake, pondering away, I'm sure. It was a beautiful sight, Sam. *You* were beautiful."

The industrial music droned on in the background along with the occasional scream of terror or cry of help from another one of Lou's past victims.

"That beautiful mind of yours," Lou continued, "does make me wonder, however. For instance, I wonder if right now, this very minute, in fact, you're using it to think things through, and... planning some sort of escape. I can't imagine why you wouldn't be, considering your mental fortitude and your physical attributes. Considering your *will to survive*."

Clang, clang . . . thoom, thoom . . . Clang, clang . . . thoom, thoom . . . Clang, clang . . .

Sam hurried with his actions. He didn't want to give the old man anymore of his attention. He grabbed his torch and went to the deceased couple. Then he set the torch into the sand again, dug out the survival tin, and retrieved the razor blade. He used it to cut away more of the man's pants, which he then wrapped around a long length of wood he'd set aside for this occasion.

When he was finished, he placed the new torch on the ground below the door, then went back to the wet wall. He took the remains of his shirt, which was now completely soaked through, and went back to his brother.

"But the will to survive is just a bloody joke," Lou continued. There was a tone of humor in his voice and, mixed with the background of incessant industrial sounds and frequent cries of terror, Sam couldn't help but feel his skin crawl. "The will to survive is a bloody joke designed to propagate that biggest joke of all... Which is, of course, the echo of God's false existence. They call this Hope, Sam, better known as Faith, and it is man's last ditch effort to salvage his life. And you know what? It has never happened. Not once in a million years." Lou cackled with glee. "Because in the end, Hope *never* prevails. And man *always* dies."

Clang, clang ... thoom, thoom ... CLANG, CLANG ... THOOM, THOOM ...

"I want you to keep this over your face, Bryson," Sam said, handing the wet shirt to his brother. "When that fire starts and that door goes up, I'm not sure how much smoke will get trapped in here. And some of the wood is treated, so it's gonna be toxic."

Bryson took the rag and nodded. "I can follow you," he said.

"No..." Sam replied. "You stay here. That old man is a tough weasel. And if he gets in here when I'm away, you play dead, alright? Let me take care of him. Now get ready to cover your face."

CLANG, CLANG ... THOOM, THOOM ...

The music droned on and the screaming undertones were now that of a male, who was begging for his death.

Sam moved swiftly, knowing that every action he now made had to be fast and without error. He took his torch and went over to the door, then carefully lit the bundle of tinder. The wood caught flame quickly, and in seconds, so too did the door. A minute later, the whole cavern was lit up by the blazing wood.

Sam took a step back as he watched the door burn away. The single barrier which had prevented his escape was now on its way to ash and cinder.

CLANG, CLANG . . . THOOM, THOOM . . . CLANG, CLANG, THOOM, THOOM . . .

"Think, Sam. *Think*." Lou giggled madly. "Put your soldier's mind to work and find the hope that I know you're looking for. Find the *real* hope!"

Under Lou's voice, a terribly long howl occurred just then, a man screaming for the release of his pain, screaming as if his entire skin was being peeled from him.

"Or keep looking for your god, Sam. Look for Him. I dare you to."

The door was fully ablaze now, and Sam could see much more of the cavern than before. He spotted the speaker above him, mounted on the stone ceiling with a trailing black cord leading to the top of the door. It wouldn't be long now, before that cord burned through and the speaker went dead.

"But just know this," the old man continued. "When you find this god—*if* you find Him—you'll be sorely disappointed. That I guarantee, Sam. Because such a monster—assuming He exists, which I'm certain does not—cares not a damn thing about you. He cares about you the same as He gave bloody bollocks for those other twenty-seven people, Sam!"

CLANG, CLANG . . . THOOM, THOOM . . . CLANG, CLANG, THOOM, THOOM . . .

Still watching the fire, Sam thought about the door's integrity, calculating how long it would take before he could bust it down.

"So you see, you cannot rely on a false being to find your way out." Eerily, it was as if Lou was reading Sam's mind. "You must rely on yourself, Sam. You must rely on your own power to overcome. And your own will to survive. A will that is not contingent upon and hampered by... you guessed it. Hope. But a will that is based solely on self-preservation."

CLANG, CLANG, THOOM, THOOM . . . CLA-CLANG, CLANG, THOOM, THOOM . . .

The entire cavern was lit up now, and it was becoming thick with smoke. From behind, Sam heard his brother coughing. Guessing the integrity of the door had weakened enough, Sam bent down and grabbed the long wooden beam.

"And self-preservation, my dear Sam, is the key to saving your life. Like that of every other animal, self-preservation—the gift that keeps on giving, the gift that comes without a bloody god to muck it up—is our true basis for existence. So preserve *yourself*, Sam..."

CLANG, CLANG, THOOM, THOOM . . . CLANG, CLANG, THOOM, THOOM . . .

Sam picked up the solid beam and lifted it over his head.

"Preserve your own life, Sam!" Lou was shouting now, and under his voice, the recording blared even louder, and the wailing of those who were dying, now a mixture of both men and women, shrilled all the more. "Preserve your life, Sam! Preserve it!"

Sam took a step forward, with the beam now completely over his head.

"Use your bloody mind and overcome this!" Lou shouted, his voice ringing with fervor.

CLANG, CLANG, THOOM, THOOM . . . CLANG, CLANG, THOOM, THOOM . . .

And Sam lunged forward three more steps, the weight of his body and the momentum of his lurch gathering together, helping him along as he hurled the wooden beam at the door.

"That's it, Sam!" Lou cried. "*You* are the god! It's in you! *You* are the *real* bloody God!"

CLANG, CLANG, THOOM, THOOM . . . CLANG, CLANG, THOOM—

With a crashing blow, the beam burst through the flaming door. The speaker above cut out, ceasing the fanatical cries from the old man, along with the crazed industrial cacophony and the maddening screams of the dying.

Seconds later, with his new torch in hand, Sam was swiftly up the stone ledge, out of his prison, and through the burning hole. His first step was into another cavern of darkness.

CHAPTER 30

Sam used the remnants of the blazing door to light his new torch. What was left of the looming darkness shrank away as he raised the cloth-wrapped burning stick. He could see before him a tunnel that ran in two different directions: one that traveled slightly upward, to his left and hopefully out of the mine; and then the other, off to his right, and probably further down into the mountain—or so he presumed.

He looked up, searching for the black electrical cable coming from the speakers. Sam spotted it easily enough, tacked onto the stone ceiling. He noticed it led down the tunnel to his left. For certain, that would be the way he would go.

His torch was solid, made from one of the thicker pieces of wood he'd found and set aside earlier. It would serve as his weapon should he run across Lou Pine. He wondered if the old man knew he'd escaped, or if he heard the crashing of the door just seconds ago. The way he'd been talking on the speaker a moment before, the things he'd said, led Sam to believe Lou knew *exactly* what was going on.

But none of that mattered now. If Sam had surprise on his side, that would be fortunate. But surprise wasn't something he could count on. And nor would he.

His movements were quick yet careful, and precise. Sam was acutely aware there might be booby traps within the mine.

Something an old SAS operative would have little trouble arranging for.

In response to this awareness, Sam kept a sharp eye on the ground and the adjacent tunnel walls as he made his way further up the passage.

The light from the torch bounced erratically off the stone ceiling, illuminating his path with a sporadic orange glow mixed with shadows. The smell of singed wood lingered in the tunnel. Sam also detected other odors now, such as the hint of burned fuel of some sort—probably kerosene, he thought—along with an ever-present smell of damp air.

He walked for almost thirty yards, then froze in his tracks a moment before it was too late. Sure enough, Sam's hunch had not failed him. One more step could have been the death of him.

He was staring at a tripwire: a thin length of fishing line six inches off the ground and strung perpendicular with the direction of the tunnel. Sam was damn lucky. His well experienced tracking eyes had caught just the faintest shimmer coming off the line, most likely being the reflection from a patch of dust that had clung to the filament.

He had seen similar traps in the caves of Afghanistan, as well as on missions in other parts of the world. The worst traps, in Sam's opinion, were the ones that triggered fragmentation explosions—not always lethal, but guaranteed to provoke mass casualties, massive pain, and a massive depletion of unit morale.

Squatting down, Sam studied the tripwire. He noticed it was connected to an improvised explosive device mounted behind a small rock against the tunnel wall. The explosive device was encased in a wooden box. And the box had a single cylindrical exit port, about an inch in diameter and facing the main tunnel.

Looking closer, Sam noticed the explosive component appeared to be that of a single shotgun cartridge, designed most likely to maim an intruder (or, in this case, a would-be escapee), as well as send a warning to Lou that something was going down. It didn't look like the trap was loaded with a large amount of explosives, which certainly made sense. Even the smallest of explosions down here would risk a cave-in.

Sam considered his options. Some traps had built-in striker springs, which would trigger the device as soon as tension was released—such as from the cutting of the tripwire. But Sam decided he would have to take his chances on this.

Knowing he planned on coming back to get Bryson, Sam stood to the side, out of the trap's line of fire, then used his torch to burn through the fishing line. As quick as the process was, it still gave him a cold chill down his spine. Thankfully, his hopes had prevailed, as the device did not contain an anti-tension trigger.

If Sam had more time, he could dismantle the booby trap further and then reconfigure it into a weapon. But that would take up too much of what precious time remained. So he pushed forward with eyes on the ground and the surrounding walls.

For the moment, his path was clear as he continued up the tunnel. He kept an eye out for more traps though, knowing that contingencies were the mainstay of a Special Forces operator, such as Lou.

Sam walked another thirty yards, then paused when he heard the faint echo of an idling engine. He knew immediately that it was the sound from a generator, no doubt used to run those speakers and whatever else Lou had wired up down here. It wouldn't be long now, Sam thought, as he slowed his pace and crept forward further.

He found the next booby trap twenty feet later, at a slight bend in the tunnel. In design, the trap was like the last one, but it was mounted on the tunnel's ceiling and aimed directly downward. Apparently, the option of simply maiming a would-be escapee was now off the table. If triggered, this device would kill a person outright.

Carefully, Sam burned away the device's tripwire, then searched for a secondary wire, just in case, before continuing onward.

The generator's engine was louder now, which helped to conceal Sam's movements. But he had to be extra alert, as the added racket would also cover up any noises Lou might make, should the old man come walking down the tunnel or be lying in wait, somewhere up ahead. Not for a minute did Sam underestimate the lunatic's skill set. He suspected Lou wouldn't have put all his strategic eggs into a simple IED basket. And also, the old man wouldn't be surprised to learn Sam had figured a way past the traps.

Considering this, Sam prepared for the possibility that Lou was hiding in the shadows up ahead, his hands on that shotgun of his and just waiting for Sam to show his face.

Fifty feet later, Sam saw a light at the end of the tunnel. It was another hundred feet out, or so it appeared, and clearly artificial, coming from what looked like a lantern. Sam considered going dark and snuffing out his torch, to avoid being discovered. But that would eliminate his ability to detect any more tripwires. Night vision goggles would be wonderful right about now, but that was obviously not an option. His best choice was to move faster. The military rule of thumb for being caught off-guard, such as from an ambush, was to bull-rush the assault force with as much speed and firepower as possible. And that was the same principal Sam decided to apply here, knowing that with a torch in hand, he was a sitting duck.

He moved faster now. Much faster, yet with his stare three feet in front of him, scanning for tripwires. Torch in hand and surrounded by darkness, he was a standing beacon for that old man, wherever he was. So speed, careful speed, was Sam's only choice.

And much to his surprise, he pulled it off.

Sam traversed the last hundred feet with no more traps to slow him down. Once he confirmed the source of the light was coming from a lantern, he quickly snuffed out his torch, putting the shield of darkness on his side as he moved forward.

The tunnel he'd been traveling through came to a crossroads, branching out into two other passageways. One passage ran off to his right, falling into more darkness, while the second went to his left for twenty feet before opening into a shallow cavern.

Sam could see the flickering lantern sitting on a box within the cavern. It was in this direction that the electrical cable above him ran. It was also where the generator sound was coming from.

One step at a time, he thought, *and leave nothing uncovered.*

Sam hurried toward the cavern, ignoring the mounting pain coursing through his body. His head still ached and so did his ribs, but he had more than enough fight left in him. Much more than his brother had, that's for sure.

Cautiously, Sam entered the cavern. It was but a small alcove containing the single lantern set on a wooden crate, as well as the generator, which was sitting on the ground and tucked behind the crate. Also, next to the lantern was another door, similar to the one he'd recently burned down. The electrical cable he'd been following ran along the stone wall and to the generator. There was another cable, a red one, which left the generator and continued on through a hole above the door.

The obvious assumption, as it occurred to Sam, was that this new cable led to Lou's audio devices he'd used to torment his victims with. But what Sam didn't know was if Lou himself was on the other side of that door. Gripping his torch like a club, he yanked free the door's latch, a single strip of leather, then quickly pulled it open.

Sam was immediately confronted with a grisly sight and a draft of cold air that stank of death. The old man wasn't in the room, but something infinitely grotesque was. Some *things*, to be precise. Many things. Appalling things. *Ghastly* things.

On the ground just past the door was an oil drum with another lantern set on it, presently lit. Sam glanced at his horrible surroundings, then reached over and grabbed the lantern from off the barrel. He raised it to get a better look.

The cavern was small, only thirty feet deep, yet lined wall to wall with a decor of lifeless debris. There were easily a dozen full size human skeletons dangling from wooden support beams spanning the cavern's ceiling. It made for a macabre maze, in which Sam slowly navigated through, the parched bones clinking as he brushed past them, announcing his passage.

He found a table at the back of the cavern—the only piece of normality in an otherwise snapshot of horror. Hanging on the walls of the cavern were more skeletons, some of which were disastrously incomplete, implying that the previous owners had been pulled apart at some point during their demise.

Mounted on the wall to his right was a single shelf displaying a line of human skulls. They were placed in an orderly fashion, ten skulls in all, and with eyes staring back at Sam in grievous wonder.

Dead humans weren't the only things on display in the cavern. On the ground near the wall sat a pile of bones, antlers, and various skulls from different animals. Several deer hides were also stacked against the wall. The head of a freshly killed bear sat on top of the hides, a long gray tongue rolled out of its mouth. Hanging by its tail from a rafter above was the pelt of a black timber wolf.

It was a sad sight Sam had discovered: Lou Pine's trophy room. This cavern of death displayed remnants of people who'd gone missing in the wilderness over the years, not to mention a host of local fauna. With a sick feeling, Sam observed some of the human victims were fresher than others, as they had not been completely bereft of their flesh.

The overriding smell in the cavern was atrocious. It alone was a grim reminder to Sam that death, perhaps even that of his own, was an elusive yet ever present reality. He thought of Lou, the crazy son of a bitch, and realized that now more than ever, the man had to be neutralized.

Sam looked again at the small table in the back of the cavern. He stepped closer, studying the piece of furniture, trying his best to ignore everything else, such as the vacant eye sockets staring back at him.

There was a small stool lying on the ground next to the table. It appeared as if whoever sat there had kicked the chair over in a quick attempt to stand. On the table were a microphone and two old-school tape recorders. Numerous cassette tapes lay scattered about. The electronic equipment was plugged into a power strip, which in turn was connected to the red cable running to the generator.

Next to the table sat another wooden crate, the top of which contained an assortment of notebooks, pencils, and a single candle set in a tin can. The candle was presently lit, and Sam noticed the recorders were stuck on "pause," making a continuous obnoxious clacking sound.

He had seen enough. Apparently, this was Lou's command post, where the old man sat in his glory amongst the artwork of human and animal detritus while he rattled off his insanities to the ears of his latest victims.

Feeling a sudden rush of anger, Sam sent the table flying with one swift kick. The recorders, microphone, and cassette tapes clattered across the ground. Then he reached over and, with a curse, yanked the electric cords from the power strip. It was then that Sam heard the *clicking* noise behind him.

Sam dove to the ground just as the shot rang out. A foray of bones and other human remains sailed through the air as the shell from Lou's homemade shotgun punched a deafening blast into the cavern. A blinding flash illuminated the room, followed by the smell of gunpowder. Instinctively, Sam grabbed the small table by its legs and swung it around, to use as a shield.

"I knew you could do it, Sam!" Lou cried. He was standing at the door, his face broken into a wide grin. The old man was wearing blue and gray camouflage pants, battle ready, the kind typically worn by urban assault teams in various parts of the world. And he had on an olive green military jacket festooned with combat webbing. On his head was a black beanie. It appeared Lou had dressed for war.

"I knew you would break out of there," he continued. "And I'm not surprised you got this far, Sam Nolan—past them traps, you bloody son of a bitch." Lou laughed. Then, in one swift motion, he ejected the spent cartridge from his gun and loaded another. He aimed the piece at Sam and said, "But will you make it any further? For your sake and mine, I certainly hope so. But you know what, Sam? I kind of doubt it."

Then Lou fired the gun.

CHAPTER 31

The blast tore another hole into the human fabric of the cavern. Sam felt the punch of the shotgun shell hit the table he was holding and the concussion sent shock waves up his arms. But he was unharmed. A sundry of shattered bone and decaying gristle rained down on him. Gun smoke instantly penetrated the air, leaving a grayish sheen that resembled a thundercloud.

"May your bloody, bollock-sucking god, bless you, Sam Nolan!" Lou laughed, then turned and ran, the door slamming shut behind him.

Sam got up off the ground, still holding the table as a shield. He lunged for the door and put his foot at the bottom, to prevent it from opening, in case Lou was still on the other side. He didn't believe the man was, but Sam could also use this moment of protection to think.

The shotgun shell had been another one of those non-lethal rounds. By sheer luck, Sam spotted rubber remnants of the bullet on the ground. He felt confident Lou was toying with him now, trying to lure him into a game of hide and seek. That was something the mad trapper would certainly get a kick out of. And whether he liked it or not, it was a game Sam would be forced to play.

He waited for another minute, his mind roping through a quagmire of possibilities. It was likely the old man had another cartridge now loaded into his gun. And it was just as likely he was standing on the other side of the door with the barrel raised. Or Lou could be fifty feet away by now, down a tunnel.

Ditching the table, Sam moved away from the door and found his spent torch on the ground. He picked it up, gripping it once again like a club, then went back and stood beside the door, his back to the wall. He used the club to pry open the door, then quickly glanced out into the cavern before yanking his head back. There was no response. So he pried the door open a little more, then carefully looked out. He saw nothing but an empty alcove and the intersection of the tunnels, illuminated by the lantern on the crate just outside the door.

"Chop, chop, Sam," Lou shouted. The old man's voice came from further away, up one of the tunnels. "I ain't got all day. If you're going to kill me, then best get moving, soldier."

Lou's distance encouraged Sam to move forward. He left the cavern and crouched down in the small alcove beside the generator. Quickly, he turned the engine off, then listened. After a few seconds, he heard footsteps in the distance, along the passage to his right—the tunnel he'd not yet traveled in. Thankfully, Lou was not heading back toward Bryson. But Sam still had to neutralize the man. And he had to do it soon.

He decided to take his chances further. With the club in one hand, he grabbed the lantern off the crate, then moved swiftly into the tunnel. Using caution, he kept in a crouched position and zigzagged forward, making his body a hard target. He heard Lou jogging up ahead and the old man was chuckling to himself, as if ruminating over some joke.

Sam traveled along the tunnel for approximately fifty yards. He spotted no more tripwires, nor did he run across Lou, hiding behind a boulder with gun in hand—although he was sure the old man was waiting for him. Cautiously, Sam crossed those fifty-yards, until he came to another fork in the mineshaft.

The main tunnel kept going. But splitting off of it, and to his right, was another passage. This new tunnel was thin and very, very dark. And it seemed to slope downward rather quickly, as if dropping into a deep pit.

Sam froze, crouched low, and listened carefully. The old man had gone quiet minutes before. Sam was now at a loss as to where his enemy had gone. Quickly, he checked the ground, looking for tracks, but there were many, which made it impossible to tell the direction Lou had traveled. Sam thought about his enemy's mind, though, and couldn't help but glance down at the tunnel dropping off to his right.

If Sam had all the time in the world, he would beat Lou Pine at his own game. Without question or hesitation. He would use the lantern to stage a false presence and then slip away into the darkness of this mountain. Maybe the old man would fall for it, maybe not. But that wouldn't matter. Sam would be invisible and he'd also be able to take his time, the sum of which would increase his chances of success.

But Sam's time was almost out. And that meant he would have to resort to a different form of action.

Thinking more on that, he recalled the golden rule for countering an enemy ambush. Once again, a fierce, direct assault was the method Sam would employ right now.

He had his doubts about the smaller tunnel, suspecting it did not lead out of the mountain. Whether Lou was down there, Sam wasn't sure. But he also suspected the last thing the old man wanted was for one of his victims to escape—especially Sam himself.

Considering this notion, along with the need for direct action, Sam glanced back down the smaller tunnel and then came to his conclusion about what he would do.

Sam turned and ran.

He ran down the wider tunnel, making as much noise as possible. He bellowed out a war cry, shouting as he went. Sam was banking on Lou hiding in that smaller passage; but also prepared for the old man to be waiting up ahead with his shotgun loaded and ready.

He kept his speed as fast as he dared, hoping also that if he triggered any booby traps similar to the ones he'd already seen, he'd rush far enough past them before taking too much damage. It was as slim of a hope as any. But it was all Sam had.

He ran for another thirty yards before seeing a light up ahead. Then his nerves ran faster than his feet, kicking up anxiety from the pit of his stomach, knowing now that he might run headlong into a blast from Lou's shotgun.

Ten more yards, and the light ahead revealed something familiar. It was about then that Sam spotted a cavern off to his left, the same cavern he'd walked into prior to first meeting Lou's monster form. The cavern with all the outdoor gear.

Sam knew where he was now. He kept running, driving into a full sprint. Twenty yards later and with a wild cry, he came out into the main cavern—the entrance of the mine, which housed Lou's library and sleeping cot, the sundry of storage items, the mud room near the mine's entrance, and last but not least, the way out of this hell.

Sam's holler stopped at the same time his body did. He paused in the middle of the cavern and looked around. As he'd hoped, there was no Lou Pine waiting here for him. But there were plenty of other things.

Things that would burn.

Abruptly, Sam threw the kerosene lantern down onto Lou's desk. It crashed with a shatter of glass and fire across a hundred paper tomes. The entire affair ignited instantly, with a hollow roar, and at once the inside of the mine was lit plain as day.

Sam saw Lou's shadow then, in the corner of his eye, coming up from the tunnel behind him. The old man had obviously been hiding in the smaller cavern a ways back. He'd fallen for Sam's trick and was now in quick pursuit. No doubt he was fearing Sam would escape.

Swiftly, Sam turned away from the entrance of the tunnel and put his back against the stone wall. He felt the wavering heat next to him—the fire gobbling up all those books and journals and other combustibles. He thought of Lou's pictures of old and how the man's history was now being consumed by smoke and flame.

"I'm coming for you, Sam!" Lou shouted. He was maybe thirty yards away and would close the gap in a matter of seconds. "Don't you worry, soldier... I'm coming for you."

It was then that Sam stepped back into the entrance of the tunnel. The fire-light behind him cast his silhouette as a strong, contrasting shadow, allowing for his body to stand out, making a perfect target.

"What's your hurry?" Sam shouted. Then he reared his arm back, preparing to throw his wooden club at Lou.

The old man fell for it. Seeing Sam about to throw something at him, Lou yanked his shotgun up and fired. But he was too late and too wide. Sam had guessed the man's actions and at the last minute, instead of throwing his club, he threw his body to the side, just as the shotgun blast roared past.

Then, with Lou now holding an unloaded gun and being only steps away, Sam swung back around and ran in for the kill. He ran in with fierce, direct action.

CHAPTER 32

"Bloody hell!" Lou cried, obviously taken by surprise. The old man raised his gun to his face, shielding himself from Sam's blow. But the strike came lower—another surprise.

"You're damn right!" Sam replied, spearing his club into Lou's groin.

The old man folded over, but was quick to recover. He snorted with laughter, then jammed the stock of his gun into Sam's broken ribs.

Sam staggered away, the pain in his lower chest searing like the fire behind him. He stumbled back, checked his stance, and instinctively held his ribcage with his free hand.

"Aha," Lou said, snickering, the glint of flames adding to the smile in his eyes. "Blimey blow hurt, now didn't it?"

Without replying, Sam pulled back with his arm. And this time, he really did throw his club. He sent the piece of stick flying toward Lou and then rushed in at the man.

Lou deflected the wooden projectile with his gun. But then Sam was on him with fists pummeling into the old man's torso.

"Oh-ho!" Lou cried humorously, as he dropped his gun and grappled with Sam. Their bodies went to the ground, a heap of thrashing fists and clawing hands.

It seemed as if the old man couldn't care less about the situation, and that he was still having fun. The notion of this sent a fleeting shiver of frustration through Sam's mind. If it was the last thing he'd do, he would make sure Lou Pine cared about the situation.

"A nice brawl, eh?" Lou said, chuckling underneath Sam's body. He was pulling defense, taking Sam's punches with his arms and elbows, his hands protecting his face.

Sam threw four fast blows into Lou's midsection, hoping to knock the wind out of him. But the old man was wiry as hell and built like a tree trunk, his body hard with muscle and bone. Sam felt the man's solid frame behind each punch. And he knew he'd have to dish out a hell of a lot more to win this battle.

"A proper kerfuffle," Lou said. "But at last, a short one." Then he grabbed Sam by the ears and dug his fingers viciously behind Sam's lobes, wedging and wiggling his sharp nails between ear and skull. As he did this, he wrapped his legs around Sam's waist and pulled him in closer, biting down on Sam's shoulder, teeth piercing to the bone.

Sam grunted against the attack. The old man was a crafty, dangerous fighter, that much was obvious. But Sam wasn't surprised. He'd expected as much, and he ignored the pain. He worked his elbows outward, breaking Lou's hands away from his ears. Then, angling from the same shoulder Lou had his teeth sunk in, Sam slammed his body to the ground once, twice, three times, until he felt the old man's clenching teeth break loose. Without so much as a pause, he grabbed Lou by his hair and started slamming his elbow into the man's face, smashing bone and cartilage alike.

And it got violent from there. Bloody violent.

"Oh, now that's scrummy, Sam!" Lou said from underneath Sam's blows. "Real scrummy." The old man pulled a short knife out then, from somewhere hidden on his body, and stabbed Sam in the leg.

"Ugh..." Sam groaned and pulled away. He stood up and stepped back, a white-hot fire blazing in his left leg.

Lou stayed momentarily on the ground, holding the knife in his hand, his face a bloody mess. And yet, he was still smiling. Always, that damn smile...

Slowly, the old man climbed to his feet. He kept his knife held straight out as a warning for Sam to keep his distance. He stood erect, then sort of casually shook his body and limbs, as if to shake off the pain, but without taking his eyes off Sam. It seemed Lou was also trying to catch his breath. "You didn't expect me to fight fair, now did you?" he said. "I'm no longer a young bloke, that's for sure. Old bones and all..."

Sam's body wracked with pain—from his head to his toes. The stab wound in his leg was bad, and he felt blood trailing down his leg and onto his bare foot. His ribs stung with each breath. And he was breathing hard, real hard. The pain in his head was now a persistent dull throb, which radiated into his neck and in between his shoulders.

But dammit to hell, Sam was nowhere close to quitting. He glanced down and saw his wooden club lying on the ground near his feet. He thought he could get to it before Lou made his next move, but wasn't entirely sure, as it seemed there was no end to the old man's surprises.

"Well," Lou said, "I'm afraid we're gonna have to end this sport sometime soon, Sam. I don't expect to have all day to entertain you, despite how much fun it's been." He was still holding his knife out in front of him as his eyes were measuring the situation, displaying with obvious detail the calculations firing off in his head. The cavern was growing hotter and filling with smoke, making it hard to breathe. As if noting this detail, Lou glanced sideways. "I am properly buggered, though. You ruined my library, Sam. That wasn't right of you. Not right at all. Bloody barbaric, in fact."

Slowly, Lou raised his knife higher and took a step toward Sam. "I think I'm gonna have to kill you now, soldier. And don't bother saying any prayers, 'cause they won't be answered!" The knife gleamed as the old man lunged forward.

But then, a gray shadow suddenly ejected out of the darkness from behind and halted Lou's lunge. A single arm, coming out from the cavern's depths, wrapped tightly around Lou's neck.

"Bryson, no!" Sam shouted, realizing at once what the shadow was.

But Sam's alarm was too late.

Lou caught Bryson's arm before he could get a firm grip around the old man's neck. Then, spinning around, knife flashing with his body's momentum, Lou drove the blade deep into Bryson's torso.

Sam panicked. He dove for his club on the ground and caught it in his right hand just as he tucked himself into a forward roll. He used his momentum to spring up and land on his feet, mere inches from Lou. Then, with all his might, he swung the piece of wood across the side of Lou's face, knocking the man out of the way.

Bryson was left barely standing, a wide slash across the top of his right arm and a knife buried deep into his midriff, just below his ribs. Blood was seeping through his shirt, blooming outward, like the petals of a flower. Quickly, Sam pushed his brother to the ground, getting him out of the way from immediate danger. Then he spun around and faced the old man.

Lou Pine staggered away from the brothers, dazed. His knife was gone, and he was now apparently without a weapon. But Sam could never be too sure.

"Well, now... I guess I didn't see that coming," Lou said, shaking his head. For once, the smile on his face looked forced and insincere. "It seems you Nolans are full of surprises."

"You got that right," Sam replied, anger welling into his chest. "And as you'll now see, we're also full of fire." He rushed in then, with his club swinging wildly and his thoughts on one thing only: to put an end to Lou Pine.

The old man was quicker than Sam expected. He dodged the wild blows and thrust a spear-hand strike into Sam's ribs. Then he ducked, spun his body to the side, and ran headlong for the cave's exit.

It was all Sam could do to ignore the pain coursing through his body and follow the guy. He cursed, bit his lip, then chased after Lou, rushing past fire and smoke as he went. The cavern was well lit by now and it was hard to keep from choking on the air. But none of that mattered at the moment. Only the elimination of the crazy trapper.

Sam caught up with Lou just as the old man reached the cave's exit. Their bodies collided against the wooden door and then they both crashed through it, knocking it off its leather hinges. A contortion of arms and legs exploded out of the cave, landing in a heap of flesh and bone and splintered wood.

Outside now, the sun was sitting low on the western horizon. There were dark clouds hovering in the sky directly above. The ground was still wet from the recent rain, and in their struggle, their bodies slid on the slippery mixture of granite and mud.

Here was the fight to the death. Both men grappled at each other's bodies, clawed at each other's faces, and wrenched viciously at one another's defenses.

The old man wasted no time with the subtleties of combat etiquette. He raked and gouged his fingers at Sam's soft targets—the neck, eye sockets, cheeks, groin, and armpits. He was obviously searching for a sensitive spot that would cause Sam to drop his guard.

But Sam was no greenhorn. He had lost his club somewhere in his fall out of the cave, but he kept his elbows in close and Lou's body even closer, holding him as tight as he could. He didn't dare let the wiry man get more than an inch of distance from which to escape.

And Sam fought back just as dirty. He got his hands on Lou's hair and cranked hard, painfully arching the old man's neck backward. Then he pushed against Lou's face with the other hand, his fingers spearing into eyelids and nostrils, scoring through flesh.

Blood was smeared everywhere, coming from both men. There were streaks of crimson left on the cold earth, with more blood on the way.

"Is this your last hope, Sam?" Lou said desperately. His voice sounded tight and forced against Sam's aggression. But the old man still wouldn't shut up. "Is this your God? *Is it!* Are you now the God, Sam? Is it you?" He got his teeth around Sam's wrist, bit down hard and shook savagely, like a pit-bull.

"Ahhh!" Sam cried. Then he gritted his teeth and shoved his wrist further into Lou's mouth, cranking his forearm up and down as he did so.

Lou gasped and turned his head to the side. "Yes," he grunted, the hint of a chuckle lining his voice. "You are a God, Sam. You're *my* fucking God." Then the old man kicked up with his knees and sprung away from Sam. He swung his legs back and planted them firmly on the ground. Then he was up and running.

But Sam moved faster.

He, too, got up on his feet. And he sprang forward and caught Lou by the waist, a classic quarterback tackle. Their bodies fell once again to the ground. Only this time, they fell just inches from the mountain's cliff side, the drop-off that looked down to the river, hundreds of feet below.

"I'm going to kill you, Lou!" Sam shouted. "If it's the last thing I do!"

"Oh, it just might be," replied the old man.

They struggled on the ground, each of them fighting for the advantage to be on top of one another. Lou kept up with his dirty tricks, landing two spear-hand strikes into Sam's armpit and one at his throat.

Sam rained fist after fist into the old man's gut and solar plexus, hoping to at last knock the wind out of him.

"You can't kill me, Sam," Lou said. He was laughing now, laughing almost hysterically. Mud covered his face, and his scraggly gray hair looked like a sopping rat's nest. "Don't you know? You can't kill the devil."

"To hell with you, old man," Sam said. He found an opening and threw a wild punch to the side of Lou's head.

Lou curled inward against the pain. But then he swung his hips out and came right back up, hands clawing viciously. He went berserk at that moment, attacking with the speed and ferocity of a mountain lion, attempting, so it seemed, to overwhelm Sam with a litany of strikes.

And it worked. Lou's fusillade successfully dropped Sam's guard, and then the old man was suddenly on top and straddling Sam's waist.

Sam had his back against the ground with his enemy on top of him, pinning his shoulders down to the cold earth. He was in a bad way now. His head was at the edge of the cliff and he could vaguely see the drop-off looming dangerously behind him. Sam knew he was in a really bad situation. But as he looked up, he realized the situation was worse than he thought. Lou was now holding a fist-sized rock in his hand.

The old man laughed and said, "I do believe I'm going to kill you now, Sam Nolan." He reached his rock-wielding hand back, cocking it for a solid strike. He had his other hand around Sam's throat and was squeezing it like a vise. "And when I'm done, I'm going to finish off your brother. Make no mistake about it, soldier boy, this is your end. So say goodbye to God, and say goodbye to Hope."

Just then, a strong wind blew across the mountaintop. Oddly enough, amongst the wicked violence of his conflict and the rising dread born from what appeared to be his impending finale, Sam's senses honed in on the surrounding wilderness. As if he were a wild animal, he suddenly detected minute details of the world around him.

Sam heard the sway of tree branches in the forest behind the entrance to the mine. He heard the lazy run of the river way below—perhaps his final resting place, once Lou smashed his head in. And Sam smelled the sweet odors of clay and sap, wet pine needles, and rain. He tasted dirt and blood, and it somehow reminded him of his home away from home, his cave in the Gila Wilderness. And while these senses flooded into his consciousness, his subconscious mind had his hand reaching out onto the ground beside him, searching for some kind of weapon. Searching for anything.

Then a barrage of thoughts, suddenly flashing through his head with the speed of gunfire, revealed to Sam a host of desperate images. He saw his mother's tears as she dropped to her knees on the porch of her house. He saw Lolo, alone in the barn, her painful heartache bringing her down, down to her knees as well. And then there was his father's grief, followed by an overwhelming vacuum of deep emptiness, which spread unfailingly throughout the lives of Sam's entire family. He saw Jenny, Bryson's wife, forever lost in the darkness of her depression. And finally, incredulously, Sam saw his long-lost partner, Ernie, standing on the side of a desert mountain, his face strapped with a dull sadness as he was waving—not hello, not goodbye—just waving.

With this overload of sensory details and mental images, it seemed to Sam that the wilderness of the Yukon was now finally speaking to him, breaching through the portals of his body and provoking him into a last will to survive.

And it was then that Sam noticed there was *something else out there...*

Something his senses had just now discovered. Something else that the wilderness had revealed to him—yet beyond sight, or smell, or taste—but of which he could only *feel*.

And what Sam felt was another presence.

He looked up and saw Lou, the old man still smiling, rock raised high, arm poised to come swiftly down, when suddenly...

Suddenly, the ground, the forest, and every tree, stone and spec of dirt, trembled violently against the longest, loudest roar Sam had ever heard.

It came from behind the men—*right behind them*—a sustained earsplitting crack of primal thunder that reverberated across the entire mountain, sending vibrations rattling into Sam's body, echoing throughout his chest, his arms, his legs, his skull, and it was a wildly animalistic roar, a roar that provoked a surreal sense of immediate, hideous terror.

But also, in this terrifying moment, was the opportunity Sam needed most.

Lou's body flinched violently from the wild scream. He was obviously stunned, and he loosened his grip on Sam as he turned a shoulder to look behind him.

Then Sam made his move. In one swift motion, he bucked his hips upward, pulled Lou's grasping hand off his throat and to the side, then reached up with his other hand and slammed home the wooden branch he'd just found on the ground. Sam stabbed Lou's face several times, with the last thrust landing deep into the old man's left eye.

Lou gave a quick gasp, followed by an agonizing whelp. He dropped the rock and threw his hands to the vicious wounds now on his face. At last, his smile and laugh were no more.

Sam bucked his hips again. Then he rolled onto his left shoulder and tossed Lou up and over—over the edge of the cliff and into a long and terrible scream of his own, lasting for the entire length of his fall, all the way down to the river.

CHAPTER 33

Sam glanced briefly over the edge of the cliff, watching the last moments of Lou's fall as the old man's body smacked heavily into the river. The sound of the splash came seconds later. Then there was nothing but the stir of the wind and the soft movements of nature around him.

He never saw the old man come back up. And Sam figured he never would. It was a long and terrible fall, which would have made for one hell of a hard landing, considering the density of water.

Done at last with the crazy Lou Pine, Sam's mind went first to his brother... and then to the colossal roar he had just heard. Or, more specifically, to the question of what had made the terrific howl. And where that thing was now.

Slowly, Sam turned back around and stood up from the ground. His stare was on the tree line, looming not more than fifty feet away. It was a moderately thick row of woods, consisting of mostly stubby pine trees, which offered little in the way of foliage. But Sam studied it anyway. He studied the trees, studied them meticulously, for the slightest hint of something wild and feral. For something dangerous.

But what Sam saw was nothing, nothing at all.

He thought about that roar and how it provoked in him a feeling of complete primordial dread. He suspected it must have been quite similar, if not identical, to the howls Andre McKinnon had talked about, the ones he'd encountered on his many expeditions.

Sam's skin crawled with anxiousness... but for only a little while. He knew the source of the howl wasn't a bear, mountain lion, wolverine, or anything else known to live out here. But Sam also knew—or suspected, at least—that whatever it was, it meant him no harm. Something in Sam's gut told him this.

His thoughts went to his brother then, and the moment became an instant rush of panic. Bryson was still down there in the mine, most likely dead—yet possibly still alive. And if he was alive, then his time was now critically close to an end.

Sam took off in a run as fast as his badly beaten body would let him. He rushed past the trees, through the pulverized wooden door, and then straight into the mine shaft. He was met with a plume of smoke and the sounds of dying flames. The fire he'd ignited had apparently failed to consume everything, and it was presently dying down. But there was still enough light to see from. And what Sam saw was his brother lying motionless on the ground.

Sam ran to Bryson's side, then crouched to his knees. The smoke was not as dense near the ground, which he was thankful for. But the knife sticking out of Bryson's abdomen put a quick damper on any sense of relief. Still, the blade appeared to be resting lower and more on the side of Bryson's abdomen. It looked almost as if it was sticking into the pelvic bone.

Sam checked his brother for a pulse and found a weak one. Deciding to wait on treating the knife wound, he reached down and pulled his brother over his back and into a fireman's carry, then walked him out of the mine and into the fresh air.

Bryson spoke up as soon as Sam set him down on the ground outside.

"Are we done, brother?" His voice was soft and feeble.

"You're damn right we are," Sam replied.

"Good," Bryson said. "That's good..."

Bryson drifted off again. Then Sam got up and moved quickly. He scoured the area, his mind set on one thing and one thing only. And he found that thing, fifty-feet down the trail leading to the mine, corralled in a small wooden stable.

Sally the mule was clearly spooked. She could probably still smell whatever had made that terrible howl. Frankly, Sam was surprised she was still alive, having not died from plain fear.

Sally quickly warmed up to him. And within minutes, he had her tethered near the mouth of the mine. Then he stooped down and studied Bryson's wound, knowing he had to get that knife out of him soon. He got up and checked the contents of the mule's saddlebags, found a roll of clean cloth and a bottle of whiskey, then went back to his brother.

"You might as well stay out of it, Bryson," Sam said, clearing away his brother's shirt and inspecting the wound. "Nothing about this is going to feel good."

With a quick yank, Sam pulled the knife out of his brother's abdomen. Then he cleaned the wound with whiskey and bandaged it up as best he could with the roll of cloth. When he was finished, he gently loaded his brother over Sally's back, then led them both over the top of the mountain and to his camp.

And through it all, Bryson did stay out of it. He didn't make so much as a peep.

• • •

Two hours later, Sam was back at camp. Two staggeringly painful hours. His whole body was a wreck, with aches abound. He might as well have been run over by a truck.

He was limping badly on the leg Lou had punctured. The only good thing was that the bleeding wasn't critical, and that it had died down some.

At least four spots on Sam's head and neck were crying out for relief. His ribs were screaming as loud as that thing in the forest had done earlier. And his shoulder, where that bastard had bitten him, throbbed like a toothache. What Sam needed right now, he realized, was one big ice bath.

But the ice bath was a moment yet in the future. For now, he settled with securing his brother into a sleeping bag near the recently lit fire.

Sam noticed Bryson's breathing was still shallow, but steady. He prayed his brother would hang in there for a few more hours, which was enough time to get them out of there. And as soon as Bryson woke up, Sam would get some electrolytes into him, hoping to fend off his existing starvation.

Thinking of this, Sam went to one of his duffel bags and opened it, hoping it still contained everything, and that Lou hadn't ransacked the bags while Sam was being held captive. Thankfully, Sam found what he needed—a bottle of water, package of electrolyte gels, can of Skoal, and one other crucial item—all of which he gathered up and brought back to the fire.

He sat on the ground next to his brother. Gently, he patted Bryson's shoulder. Although still worried, Sam was thankful for the present outcome. He drank from the bottle of water and crammed a fat wad of tobacco under his lower lip. Then he quietly surveyed his surroundings as he considered his thoughts.

Everything in the camp looked the same as he'd left it, with one exception: his brother was now with him. A light wind pushed at the grassy meadow. And beyond, the nearby line of trees resembled a troop of tall creatures standing in the shadows. The smell of burning wood was a much needed, welcomed comfort. In the far distance, and from the surface of Earl Lake, came the solitary cry of a loon. And that, too, Sam found comforting.

It seemed the dark end of a long and terrible day had finally come to greet Sam. It was quick to stir and lull him toward his impending finale—a finale not of death after all, but of deep sleep.

But before he finally drifted off, Sam did one more thing.

He pulled from his lap the other item he'd taken out of his duffel bag—the crucial item—which was a handheld DeLorme Satellite Messenger unit, complete with a GPS tracking system and personal emergency transponder. And with a deep, relieving sigh, he pressed the S.O.S. button.

And then Sam was lying on the ground next to Bryson, with the steady pulse of his brother's breathing being the best and last thing he would think about that day.

CHAPTER 34

It took two months before Sam finally made a full recovery. His mother's good cooking and never-ending care expedited that time by a month, or so he figured. It was good to be back home. And it was damn good to be around his family, friends, and the many animals of the ranch.

Presently, Sam was riding Dee, the blue roan mare, and staring out at what had to be the finest New Mexico sunrise he'd ever laid eyes on. He'd gotten up damn early, earlier than his dad, which might have been a first. And that's because Sam's mind wouldn't quit. It *couldn't* quit—as it kept gnawing away at what seemed like a hundred different concerns, some good, some bad, and all of which he couldn't get a grip on.

Partly, he kept thinking about his lost partner, Ernie. The man's fate had never revealed itself to Sam, which left a wicked feeling in him. He had talked to his father and Nali about this—finally, Sam had talked—and both men had counseled him wisely, recognizing his feelings yet reminding him that some questions in life will always remain unanswered.

Interestingly enough, rescuing his brother had filled Sam with a renewed sense of pride. The feeling was something he didn't know he'd been missing, and he was grateful for its return.

Sam thought about his brother and smiled. After they'd been rescued, strangely enough, Bryson stayed wide awake for the duration of the plane ride back to Carmacks. Adding to Sam's persistent migraine were Bryson's persistent requests for all the details regarding Sam's trek up north, his subsequent tracking efforts, and the harrowing conflict that followed. It was a long plane ride back, physically painful and annoying as hell. But it was also an experience Sam would gladly never forget.

Of course, Bryson had made a quicker recovery than Sam, damn him. His brother had stayed on at the ranch for a few weeks, but he and Jenny were now home, up in Seattle.

With fondness, Sam remembered the tears that had burst out of the woman's face once she laid eyes on the two of them. Jenny damn near squeezed the last of Bryson's breath out of him with the hug she gave. Sam received a powerful hug also, which was something else he would never forget.

Gently, he pulled on Dee's reins, directing the horse to the north, where the distant mountain range of the Gila Wilderness loomed. Sam was now thinking about future preparations, setting store for the upcoming winter, hunting elk and small game, gathering tinder, stock-piling miscellaneous provisions, and cutting firewood... These were all the things he would not be doing anytime soon. (Although he suspected cutting firewood would find its way on his list of ranch chores in due time, now that he was on the mend). Sam smiled again, then reached out and patted Dee on the neck.

"Looks like we've got a few more rides ahead of us, girl," he said. The mare flicked her head and snorted, as if she couldn't agree more.

Sam laughed. It *was* good to be back. *Damn* good.

He rode the mare farther up the meadow for a time, edging along the creek and catching the distinct odors of sage and grama grass on the wind. Resting in a thicket of birch on the other side of the creek were four Herefords. The cattle stared curiously at Sam. He wondered briefly about them. And then, in an unsettling way, the sight gave him the shivers.

Sam was suddenly reminded of that undiscovered creature up there in the Yukon. The evidence he had come across by his own accord was startling enough. The footprints, the awful smell, and the undeniable presence of something—which he'd detected not once, but twice. And then that god-almighty howl. All of this evidence had left a never-ending nagging voice inside Sam's head, a voice that whispered a sliver of doubt into his *own* doubts as to the existence of such a legendary beast.

When they'd arrived back in Carmacks, Sam had a long talk with Andre McKinnon. Like Bryson, the man was dying to learn about Sam's harrowing adventure. And sure enough, Sam's accounts and descriptions had validated all the more Andre's notions and harebrained ideas regarding the legendary creature supposedly stalking the vast wilderness of the Pacific Northwest.

Sam explained everything to Andre, as much as he could recall. But he also tried to focus mostly on his encounter with the crazy trapper, and of his rescue of Bryson. And Sam explained this part to the Canadian Mounties as well, who were quick to deploy a search and recovery mission to the area.

In the days and weeks that followed, Sam learned the Mounties had recovered the remains of fifteen human bodies from the abandoned mine shaft, along with a wide assortment of personal effects, such as coats, fishing rods, backpacks, lanterns... All gear which Sam had already discovered, while in the mine. However, if Sam's memory served him well, the crazy trapper had mentioned killing twenty-seven people while living in the Yukon. And that meant there were at least a dozen souls still lost in the wilderness. A dozen souls still missing and still causing heartaches to their loved ones left behind.

And, as Sam hated to admit, there was also one more soul to add to that number of missing persons.

Lou Pine himself.

The Mounties had never recovered the old man's body from the river. But they announced publicly that Lou had most certainly died from his fall—a fall that lasted for one-hundred and fifty-seven-feet. They had searched portions of the river, both in the spot Lou had landed and then further downstream, but ultimately found nothing. Even so, the Mounties eventually declared that the ruthless serial killer of the Yukon Territory was officially missing and presumed dead.

But Sam wasn't so sure.

The fact that they had never found a body left a seed of doubt in his mind. And it was with an only semi-convincing assurance that Sam told himself Lou was long gone, as he considered what he did know: Lou Pine was a horribly wounded old man who had fallen over one hundred and fifty feet off a mountain, and into a cold rushing river in the heart of one of the most desolate places on earth.

But still...

Sam considered these known facts. But he also knew a person could conceivably survive a fall from that height. And if a person could survive that fall, if *anyone* could, well then...

It was a notion he found hard to shake—hence, the nagging doubt which kept his thoughts churning. But it was a doubt Sam would have to learn to let go.

Dee snickered then and jerked her head to the left. There was a southern wind crossing the prairie, and she'd caught the scent of something coming up on them. Sam turned and looked, then spotted a rider on a horse about a hundred yards off.

He recognized the horse; it was Paul. And Paul was carrying a long-haired Apache woman on his back. And that horse closed the distance between the two riders in a matter of seconds.

"I thought I'd find you out here, cowboy." Lolo was wearing a white Stetson Stallion, which contrasted nicely against her crow-colored hair. Complimenting her hat was a brown leather coat, denim jeans, and chestnut Laredo boots. She pulled her horse up next to his, smiled, and gently slid her hat off. Then she exchanged it with Sam's hat and laughed. "See there; it looks good on you."

Sam chuckled. "I bet it does." He nudged the hat further on his head. "But of course, anything coming from you has got to look good."

Lolo lifted her chin, gesturing to the north. "You know there's a barbed wire fence up there... Just in case you're considering some bad idea."

Sam smiled. Then he turned in his saddle and looked squarely at her. "Don't you worry, ma'am. I ain't going anywhere. Just a ride, is all. A short, relaxing ride."

They were the words she had been waiting a long time to hear and the words Sam had needed to say. And they came out of his mouth as smooth as a breeze on the trees.

EPILOGUE

Six Months Later

Eugene Beaumont Legrand climbs off his snowmobile and steps knee-high into the snow, cursing his luck. It's a broken drive belt again, dammit. He just replaced the thing last month, which means there's something in the drivetrain causing too much heat. But right now, that's the least of Eugene's problems. The worst is that he doesn't have a spare belt with him and he's stranded in the middle of nowhere.

He turns and looks out at the wide landscape of snow. He has a good idea of his location—twenty miles north of Whitehorse—with nothing but a cold winter in between. This would be a death sentence for a lesser person. But Eugene is a hardened woodsman with thirty years of fur trapping under his belt. He can survive in the worst of conditions (pretty much what he's in right now) but damn if he wants to walk twenty miles back to civilization. Not tonight, at least.

He thinks about where he's at, the area, and then remembers there's an old hunting cabin east of here, perhaps three miles away, maybe a little more. It'll make for a rough trek. But at least he'll have some shelter for the time being. He's been traveling for ten hours already, and the thought of resting his weary bones is all he wants to think about right now. In the morning, he can dial up his GPS unit and call in for help.

With a sigh, Eugene grabs his snowshoes and fastens them to his feet. Then he secures his daypack, loaded with a few essential items, onto his back, and starts walking. He's got a .357 Magnum holstered on his hip, but he's not counting on using that anytime soon. The dead of winter in Canada's Yukon Territory is a time when most dangers, such as bears, are also dead asleep.

The sky is set a deep plum color, almost black, but not completely dark. It is a clear night, and the infinite stars of the Milky Way bathe the winter landscape in a surreal, shimmery light. There's an eerie stillness hanging in the air, as if the world itself were hibernating, or perhaps holding its breath in fear of some impending doom.

Eugene notices the deathly calmness surrounding him and it hardly fazes the man. Mostly, he's grateful for the lack of weather, knowing that a snowstorm would add a dreadful wrench to his brief journey.

He walks for two, maybe three hours, and knows he has made good time. Eugene also knows he is getting close to the cabin. He's still confident with his location, such that he doesn't even bother to check his GPS unit.

Another ten minutes of walking and Eugene's nose catches the distinct odor of burning wood—the stove at the cabin. Yahoo! This is good fortune. Good fortune indeed. Burning wood means certain comfort, possibly some hot food, and maybe even a little something to drink. For damn sure, it means he's no longer stranded. Hell, if the stars above are aligned properly, maybe Eugene will get his hands on a new drive belt for his snowmobile. Perhaps whoever's in the cabin has an extra. Then he won't have to call for help in the morning.

He walks another ten minutes, then comes up to the ramshackle building. There's a light in the window and just outside, standing in the snow, is a man, smoking what looks like a cigarette. Eugene's nose detects the smell of cooked meat and his mouth waters at the prospect of hot food.

"Hey, there!" he calls out, taking care to alert the man to his position, just in case he's mistaken for a wolf and drawn down on. "Hello, friend."

"Well, hello to you." The man seems surprised to see Eugene, and rightfully so. He drops his cigarette into the snow and wraps a scarf around his face. "What the hell are you doing out here?" he says.

"Broke a belt on my snowmobile," Eugene replies as he approaches the cabin. "Over the hill, a few miles yonder."

"Well, come on in, then. Get yourself out of the cold. I got some venison stew on the stove. I'll feed you well enough. And then you can rest some."

Eugene unbuckles his snowshoes at the door, then follows the man into the cabin. The warmth of the place is a pleasant shock to his system. He unloads his pack and peels out of his outerwear before taking a seat beside the wood-burning stove. Smiling, he glances around the room as he rubs his hands over the heat.

"I got a little whiskey, if you're of a mind," the stranger says. He brings Eugene a bowl of hot stew and sets a bottle of Jim Beam on the table next to him.

"I sure *am* of the mind," Eugene replies happily. "Mighty thanks, mister. It's been a long, long day."

"Oh, I bet it has," the man says, walking again to the small kitchenette. He serves himself a bowl of stew, then comes back and sits in a chair across from Eugene.

"Damn, I'm hungry," Eugene says, after a few bites. "And this might be the best meal I've had in a while." He glances up, noticing that the man—the old man—has taken off his scarf. Eugene then freezes, his spoon halfway to his mouth. "Lord, almighty, what in the hell happened to you?"

"Well, now, mate, that's a good question. A *bloody* good question."

Then the old man's horribly disfigured face breaks into a great big smile.

THE END

AUTHORS NOTE TO READERS

As a lifelong fan of the Sasquatch mystery, admittedly, I had a world of fun writing this novel. I've always been a sucker for the unsolved and the unexplained. As well, it was through my personal research of the legendary creature that the inspiration for this novel came to mind one day. The question that hit me was what if Bigfoot really exists... and it's not too friendly?

That query got me started. And after a good deal of research, and a novel later, of course, I still have no definitive answer. But allow me to share a few of the details and authentic anecdotes I uncovered during my research, some of which went into the writing of this story.

Bryson Nolan's rugged, outdoorsman lifestyle, and the events leading up to his abduction at Earl Lake, is based on the actual life and tragic fate of the 49-year-old hunter and renowned woodsman, Bart Schleyer. Known for trapping grizzlies and other large predators, Bart went missing on September 14th, 2004, while solo-hunting for moose in the Reid Lakes area of Canada's Yukon Territory. Some of his remains and gear were eventually discovered in the area, but to this day, it is unclear what actually happened to the man. For starters, no environmental disturbances were found, which would have almost certainly been the case had Bart been attacked by a bear, or other known predator. Given Bart's experience and the lack of evidence surrounding his fate, many of those who knew the man remain baffled as to what really happened to him.

The case of Bart Schleyer is just one of thousands of similar unsolved mysteries regarding people who have gone missing under bizarre circumstances, throughout the wilds of North America. For more information on these eerie accounts, consider reading the *Missing 411* books by David Paulides.

Most of the tracking techniques employed by Sam throughout the novel are genuine practices, which I picked up from my research. Derek Randles, a tracker, hunter, and Bigfoot researcher in Olympia, Washington, was invaluable to the imparting of some of these techniques. Also, the book *Fundamentals of Mantracking*, by Albert Taylor and Donald Cooper, was just as important.

I've read a host of books and watched countless videos, all pertaining to the Bigfoot phenomenon (my poor wife can attest to this). One book in particular, *Sasquatch: Legend Meets Science*, by Dr. Jeff Meldrum, proved indelible to my research. Also, a big shout-out goes to my friend James "Bobo" Fay for his research connections, as well as tubular stories.

Much of the experiences and theories provided by Andre McKinnon's character are indeed based on actual events and conjectures among the Bigfoot community. Andre's terrifying encounter with several of the creatures while camping with his friends in Montana, however, was entirely from my imagination.

Another invention of mine was the existence and history of both Earl Lake and Earl Clemens.

For the scenes and samples of the Southwest, genuine as they are, yet limited as it relates to the true richness of the area, I am forever grateful to my family heritage. I've spent enough time in the Southwest to appreciate just how enchanted it is.

A long-awaited thank you goes to Matthew Oler for teaching me all that I know about cattle ranching, as well as the hidden curiosities of the Gila Wilderness. Real cowboys still exist, I'm glad to say, and they are just as competent as Sam Nolan.

Last but certainly not least, I owe much gratitude to Jacques de Spoelberch, whose kind support and editing talents came as a tremendous gift in the writing of this novel.

As a final note, I would like to offer a bit of advice. Embrace the outdoors, now and forever. Although Denali is a fictitious character, it would be remiss if his wisdom were overlooked. I do believe there is powerful medicine that comes with being close to nature. But while adventuring in remote areas, just be cautious, and use common sense. Consider bringing bear spray, a personal transponder, and someone you can trust. I would also caution against hiking alone, unless you are absolutely confident with your skills. Unless you're Sam Nolan. But even then...

And with that, let me end with one more nugget of curiosity: The "very loud and very long scream" referenced several times throughout this book, and suggested to be made from a Sasquatch, is an exact description to a sound I heard not once, but twice, while camping in the Sierra Nevada Mountains. It is a scream that keeps me wondering to this day.

ABOUT THE AUTHOR

Chris Riley lives near Sacramento, California, vowing one day to move back to the Pacific Northwest. In the meantime, he teaches special education, writes stories, and hides from the blasting heat for six months of the year. He has had over 100 short stories and essays published in various magazines and anthologies, and across multiple genres. He is the author of the literary suspense novels *The Sinking of the Angie Piper* and *The Broken Pines*. For more information, go to www.chrisrileyauthor.com.

OTHER TITLES BY CHRIS RILEY

The Broken Pines

NOTE FROM CHRIS RILEY

Word-of-mouth is crucial for any author to succeed. If you enjoyed *Went Missing*, please leave a review online—anywhere you are able. Even if it's just a sentence or two. It would make all the difference and would be very much appreciated.

Thanks!
Chris Riley

We hope you enjoyed reading this title from:

BLACK ROSE writing

www.blackrosewriting.com

Subscribe to our mailing list – *The Rosevine* – and receive **FREE** books, daily deals, and stay current with news about upcoming releases and our hottest authors.
Scan the QR code below to sign up.

Already a subscriber? Please accept a sincere thank you for being a fan of Black Rose Writing authors.

View other Black Rose Writing titles at www.blackrosewriting.com/books and use promo code **PRINT** to receive a **20% discount** when purchasing.

Printed in the USA
CPSIA information can be obtained
at www.ICGtesting.com
JSHW081044081023
49625JS00001B/35

9 781685 133658